The Stillness Broken

A Maxwell Graham mystery thriller

Lawrence Falcetano

The Stillness Broken
A Maxwell Graham mystery thriller

Copyright © 2020 Lawrence Falcetano

First Edition

"Startled at the stillness broken..."
Edgar Allan Poe—the Raven

Lawrence Falcetano

Dedication

To my wife, Susan, who knows why.

Lawrence Falcetano

Chapter 1

"The thousand injuries of Fortunato I had borne as best I could; but when he ventured upon insult, I vowed revenge."
Edgar Allan Poe—The Cask of Amontillado

I was sitting at my kitchen table enjoying a beer and thinking about murder. Most psychoanalysts agree that anyone can commit murder. Even those who believe they're incapable of it can be driven to it by circumstance. Human beings murder for a myriad of reasons: greed, hatred, profit, power, revenge, lust, and some time for the sheer pleasure of it, and often with meticulous planning, or in the heat of anger, but always with malice aforethought. Nonetheless, the result is the same—people killing people.

My reason for wanting to kill Drew Flannery was pure hatred. Hatred which festered out of the indignation I felt for the treasonous thing he had done to me. I was sure, at the time, the only satisfying course of action for me was to terminate his existence.

I finished my beer and hook shot the empty can in a wide arc toward the wastebasket by the sink. It bounced off the rim and landed on the tile floor. I left it there. Turning back to the small photo album on the table in front of me, I continued flipping through pages of photographs of my college years. The faded color images passed before me like an old movie, mixed with memories of good and not so good times. About halfway through the album, I came upon a photo of Drew and me smiling happily into the camera, while my then best friend, Ray Deverol, snapped the picture.

I'd logged in a lot of time with Ray and Drew during our college days. We stayed out later than we should have, consumed more alcohol than was considered healthy, and chased more girls than we knew we could handle. We kept each other's secrets, wore each other's clothes and relied on each other's friendship. In short, we were typical college friends, endeavoring to get an education and determined to have a good time doing it...until I decided to kill Drew.

"Are you out of your mind?" Ray said, after he had cunningly coerced from me my malevolent intentions, and realized I wasn't kidding. "If you're even remotely serious, you'd better forget it."

I punched the top of my desk where I'd been sitting. "The bastard deserves it!" I said. Ray looked straight into my eyes. He had a way of demonstrating his anger, yet letting me know he was looking out for my welfare, much like a loving father chastising his child. "Forget it!" he said.

Of course, Ray had been right, but blinded by hatred, I couldn't make him any promises. For several nights after, I lay in my bed thinking of ways to end Drew's life. There were the conventional means: shooting, stabbing, poisoning or strangulation, but they seemed too messy and I wasn't sure I had the courage to go through with them. I thought of more than one way to make it look like an accident, and although I surprised myself with my own inventiveness, I quickly gave up the ideas, fearing something might go wrong due to an oversight in my planning. I even thought about hiring someone to do the job, but how does a financially strapped college student pay for that service, and where would I find such a person?

It took nearly two months for me to get over the idea of wanting to exterminate Drew. Since then, a couple of decades and the onset of maturity have dispelled my urge.

Taking Ray's advice would have been the smart thing to do. We were allies, looking out for each other. That alliance became a deep loss for me when Ray disappeared from the radar not long after graduation. It wasn't easy living with the burden of not knowing how or why your best friend suddenly dropped off the earth. When we last spoke, he phoned to tell me he had joined the Peace Corps and would travel the world. He promised to stay in touch. I wished him good luck and never heard from him again. After a while I made inquiries, asked questions, and followed leads to find him, but each one brought me to an agonizing dead end. I accepted the reality that Ray vanished and I was helpless to do anything about it; time and the course of human events, inevitably pushed Ray's memory to the back of my mind. I held on to a glimmer of hope that one day I would see him again.

Although Ray's absence left a void in my life, the ensuing years kept Drew Flannery's memory in my daily conscientiousness. Drew's name appeared in the city papers regularly, and I occasionally read the measures of his medical achievements with a sense of indifferent curiosity. Cultivating a lucrative practice in the northeast for nearly two decades, he had become "Dr. Flannery" with a status among the medical community fast approaching sainthood. Although he had become head of surgery at Andover Medical, a hospital located within my precinct—our paths hadn't crossed in twenty years.

Drew's accomplishments came as no surprise to me. With a genius IQ and a steadfast direction of purpose, it was evident he'd succeed in anything he chose to do. What *did* surprise me was that he had become a socialite, rubbing shoulders with the area's highest citizenry, hosting banquets and testimonials at his lavish Long Island home. This wasn't the college classmate I remembered. Drew had always been shy and reserved around strangers and had no real friends at school—except Ray and me.

I turned a few more pages of the photo album until I came to a small photo of Sherilyn Fasano and me on a Seaside

Heights, New Jersey beach. We were smiling into the camera, each holding a can of Miller Lite in the air above our heads. I was surprised to see the photo since I thought I had destroyed all vestiges of Sherilyn to obliterate her memory, forever.

I went to the fridge for another beer, retrieved the empty beer can from the kitchen floor and dropped it into the wastebasket. I took my seat again at the table, popped open the beer, took a long pull, then closed the album cover, avoiding a second look at Sherilyn and feeling good about myself for not ripping the photo from the album and tearing it to pieces. Nineteen years as a New York City cop has taught me a bit about self-control. Although I'm still working on that cardinal virtue, having worked twelve years as a Homicide Detective, the gains I'd made in self-restraint were supplanted by my inordinate degree of cynicism, not only because of the inherent nature of police work but because one discovers, very quickly, the dark recesses of the human mind and its evil capabilities. The main tenet of being a cynic is to "doubt everything." To most people this can be a detriment, for me, it's an asset. Years of police work have nurtured my cynicism so that now I use it almost daily as a defense mechanism against uncertain situations and people with whom I'm not comfortable. It has saved my life more than once.

My cynicism kicked in the morning I discovered an envelope from Drew Flannery in my mailbox at headquarters. Inside, was a handwritten note inviting me to Drew's Long Island estate to spend an afternoon rehashing old times with him and Ray. I was surprised and overjoyed at the prospect of seeing Ray again and wondered why, after twenty years, I should receive the news from Drew that Ray had returned, especially after what Drew had done to decimate our relationship. The prospect of my ever becoming "close" again with Drew vanished with his single act of treachery. Ray and I had more in common, and if the term, "best friends" applied, it would have been between us, particularly since it was Ray who saved my life during our senior year at school. After a quick check of Drew's credentials, I became satisfied the note was genuine. Drew had left his address and phone number at the bottom of the note (along with scanty driving directions) and asked me to call.

Elated that Ray had resurfaced—presumably, well, and in one piece, and motivated by curiosity and nostalgia, I phoned Drew to accept his invitation. When we spoke, he sounded genuinely magnanimous. I was cordial but cautious. The truth was, I didn't care if I ever saw Drew again, but I did want to catch up with Ray.

I finished my beer and took another hook shot at the wastebasket with the empty. Missed...

***

My Chevy Nova struggled up the winding road toward Drew Flannery's mansion, reminding me, with each cough and sputter of its engine, that it was time for me to buy a new car, but my recent divorce and double child support payments quickly negated that luxury.

The gravel road inclined upward from the gated entrance at the street, wide enough for two vehicles to pass but densely populated on either side by a variety of trees and shrubbery. It took me through a wooded tract until it leveled out into several turns, then continued to a parking area by the front entrance.

As I came around the last turn, the mansion appeared suddenly from behind a stand of tall Oaks and Evergreens, silhouetted against a brooding gray October sky. An imposing structure with spires and cupolas and at least twenty rooms, it stood surrounded by well-manicured acreage and a black wrought-iron fence and elevated high above a quiet suburban street.

I pulled to the curb by a front portico behind a silver Jaguar and an older Nissan and turned off the engine. In the sudden stillness, I remember thinking; *it's too quiet, too peaceful*, almost like the unsought serenity of a graveyard. There were no sounds from birds or insects, and the occasional breeze that whistled steadily over the rooftops only added to an already eerie atmosphere.

Although the grounds were richly landscaped, the house itself appeared dismal and uninviting. Its facade was constructed of gray stone, with an abundance of English Ivy climbing to the roofline and clinging to the enormous stone chimney that rose from the foundation up through the gable end roof. I looked up through my windshield at the tall trees surrounding the structure, their skeletal limbs reaching down above the spires and swaying in the afternoon breeze like searching human arms. Iron bars covering the windows on the first floor didn't do much to make a visitor feel welcome. Despite the outward gloominess of the place, its enormousness was a testament to Drew Flannery's wealth and influence.

I closed the door of the Chevy, gently, out of a coerced reverence for the silence, and buttoned my blazer around the Colt Defender I carried in a belt holster on my hip. I'd auditioned many service pistols during my career, including 9mm's and .38's and although the Colt was a bit cumbersome because of its size and weight, I felt comfortable relying on the larger caliber. *The bullet that makes the biggest hole wins!*

As I walked under the portico toward a pair of massive Oak entrance doors, I looked curiously at a carving centered in the upper panel of the right door, depicting what appeared to be the face of a devil or demon. Its bulging eyes cast a portentous stare at an unsuspecting visitor, while its hinged metal jaw, with its pointed teeth, served as the doorknocker. I left the maleficent spirit undisturbed and pressed the chime button on the doorframe. Three melodic tones broke the silence inside the house. Before the third tone faded, a door swung open and Drew Flannery appeared, drink in hand, his bright white teeth filling that phony smile I remembered all too well. He was dressed entirely in black, from his polished shoes to a satin long sleeve shirt, which he kept buttoned at the wrists and collar but with no tie. Drew had never been eccentric in his dress, and I didn't expect such a morose appearance, given his present-day stature. His skin was smooth and taut but appeared sallow, almost unhealthy. His black hair was full and neatly parted, and although he was my age, I couldn't see a strand of gray in it. A thick black mustache sat beneath his nose and followed obliquely the contour of his mouth. Dark areas beneath his eyes attested to a lack of sleep.

"Jet," he said, "Glad you made it." I hated the nickname, but it stuck from my years of running track at college. My speed and athletic ability had earned me the handle, and I'd lived with it throughout my school years. It felt strange to hear someone use it again. Neither Drew nor Ray had acquired a nickname at school, although Ray had his moments of glory as captain of the soccer club. Drew had been less enthusiastic about sports; his idea of competition had been the college debating team. It didn't matter that Drew wasn't a member of the "Jock Club", he owned the Pontiac and weekend "partying" was downtown more than five miles off campus.

"Hello, Drew," I said without a smile.

"Ray arrived a while ago," he said.

He didn't offer a handshake, but made a gesture, which I interpreted to mean, "Come in." Despite his big smile, I wasn't convinced he was glad to see me.

I stepped into a two-story vestibule and we entered through a second doorway and started down a long corridor over a polished terrazzo floor.

"I trust my directions were precise enough," Drew said.

"The wonders of GPS," I said, even though I didn't own one, or wouldn't know how to use one if I did.

I was immediately impressed by the surrounding opulence. Polished brass sconce lamps decorated the rich oak-paneled walls on either side of us as we walked under three large crystal chandeliers hanging between massive wooden rafters. None of the fixtures were lit, and we depended on the daylight that shone through the stained glass windows set close to the high ceiling to light our way.

As we were approaching the end of the corridor, it was hard not to notice a bigger than life painting hanging on an end wall. Within the ornate gold frame, a young woman in a flowing blue gown sat comfortably on a red velvet divan, her hands resting delicately on her lap. Lengths of blonde hair fell over her bare shoulders, partially concealing the string of white pearls she wore around her neck. Her luminous blue eyes seemed to follow us as we continued toward her. I couldn't help staring at the beauty of the woman and the painting. Drew noticed my interest. He paused and looked up at the portrait. "My wife," he said, "some time ago."

I nodded my approval and thought; *Drew did all right in that department, as well.*

He offered no more about it as he led me through a pair of double doors and into a large room, which was the library. Despite the warmth of paneled wood, there was a coldness in the atmosphere, as if the room had little or no history of human occupancy. It was just *there*, as empty and uninviting as the mansion itself.

My eyes were immediately drawn to a wall of windows that looked out onto the rear grounds and surrounded a pair of French doors, which opened to a brick patio. The opposing wall was adorned with books on built-in shelves that reached almost to the vaulted ceiling. A wooden ladder on rollers, attached to a brass rail, stood in a far corner affording access to the highest shelves. Two tan leather wingback chairs stood on either side of a huge fieldstone fireplace, and a matching leather sofa stood opposite them atop a multicolored Persian rug. On one end of a decorative oak mantel sat a life-size bust of an author I immediately recognized as the poet and mystery writer, Edgar Allan Poe. At the opposite end, a gloss black replica of a Raven perched on a twisted tree limb looked out over the room with intrusive red eyes.

In a chair in front of the fireless hearth, Ray sat comfortably, nursing a tall drink. When he saw us, he stood and greeted me with that warm smile I well remembered. "I never thought I'd see you again," he said, pumping my hand so vigorously he nearly spilled his drink. He swung one arm around my neck and pulled me close in an affectionate squeeze.

Time had been good to him. The silver-gray that lightened his hair only served to enhance the handsome features he'd always had. He hadn't lost his athletic physique, and despite his deep tanned complexion, I could still see the crescent-shaped scar on his right temple, a memento of that night on Schooly's Mountain when he'd saved my life.

"What are you drinking these days?" Drew said on his way to a well-stocked bar beside the fireplace.

"Beer's fine," I said.

From a small refrigerator behind the bar, Drew removed two frosted mugs and a couple of bottles of Sam Adams. He filled the mugs and carried them to the sofa. He handed me mine.

Ray took his seat again, took time to drain his glass, then said, "Great to see you, Max. You haven't aged a bit."

"I keep a picture in my attic," I said.

I wasn't sure Ray got it.

"I've been following your career," I said to Drew, trying not to sound too friendly. "Your name's been in the papers often enough." I took a sip of beer. It was so cold it made my teeth chatter. Probably not the best choice for October, but it felt good going down.

"It's nearly impossible to be successful and keep one's anonymity," Drew said, as he took a seat on the sofa, "especially in a metro area like this."

"Don't believe him," Ray said. "He eats it up with a spoon."

Ray made his way to the bar and took his time mixing himself another drink. When he was satisfied with the potion, he held his glass up, contemplating its contents against the light coming from the wall of windows. It was easy to see he had already downed more than a few. Ray had had a weakness for alcohol at school. I hoped it hadn't gotten the better of him.

"Top shelf stuff," he said to Drew.

"Only the best," Drew remarked with that degree of arrogance he had acquired and I had come to hate most about him.

"You've been in the news yourself," Ray said to me as he ambled back to his chair. "A recent celebrated case you'd solved." He raised his glass in a mock toast. "Maxwell Graham," he said, "the Sherlock Holmes of Midtown South." He smiled. I smiled. Drew didn't. Ray always had a knack for ball-busting.

"That's how I got the idea of getting us together," Drew said, "when I read your name in the *Times*."

"Why'd you choose NYPD?" Ray said. He gulped a good portion of his drink without waiting for my answer, which gave me time to reposition myself in the awkwardly shaped chair in which I was sitting. Whenever I tried to find a comfortable position, its high back pushed against the back of my head, causing my chin to touch my chest. In the five minutes I'd been sitting in it, I was already beginning to feel an ache in my spine. Ray was sitting in the same type of chair and seemed not to be having a problem. It looked like he'd found his position, a slight slouch with an awkward lean to the left. I tried to duplicate it but couldn't. I guessed I needed to drink some of whatever Ray was drinking to make that happen. There was nowhere to set my glass down, so I balanced it on my knee and sat upright before I spoke.

"After walking around with a degree in criminal justice under my arm, I joined the force, opting for the adventures of working the streets, rather than sitting behind a desk. After twenty years, they put me behind a desk, anyway."

Ray laughed, and we clinked glasses. "Well, the years haven't taken much from us," he said. "At least we all still have our hair...unlike Professor Calloway."

"Sociology 101," Drew said. "I aced his class."

"You aced every class," Ray said.

"He was as bald as a baby's ass," I said, "except for the tufts of hair at the sides of his head.".

"Remember the time we collected hair off the barbershop floor," Ray said, "and put it in an envelope and left it on his desk? He went ballistic when he opened that envelope in front of the class. I still remember his face and the top of his head pulsating red from anger."

"*Your* brilliant scheme," Drew said to Ray.

"Of which you were a willing participant," Ray reminded.

"It was amusing," Drew admitted, "but we almost got suspended."

"But we didn't," I said, "and we had a good laugh for a long time after."

"I never thought I'd be laughing about my school years," Ray said. "They weren't the best years of my life."

"They were hard but good," I said.

"And easy for some," Ray said, directing his comment toward Drew.

"Simply a matter of application," Drew said, sounding a bit tutorial.

"Here's to fond memories and rekindled friendships," I said.

We raised our glasses to our lips again to celebrate our memory. Over the edge of my glass, I watched Drew's eyes as he drank. I could almost read his mind behind them. I anticipated the impending deception I knew he was adept at executing. Was there something hiding behind those dark eyes, or was I a victim of my own cynicism? I downed the rest of my drink and waited.

Chapter 2

*"So sweet the hour, so calm the time,
I feel it more than half a crime."*
Edgar Allan Poe—Serenade

Ray hadn't offered any biographical information, and I was sure I'd grow old, or crippled, sitting in that chair waiting, so I decided to prime the pump, so to speak. "Tell me what roads you've been down, Raymond," I finally said. He'd never liked me to call him Raymond, but I had to "bust" him back a little. He didn't answer right away, but took the time to organize his thoughts by gazing into the top of his glass and circling the rim with his index finger. I got the feeling he was hesitant to open the gates to his recent past, but it might have just been the effect of too much alcohol.

"Settled down on the West Coast after my stint with the Peace Corps," he finally said. "I got lucky enough to land a position in sales with a pharmaceutical firm in Los Angeles."

I wanted to ask him why he never contacted me, but let it go. There'd be time for that later, without Drew's presence.

Ray had struggled with the usual ups and downs at college until he finally emerged with his degree in business. I'd told him more than once he'd make a great CEO, but his sights weren't set that high back then. Guess he hadn't changed his mind.

"Last year, they transferred me here to their main facility."

"That's how Ray and I got reacquainted," Drew said, "through his sales to the hospital. He'd come to the hospital hoping to expand his accounts, and providence directed him to me. Imagine my surprise," Drew said.

"The market's bigger on the East Coast and they needed their *top* salesman to oversee things," Ray added, with a wry smile.

"Perennial modesty," Drew said.

Now that the gates were open, I pushed Ray a bit further, "Is there a better half?" I said.

Ray smiled. "Came close once," he said. "But I bailed."

"The contented bachelor," Drew said.

"I'm not against it," Ray said. "Just never felt the time was right."

"It rarely is," Drew commented over the top of his glass. "Matrimony is a courageous venture."

He threw back the rest of his drink, then got up and walked back to the bar. I watched curiously as he set his glass down and walked across the room to the wall of books. His demeanor changed suddenly from cordial host to a man self-absorbed in his own concerns as he stood examining a row of books It reminded me of how quickly he had turned on me that last year at school.

From where I was sitting, I could see titles in the mystery and horror genres, books on the occult and several historical novels. Drew ignored these volumes and approached a section of shelving where he stopped to admire a group of books that had been protected behind a pair of glass doors. "My Poe collection," he said, with noticeable pride.

"You were big on Poe at school," Ray said.

"I see you still are," I said, indicating the ornaments on the mantle.

Drew's eyes scanned the books in front of him as he removed a key ring from his pocket, which was attached to a gold chain secured to his belt. He used the single key on the ring to unlock the glass doors. "First editions of Poe's works are nearly impossible to find," he said, opening the doors carefully. "I've been lucky enough to obtain several at a fortune in cost." He pointed to the first book without taking it from the shelf. "A First edition of, *The Narrative of Arthur Gordon Pym*, published in 1838, the author's only novel, collectors would give a year of their life for a copy of this." He spoke without taking his eyes off the books and without turning to look at us. As he continued, he ran his fingers along the binding of a second larger book, "*The Raven and Other Poems*," he said, "1845, first edition. There are only two left in existence. This is one of them."

He moved his hand further along the shelf until he found and removed a thick leather-bound volume from the very end. He brushed his hand delicately over the front cover several times as if he were polishing a precious gem. "*Collected Works*," he said, "a volume that's not as valuable as the others but previous to me just the same."

He turned and looked admiringly at the mantel. "That's a life-size bust of Poe," he said, "with correct proportions down to the exact millimeter." He stepped closer to the blackbird. "And this, of course, represents his most famous work, 'The Raven'." He stroked the nape of the figure with affection, as if it were a living thing. "It's a tribute to his genius."

He sat on the sofa again and balanced the book on his lap. "Edgar Allan Poe," he said, without taking his eyes off the front cover, "indisputably the best writer of the genre. I've read everything he's written, each tale a venture into the mysterious and macabre, each poem a rhythm of sorrow." He looked up at me. "You know, he's the inventor of the detective story. You might learn a few things from him."

Verbal jab!

"He might've learned a few things from me," I said.

Return jab!

He opened the tooled leather cover with what seemed to me to be an inordinate amount of reverence. Delicately flipping over a length of gold ribbon that served as a permanent bookmark, he began carefully turning pages while mentioning a few story titles that were his favorites. Twenty minutes and several drinks later, we were still listening to Drew's exposition of the literary accomplishments and personal life of Edgar Allan Poe with only scant offerings from Ray or me. I hadn't joined any discussion on writers since my membership in the Literary Club at college, and with the passing years, my literary interests waned. It wasn't long before I had my fill of Mr. Poe.

As I was draining the last of my drink, I noticed, over the top of my glass, a sleek "knockout" of a woman as she appeared in the doorway across the room. Folds of blonde hair cascaded over her shoulders onto the pink workout suit she wore, which clung to every part of her shapely body like a second skin. Her complexion was healthily tanned and her slender fingers were tipped with meticulously manicured nails painted pink to match her outfit. She swayed her hips a bit too much, I thought, as she walked toward us, her bright white Reeboks squealing on the polished wood floor.

"The boys from school," she said, with a hint of sarcasm.

Drew stood and tucked the Poe book under his arm.

"My wife, Monica," he said, matter-of-factly.

"Don't get up," she said, as she offered me her hand. I took her delicate fingers gently in mine, being careful not to touch her nails. She responded with a limp wrist. Although the earmarks of time were evident on her face, those luminous blue eyes told me the woman in the painting had come to life.

"You're the detective," she said.

I nodded with a half-smile.

"Of course, you know Ray," Drew said.

Ray gave a polite nod on his way back to the bar as she continued her attention to me.

"I've heard a few things about you," she said.

"I'll deny it all," I said with a smile—then felt dumb for saying it.

"I've never met a real detective," she said. "Must be exciting."

"It can be," I said.

She forced a patronizing smile.

"Would you like a drink?" Drew interrupted with what seemed to me to be an inept effort at congeniality.

"No. thanks," she said. "I'm off to the club for my afternoon workout. I'm sure you boys would rather reminisce without me hanging about."

With that much attention paid to her fingernails, I wondered just how much of a "workout" she thought *was* a workout.

Drew offered no more as she turned with a slight pirouette and walked away. "Don't wait up," she said, rattling a set of car keys in the air above her head, "I'm taking the jag."

Drew put on his phony smile again as we watched her walk away and through the doorway. When she was out of sight, he dropped the smile and said, "A courageous venture." It was easy to see there was trouble in this paradise. The sudden change in his demeanor reminded me of his talent for deception.

Without further concern, Drew returned the Poe book to its place on the shelf, being careful to close and lock the glass doors.

We spent the rest of the afternoon drinking, laughing and telling small lies about our lives until Ray asked Drew to give us a tour of the mansion. Drew agreed enthusiastically and led us out of the library.

After another round of drinks in the library, Drew offered to set out something to eat, but I declined. It was getting late, and I wanted to beat the Saturday evening traffic I knew I'd have to fight driving through the city to get to my apartment on the other side of the Hudson.

"We'll do this again," Drew said, as he escorted us toward the front entrance. "Next time, I'll show you the rear grounds. I've got a tennis court and nine holes of golf back there."

We walked through the two-story vestibule and paused under the front portico. Although the abundance of trees on the grounds kept the area in shadow, it was easy to see Ray's listless eyes; his condition was far beyond safe driving. Drew had been thinking the same. "Perhaps you could drive Ray back to his apartment?" he suggested. "He can leave his car here and pick it up at his convenience." Of course, I agreed, it was the right thing to do and it would give me a chance to get reacquainted with Ray without Drew's presence, but as I helped Ray into the front seat of the Chevy, his head dropped back onto the seat back and he closed his eyes. *There won't be much conversation during this ride*, I thought.

Drew gave me verbal directions to Ray's apartment after I slid in behind the wheel. When I turned the key, the Chevy choked a few times, then started with the usual embarrassing belch of blue smoke. I turned the car around in the parking area and headed down the road away from the house. Through the rearview mirror, I saw a smiling Drew give a quick wave. Maybe it was my cynicism or my mistrust for him, but despite that grinning face, I couldn't shake the feeling there was something more behind our friendly visit, something I couldn't put my finger on.

Drew was not a happy camper. Whatever problem he was having with his wife was obvious, but we all have woman trouble at some point, married or not. My instinct told me there was something behind the facade.

As I followed the road back to the main gate, I kept thinking how Drew had evolved from the shy, unobtrusive, intellectual college student I once knew, to a highly regarded medical professional. The fruit of his labor had been fame and fortune. But that familiar smile couldn't hide the affliction in his face; a face I had learned twenty years ago was capable of deceit.

Chapter 3

"This is a question which, oh Heaven, withdraw
The luckless query from a member's claw."
Edgar Allan Poe—O,Tempora! O, Mores!

I work out of the Midtown precinct building on West 35th
Street. The detective bureau is made up of desks situated in
rows in one large room. Each detective is assigned to a desk
according to his or her seniority. Although the room afforded
little privacy, I had been relegated to a far corner flanked by
two windows, a location well out of earshot and much to my
liking.

I was at my desk writing the monthly check to my ex-wife.
I'd been late with the check once or twice, but so far, Marlene
hadn't made a big deal of it. I suppose electronic transfer
would have made things a lot easier for the both of us, but I
wasn't comfortable with that, psychologically it seemed to me
like Marlene was taking rather than I was giving. Anyway, I
chose to stay with paper and pen. Marlene and I had been
bitter divorce adversaries but came to the understanding that a
civil tolerance of each other was the better way to go for the
sake of our daughters. I didn't want to rock that boat, so I tried
to keep the checks on time.

Christie and Justine sat in a framed photograph on my
desk and smiled out at me daily. The rigors of raising two
daughters far surpassed anything I'd experienced in police
work. They were the treasures of my life, and I missed them
every day since Marlene moved to south Jersey. I had
visitation rights: Mondays and Wednesdays and every other
weekend, but it wasn't easy, and it's an expensive and ugly
business to keep fighting in court. Only the lawyers come out

ahead. So I learned to deal with it and see my daughters whenever it was practical.

Marlene wanted out of our marriage after nineteen years. I guess I was too busy, or too stupid, to see it coming. Living with a cop is no picnic, I suppose. There were the years of shift work and weekend work and vacation work that stretched her tolerance to the limit. And she had to suffer the daily uncertainty of whether her husband would come home safely, or come home at all, for that matter. We had loved each other as much as any normal married couple and our union had produce two beautiful daughters. But near the end, the bickering and nagging took a toll on me as well, and I conceded to the divorce. No one was to blame, certainly not Marlene. She had the marriage, and I had a career, and sometimes it's difficult to balance both. I've always loved Marlene, and maybe I still do. The idea of rekindling our marriage was an unlikely possibility that lingered in the recesses of my mind, but I don't think Marlene will ever have me again. I'd have to bring with me the same baggage that I'd had before: uncertainty, insecurity, worry, and fear, all emotions that Marlene would have to deal with just to be married to a cop. I think she'd had enough.

I slid the check into the envelope and sealed it. As I was writing the address, I thought about how good it was to see Ray again, and although my feelings for Drew weren't amicable, it was interesting to see, first hand, just how successful he had become.

My desk phone rang. When I answered it, a voice said, "You're a difficult man to reach."

It was Drew Flannery.

"Heavy caseload," I said.

"Have you spoken to Ray, recently?"

"Not since we were with you."

"I'm concerned," he said. "He never returned for his car. I called his cell numerous times but received no answer."

"Maybe he's away on business. He *is* a salesman."

"Ray never goes on business trips. All his selling is done right here. And don't you think after a week, at some point, he might need his car?"

"Have you called him at work?"

"They won't give out information about employees. I'm afraid something's wrong."

I had left Ray off by the front steps of his apartment after I'd given him a ride back from Drew's. When he assured me he was fine and promised to call, I watched him climb the steps and disappear inside. Telling myself he'd be okay, I drove back to my apartment half satisfied, but Drew was right, I didn't feel comfortable with this.

During the twelve years I'd been assigned to the detective bureau, I'd hung on to the hope of one day doing my own private investigating. Despite what one might think about the adventures of being a Manhattan detective, the daily duties soon become ordinary and routine, filled with phone calls, report writing, and tedious interviews. My idea of detective work meant working for myself, choosing my cases and investigating them my way, without the constraints of departmental regulations. In the past, I'd pushed the envelope more than once and caught Hell for it, but my *modus operandi* had almost always brought me a conviction, and I had no intention of changing it. Conversely, the salary and benefits the department offered were essential to a guy with a wife, two kids, and a thirty-year mortgage and to give up the retirement pension that awaited me would have been insane.

There had been occasions over the years, when I'd provided clandestine investigations for friends or acquaintances, strictly pro bono. I enjoyed a greater sense of satisfaction and achievement during these investigations and they helped me keep my dream alive. I hoped now there would be a simple explanation for Ray's disappearance. If there weren't, this would be one investigation I'd undertake with mixed feelings.

"I'll see what I can find out," I said to Drew.

I ended the call, dug Ray's cell phone number out of my wallet, and punched up the digits. It rang for a long while, but no one answered. Receiving no answer on the second try left me no choice but to drive out to Ray's.

Ray lived in a four-story apartment building in the Williamsburg section of Brooklyn. The house looked old, but well kept. It was painted bright yellow with white trim and had white wooden shutters on the windows.

An elderly woman was sweeping debris off the front steps of the building as I parked at the curb. When I got out and approached her, she said, "I ain't interested in buying nothin'." I smiled and showed her my shield and ID. "I'm looking for Mr. Deverol," I said, "Ray Deverol."

She was short and frail. Her silver hair was streaked with yellow and wrapped in a bun at the back of her head. She wore a flowered apron over a pink housedress, and it was hard not to notice she was missing several front teeth.

"He in trouble?"

"He's a friend," I said.

She took her time leaning her broom against the stair rail before she said, "I'm Addie Kellerman. I own the building."

I put on my best polite and patient face before I said, "Nice to meet you, Mrs. Kellerman. Is Mr. Deverol in?"

She leaned closer to me and lowered her voice. "I ain't seen him in more than a week. I hope nothing's happened to him. He's a good tenant—quiet, polite, never late with his rent."

"Is it usual for him to be away for a long while?"

"Sometimes he spends time with his brother, but he always lets me know when he's leaving and when he'll be back. Do you think something's wrong?"

I ignored her question and said, "May I see his apartment?"

She thought about that for a moment, then put a slender hand into the pocket of her apron, pulled out a key ring with a single key on it and handed it to me. I wasn't feeling good about things and almost afraid to go inside.

"First floor to the right," she said.

I climbed the steps and pushed open the front door. The main hallway was immaculately clean and smelled of disinfectant and fresh paint. A row of mailboxes was behind the door to my left. Inside Ray's box, I found a fitness magazine, several supermarket circulars, and an electric bill. I tucked them under my arm and walked to Ray's door at the end of the hall. I turned the key easily in the lock and I went in. The apartment was small but tidy. Ray was meticulous, as always. We'd had the neatest dorm room on campus. He had always kept his clothes neatly folded and his desk organized for studying. When he was through with his studies, he would carefully return his textbooks to a wall shelf where he kept them in alphabetical order. Occasionally, if I got back to the room before he did, I would mess up his clothes and rearrange his books just to gratify myself.

I gave the living room a cursory check; nothing seemed unusual. I dropped Ray's mail on a desk in the living room and walked into the bedroom. The bed had been neatly made. When I swiped my finger over the headboard, the accumulation of dust on my fingertip told me Mrs. Kellerman was right. Ray hadn't been there for a while. The drawers of his dresser were filled with underwear and shirts, and half dozen suits were hanging in his closet where several pairs of dress shoes and a pair of running shoes were lined up neatly on the floor below them. His cell phone was on a night table beside the bed. It seemed strange that a salesman would go anywhere without his cell phone. After trying a few buttons, the screen came to life. I checked his received calls and text messages and found several of the same numbers I recognized as Drew's, and the two calls I had made from the precinct before I had left. Other than those, Ray hadn't received any calls for at least a week. I closed the phone and left it where I'd found it, then went to the kitchen.

The kitchen was hygienic, everything in its place. On a wall calendar hanging behind the kitchen door, Ray had diligently marked off the days with an X, the last having been marked with the name *Drew*—the day we'd visited Drew at his mansion.

At the desk in the living room, I scanned through some of Ray's personal effects. I skimmed the pages of a small address book I'd found in a top drawer that contained company names, addresses, phone numbers and personal names of Ray's business contacts. As I flipped through the pages, a scrap of paper fluttered to the carpet. I picked it up and read the hasty scrawl—it was Drew Flannery's address. Below it was the address and phone number of "Island Health Club" on Long Island. Ray had always kept himself in good shape so it wouldn't be unusual for him to join a health club, but why out on Long Island? He could have his pick of gyms and fitness clubs closer to his apartment. I slipped the piece of paper between the pages of the address book and dropped it into my pocket. Back at the front steps, I returned the keyring to Mrs. Kellerman. I gave her my card after writing my cell number on the back, thanked her, and asked her to call me if she heard from Ray.

I wasn't satisfied with what I'd found or didn't find, so I decided to head out to the health club on the Island to see what I could find there. It took me more than an hour and I had to stop and ask directions a couple of times, but I was finally able to find it.

The place was a sprawling low-level building painted red with a blacktop parking lot on three sides. I parked the Chevy and walked across the lot to the front door. Inside, the main entrance looked like the lobby of a lavish resort hotel: palm tree planters stood in each corner of the room atop a glossy marble floor, six granite pillars held the vaulted ceiling up over a plush red circular sofa in the center of the room, which surrounded an effervescent fountain. Several full-length mirrors lined one wall, and several upholstered armchairs had been placed strategically between marble statues of Roman soldiers in full battle array. Above it all hung an elaborately designed brass and crystal chandelier. The thing was so expansive it nearly took my breath away when I looked up at it. I stood for a moment, not amazed by the lavishness that surrounded me, but by the menagerie of golden-bodied men and women passing through the lobby, strutting their physiques. No one could pass a mirror without admiring his or her self with unabashed adoration.

I walked to the reception desk on my right and waited for a young man behind the counter to finish his phone conversation. He was thin and pale, with short-cropped yellow hair. He certainly wasn't a billboard for the club's services and definitely not a member. I wondered whom he knew or did to get the job. He hung up the phone and turned to me with a friendly smile.

"Interested in membership?" he said.

"No thanks," I said. "I'm more of a 'Y' man."

He lost his smile and said, "How may I help you?"

34

I showed him my ID. He took it from me, brought it close to his face and squinted at my photo, then looked at me again, then back at the photo.

"I had fewer gray hairs then," I said.

"We have lots of members that are policemen," he said, handing my ID back to me. "Some are my friends."

"We're a friendly bunch," I said.

"What can I help you with?"

"I'd like to see your membership list."

"Do you have a warrant?" he said. I think he believed it was part of his job to ask that.

I leaned closer to him, and said, "Does a friend need one?"

He offered me a broad smile, then turned and walked to a computer at the end of the counter. I followed him and waited while he pecked at a keyboard in front of a computer monitor. When he finished with the keys, he slid the mouse to me and turned the monitor screen for me to see. I began to read a long list of names and addresses, both men and women, while my new friend leaned on the counter, smiling and looking at me more attentively than he needed to. I was beginning to feel uncomfortable and wondered what he was thinking.

I started at the top of the list and scrolled down slowly. When I reached the D's, Ray's name didn't appear. "Is this list up to date?" I said.

"Always," he said.

I continued scrolling until I came to a name and address I recognized. I scrolled through the rest of the list, and then turned the screen back toward him.

"Find what you're looking for?" he said.

"Yes," I said. "Thanks for your help."

"Anytime," he said. "If you change your mind about the membership, I'll be glad to handle you personally."

I nodded with a half-smile as I headed for the door, almost stumbling over a floor planter on my way out.

Back in the Chevy, I removed the address book from my pocket, took the scrap of paper from between the pages and read the address again; to be sure I was at the right place. I was. The trip hadn't been in vain. Ray's name wasn't on that list, but Monica Flannery's was. During the drive back to Manhattan, I kept asking myself, if Ray wasn't a member of the club and Monica Flannery was, what was the connection?

Traffic was heavier during the ride back. It took me almost two hours. When I arrived at the detective bureau, Monica Flannery was waiting for me at my desk. She looked even better than she had the first time I'd seen her. A tight skirt and heels make a man raise his eyebrows and look a little harder.

"Sorry," I said. "I wasn't expecting you."

I motioned for her to sit as I took my seat behind my desk.

"I decided to come at the last minute," she said.

She sat in a chair beside my desk and crossed one magnificent leg over the other.

"I'm concerned for Ray," she said, without the friendly smile she'd had before.

"We all are," I said.

"I don't know where to start."

I wasn't going to say, *try the beginning*, but I did.

She scowled at my sarcasm, got up and walked to the window and stood staring down onto 35th street for a long while. I leaned back in my chair and waited. There was something about her I didn't trust. I told myself to be careful.

"Ray and I are having an affair," she finally said, without turning.

I suppose I should have been shocked, but over the years I've heard it all and even a good friend's troubles become part of the routine.

"How long?"

"Nearly a year."

"Does Drew know?"

"We were careful," she said, "until a month ago when he became suspicious and confronted me. I denied everything at first, but when I realized he wasn't buying it, I confessed."

"What made him suspicious?"

"I don't know."

She came back to the chair, sat and crossed her legs again.

"I'm not here to confess my sins to you," she said. "I want to find, Ray. I'll pay whatever you ask."

"I'm not a private detective," I said.

I was having a tough time looking at her and concentrating on what she was saying. Her crossed legs were smooth with all the right curves and went all the way up to her solid hips and slender waist. My eyes kept wandering from her lips to her ample breasts, which quivered each time she made the slightest move. I was enjoying the show but beginning to feel self-conscious. I changed the subject quickly to mitigate the distraction.

"How long have you been a member of the Island Health Club?" I said.

She wasn't expecting that one.

"You've done your homework," she said.

"I'm trying to find Ray."

"I've been a member forever," she said.

"Is Ray a member?"

"It's an exclusive club."

"You mean just for the wealthy," I said.

She didn't react to that but instead, said, "Ray and I have met there on several occasions."

"A clandestine rendezvous," I said.

"I'm afraid for Ray," she said.

Chapter 4

"Two separate—yet most intimate things."
Edgar Allan Poe—Tamerlane

The Nova was the first new car Marlene and I purchased during our marriage. It became mine as part of the divorce settlement. Marlene got the Volvo. During her heyday, the Chevy made innumerable trips to school, Girl Scout meetings, music lessons and countless runs to the grocery store. Her silver paint had faded to a dull gray, and the dents and scrapes on her body were a testament to her years of loyal service. I had lost the front hubcaps long ago, but the rear ones were still shiny new. She was the only ride I had or could afford, so I babied her whenever we hit the road together. I had developed a genuine attachment to her and wondered when the time came if I'd be able to give her up. It might be like going through a second divorce.

After thirty minutes of inching my way through the Lincoln Tunnel and hoping the Chevy's engine wouldn't overheat, I finally emerged on the New Jersey side of the Hudson River and headed for Green ridge Borough, a small community in North Central New Jersey where I lived. Green ridge sits in the shadows of the Watchung Mountains, just north of Route 78, and prides itself on its revolutionary war history. I spent the first twenty-five years of my life there until I married and moved away. After my divorce, it seemed only natural to go back. After a nineteen-year absence, I discovered Green ridge hadn't changed much from the years I'd spent there growing up and I quickly found myself feeling like I had never left.

My apartment was on the second floor of a two-story building situated on a quiet street, not far from where I'd once lived. It was a convenient drive to Route 78, which took me east into Manhattan and to work each morning. Mrs. Jankowski, the widow who lived below me, owned the building. She had given me the apartment at a better than fair rent as a gesture of friendship to my mother, whom she played "Bingo" with every Friday night at St. Michael's Church. Besides, she'd said, she felt safer with a policeman living upstairs.

I needed the apartment since my divorce left me with no place to live. Marlene and I had sold our home of fifteen years, cleared our debts and split the remaining cash. The apartment consisted of a large front living room, a small kitchen, a bathroom, and one-bedroom at the rear. I'd furnished it according to my modest needs; although after I'd met Sandy, she suggested the apartment was cold and added a few things, like a ceramic vase with artificial flowers in it for the center of the coffee table, a large framed oil painting of the Italian Riviera for the living room wall, and a couple of black and white photographs to hang in my bedroom over my headboard. In the bathroom, she'd place several colored soap pieces in a seashell-shaped dish on the top of my toilet tank that she said would add fragrance. She assured me that all these things would give warmth and ambiance to the apartment.

As soon as I unlocked and opened the apartment door, I spotted Sandy in my kitchen working over the counter by the stove. She was wearing a pink sleeveless blouse and sandals. A kitchen towel was wrapped around her waist like an apron, and for an instant, it looked like she might not be wearing anything beneath it. She sometimes teased me that way when she was feeling frisky. Her auburn hair fell in soft folds against the milky whiteness of her shoulders and I felt that tinge of excitement, as I always did, whenever I saw her.

Sandra Sullivan was of the Connecticut Sullivan's; her father had been a prominent judge and her mother a rich wife. As an only child, she conceded, both parents pampered her until her father's untimely death brought a falling out between her mother and herself over the distribution of the estate. Things had soured so badly between them that she viewed it as a blessing when she was accepted into Harvard and was able to live away. I often wondered how a girl of Sandy's temperament could hook up with an average "Joe" like me. I suppose love is blind and opposites do attract. I gave up trying to figure it out. I only knew our relationship "clicked" in the short time we'd been together, and I was playing my cards right. I didn't want to screw it up.

I'd met Sandy during the several court appearances we'd been a part of over the years. As a defense attorney, she'd grilled me to toast more than once on the witness stand. Some men might be wary of a woman like Sandy, threatened by her good looks, independence, and intelligence; but it was those very attributes that attracted me to her, that, and the inexplicable good feeling I got whenever we were together.

Our first casual conversation, over lunch, had been more antagonistic than friendly. She told me she held a firm belief in civil obedience, which is why she decided to practice law. I told her, her beliefs probably stemmed from her Irish-Catholic upbringing and that I saw society and the law in a more realistically cynical way. She said I had a lot to learn about human kindness. I told her I didn't see much of that in my profession.

I closed the door behind me and walked toward the kitchen.

Sandy turned and flashed me a big smile, "Hey, Lovey," she said.

"Hey," I said.

In the ten months we'd been together, she'd persisted in calling me "Lovey" despite my objections. I already had one nickname I disliked and didn't want another. Just hearing the tag drained a bit of manhood from me, even coming from Sandy.

"It's just between us," she'd insisted. "It's affectionate and cute and it has meaning to me."

I relented.

So, "Lovey" went to the fridge to look for a beer. I found a can of Bud behind a quart of orange juice, popped the tab and leaned over and kissed Sandy on her cheek. A furtive glance at her rear revealed a pair of khaki short-shorts. I walked to the kitchen table, trying to conceal my disappointment.

"Why are you here?" I said. "And, what are you doing?"

All the while she'd been mixing something in a glass bowl with a wooden spoon.

"Court adjourned early," she said, "didn't feel like being alone."

Sandy and I hadn't gotten to the point in our relationship where one of us was willing to give up their apartment and move in with the other permanently, although there have been occasional sleepovers. Having been married for nineteen years, I wasn't averse to having someone share my bed, but since the divorce, I must admit, I enjoyed sleeping alone and felt a sense of freedom and territoriality that I relished, although I'd never mentioned this to Sandy.

I unbuttoned my shirt collar, removed my tie, hung it on the back of the chair and sat down with my beer. I took a swallow then said, "What's in the bowl?"

"Cookie dough, I'm making us chocolate chip cookies."

"There's a full box of Chips Delights in the cabinet right above your head," I said.

"It's not the same," she said.

I unclipped my gun from my belt and put it on the table.

"They say dark chocolate is an aphrodisiac," I said.

"I don't think that's been proven," she said.

From my pocket, I removed the address book I had found at Ray's apartment. If it became necessary, I'd run down every name and interview every person in it. It was an option I left open for now. On the inside front cover, I read the name, Allan Deverol, whom I remembered was Ray's brother. I closed the book, took a swallow of beer and rubbed my eyes with the heels of my hands.

"Caseload catching up?" Sandy said.

I tried not to discuss my work with Sandy, she hears enough of everyone else's problems all day, every day, but this was more personal and her advice had always been valuable to me.

"Remember that invitation I got a couple of weeks ago?" I said.

"Your friend Flannery," she said, "the surgeon."

She wiped her hands on her towel-apron and came up behind me and began massaging my neck and shoulders. It felt good. Her hands were small but strong. I rotated my neck to help relieve the tension.

"My buddy, Ray Deverol and I spent four years with him at college," I said.

"And?"

"And now, after not knowing where Ray's been for twenty years, he shows up in my life again and suddenly, he's gone."

"Gone How?"

"Gone, like—with the wind."

"Are you sure?"

"His car's been parked at Drew's since the night he drank too much and I drove him home. Drew called me this morning, said Ray never came back for the car and he'd been unable to reach him all week. That was enough concern for me, so I drove to Ray's apartment this afternoon. He had not been there since the day we were at Drew's."

"How close were you and Ray back then?"

"He saved my life during our senior year at college."

"That's a story I'd like to hear," Sandy said.

***

Twenty years ago, and I could go back to that night like it happened yesterday. I remembered every detail, like the bright amoeba shapes floating in the darkness, just a few at first, like tiny particles in the night sky, multi-colored and undefined, and how they increased in numbers, growing larger and more mottled, moving randomly in every direction and gradually changing the darkness from black to a dull gray. When I forced my eyes open, I found myself looking through the rear window of the Pontiac at an upside-down world. Through the cracked and snow-smeared glass, I saw Ray and Drew standing in the moonlit snow about thirty feet away, staring at the wreckage, wide-eyed with disbelief.

"Run back to the highway and get help!" I remembered Ray shouting.

Drew stood motionless, unable to take his eyes off the mound of twisted metal that was once his ride until Ray shoved him hard on his shoulder. "Go, now!" he said. Drew ran for the roadway, slipping and sliding a few times until he made it over the top of the embankment and vanished into the darkness.

I felt a throbbing and dizziness in my head and a biting pain in my back as I teetered on the brink of consciousness, trying to piece together the events of the past few minutes. Bleary images of Drew maneuvering his Pontiac Grand Am down Schooly's Mountain at a perilous twenty miles over the speed limit flashed seamlessly across my mind. I could see the thin covering of snow that blanketed the roadway and the occasional street lamp, which didn't do much to light the hairpin turns.

"Take it easy. I'd like to get there in one piece," Ray said to Drew.

"If we get there," I said from the back seat.

Drew's foot stayed on the accelerator.

"Cut the crap!" Ray said, this time meaning it.

Drew laughed. "I thought you jocks were the competitive type," he said.

We were on our way to the Stony Brook Tavern to celebrate my twenty-first birthday. I'd phoned my girlfriend, Sherilyn, and she'd agreed to meet me there by eight. When I told Ray and Drew she was bringing along her roommates, they became energized over the prospect of a night of carnal pleasures, a fantasy in their minds that had little to no chance of becoming a reality.

The beginning of our senior year had been our best time together. With the certainty of graduation in the coming months, and the hardest work behind us, we were all looking forward to the adventures of our lives ahead and as a result, concentrated a bit less on studying and a bit more on partying.

After Drew eased off on the accelerator and the Pontiac slowed to a reasonable speed, Ray looked back at me with hopeful exuberance. "Are they hot?" he said.

"Who?"

"The girls."

"They're Sherilyn's roommates," I said.

"So what?" Ray said. "She could have dogs for roommates."

"They're hot enough," I said. "But they won't be looking at you, even if you are wearing your American eagle jacket."

Ray's jacket was his prized possession. It was a brown leather Navy pilot's jacket his brother had sent to him from South Korea. Ray wore it only on special occasions or when he was trying to make an impression. In profile, on its back, was an American bald eagle, wrapped in the vibrant colors of Old Glory. I knew how much that jacket meant to Ray and liked to tease him about it.

"This jacket brings me good luck with the ladies," Ray said, adjusting the collar and brushing off specks of nonexistent dust from the front of it.

"Along with the lies you tell them," Drew said.

"Let me wear it tonight," I said, "as a birthday gift."

"No way," Ray said. "Nobody wears this jacket but me."

We sat in silence for almost a full minute, watching Drew negotiate the curves of the mountain roadway until Drew finally broke the silence. "I'll bet they won't show," he said.

"He means the girls," Ray said to me.

"Why would you think that?" I said to Drew.

"He's hoping," Ray said, "because he's afraid of girls."

"I wasn't afraid of your sister," Drew said.

Ray didn't have a sister, but he whacked the back of Drew's head, anyway.

"They'll be there," I said. "Just drive."

The last rays of sunlight had already faded behind the mountain crest, and I could see the fine snowflakes in the Pontiac's headlights. The car's big engine roared, and the occasional pothole shook the vehicle like an amusement ride. As we made the last turn at the bottom of the hill, I saw Ray stiffened his arms suddenly and take hold of the dashboard. At the same time, I felt the Pontiac swerve out from under us and I saw Drew turn the steering wheel hard, trying to regain control. But the slick roadway and inertia kept the car going straight off the road and into the woods. I grabbed the door handle and held tight as we started down an embankment, bouncing over a few large rocks and tree stumps. As I held on for my own life, I saw Ray slide helplessly across the front seat toward the passenger door and smack his head hard against the window, causing a web design to explode in the glass. I remember Drew pulling his body close to the steering wheel just before my head banged against the interior roof and everything began to spin. But the spinning wasn't in my head. The Pontiac was tumbling sideways down a steeper slope. I tried to grab for anything, but my arms flopped loosely in the surrounding space. Instinctively, I let out a scream, the shrillness of it mixing with the shouts from Ray and Drew and the sound of breaking glass and crunching metal and twigs and frozen branches snapping around us. I began bouncing around inside the car like a steel ball inside a pinball machine as we continued down the slope, until the car slid on its side, flipped over onto its roof and stopped. My last moment of consciousness was just after the back of my head slammed into the rear window.

When I looked down at my legs, I saw they'd been pinned between the twisted front seat and the side door. They felt like they had been buried in an anthill, not a welcomed sensation for a third-year track and field star. I tried pushing to free myself but was wedged tight. My arms were free, but it was a million miles to the door handle. I remember thinking: God, this can't be happening. Am I going to die? Am I paralyzed?

As I pushed hard with my arms, trying to squirm closer to the door, I heard a dull pop and a crackling sound. I looked away as blinding flames exploded under the car's hood, lighting the surrounding area and turning the snow a bright orange. The heat of panic surged through me even before the hot flames slapped against my back and spread into what was once the front seat. I saw Ray run toward the wreckage. I could hear him kicking at the side door while fighting the choking black smoke that filled the interior compartment and billowed out through the broken windows. I squeezed my stinging eyes shut and took short gasping breaths. Ray continued kicking at the door and began shouting to me that it would be all right just as the searching flames caught my jacket sleeve and travel up to my collar. I heard glass breaking and the grating of metal as Ray yanked the door back enough to reach in and slide his arms under mine and pull me through the hot steel. When I was free, he rolled me in the snow several times until the flames were extinguished. "It's okay, buddy," he said. "You're going to be all right."

The heat from the car interior quickly changed to a bitter chill as he dragged me over the cold ground away from the growing inferno. Although I was lying in wet snow, I could feel warm blood on my back, soaking through my shirt and jacket.

"Where you hurt?" Ray said.

"My back."

"Can you move?"

I nodded and sucked in several breaths of fresh air as Ray dragged me to a safe distance and propped me against the base of a tree. I helped as much as I could while he peeled off my burned and bloody jacket. My head was still spinning, but I was cognizant enough to realize it was no illusion when Ray removed his American eagle jacket and draped it around my shoulders. With blood oozing from the open wound in his right temple, his only concern was for me as he zipped the jacket up to my chin and raised the collar around my neck.

"Drew's gone for help," he said. "We'll be okay."

He sat beside me at the base of the tree with his arms wrapped around himself against the cold, wearing only his school sweatshirt, while I sat wearing his treasured jacket. We waited together; breathing hard and watching the flames engulf the Pontiac as the distant blare of sirens filled the night air.

***

"Wow. Sounds just like a scene out of a movie," Sandy said. "Some friend."

She walked her fingers down the side of my neck and worked them into my left shoulder.

"Ah, right there," I said.

She pushed her thumbs hard into a muscle in my upper back. I could feel it loosening. After a minute, she said, "Couldn't Ray have taken a vacation?"

"His dresser drawers are full, and his suits are hanging in his closet."

"What about a short business trip?"

She was trying to be helpful, but I turned and gave her a look.

"Sorry," she said.

She stopped massaging me and walked back to the stove, only slightly indignant.

"Ray's landlady told me she hadn't seen him for at least a week and he usually lets her know when he'll be out of town."

"Still listening," she said. I watched her butter a cookie sheet and begin to drop small mounds of cookie dough in several rows on the sheet using a tablespoon.

"Flannery's wife came to my office this afternoon and dropped a bomb on me. She and Ray—by her own admission—are having an affair. She blames Ray's disappearance on her husband, claims he threatened to kill Ray when he found out they were fooling around. She acted genuinely concerned."

"Do you think he'd kill Ray?"

"She thinks so."

"But do *you* think so?"

"I don't know."

"Have you confronted Flannery?"

"And accuse him of killing Ray?"

"That's not what I mean. Feel him out. Read his body language. If there's any guilt in him, you'll see it. You're good at that."

"Maybe," I said. "But I already know he's hiding something, the fact that his wife is involved with Ray. He'll look guilty to me no matter what."

"Cheating is immoral," she said, "but not a crime."

"True. But the question is—did he kill Ray?"

"Maybe he didn't kill Ray," she said.

"What do you mean?"

"Maybe he *had* Ray killed,"

"It's the same thing," I said.

"From the viewpoint of the law," she said. "But it's a lot less messy if someone else does it for you."

"True," I said, "but I'm having a tough time believing either."

"You're letting your emotions muddy your thinking."

"I know better. I'm not new at this."

"Nevertheless, you're letting it happen."

She was right. I felt myself struggling against it with every thought.

"Do you believe in his wife's story?"

"I can't discount it."

I finished my beer, got up and tossed the can into the wastebasket.

"If I don't come up with something tangible," I said, "I might have to believe her."

I took Sandy gently by her waist and pulled her close for a kiss. Before our lips met, she reached up with her spoon and playfully swiped a blob of cookie dough down the front of my nose. I wiped it away with my finger and spread it sensually across her mouth, then pulled her lips into mine. We kissed long and slow, smearing cookie dough over our lips and licking it off each other's face, absorbed in the passion of love and the sweetness of dark chocolate. When it was over, we were both breathing heavily.

"I need to put these cookies in the oven," she said, "ten to twelve minutes."

"Time enough," I said.

Chapter 5

*"These escape observation by dint of
being excessively obvious."*
Edgar Allan Poe—The Purloined Letter

Sandy didn't expect to stay the night, but she did. We made love, had chocolate chip cookies and milk, watched TV, made love again, and then fell asleep in each other's arms. In the morning, she rushed out of the apartment in frenzy, hoping to keep an eight o'clock court appearance. After she left, I shaved, took a quick shower and jumped into my street clothes. I was scheduled to work the four to twelve shift and was hoping to spend my day relaxing and rearranging my thoughts about Ray. I had just started a fresh pot of coffee when my cell phone rang. It was Drew.

"Did I wake you?" he said.

"Yes," I said.

"Sorry," he said, without sounding like he meant it. "I'm plagued by Ray's disappearance and was thinking we should get together to try to make some sense of it, from a personal standpoint, I mean."

"Did you remember something that might be helpful?"

"No. I just thought if we discussed things one on one, we might come up with something useful. Can you meet me at my home around noon?"

Drew was showing a natural concern for Ray, and at this point, I had no reason to doubt his sincerity, so I agreed to meet him. If he wanted to discuss the situation, I'd let him. Words can be powerful disclosures and I've learned that letting someone talk when they want to, often reveals more than was initially intended, if one knows how to listen.

It was a little before noon when I arrived at the mansion. Drew led me through the library to the patio at the rear of the house. He was dressed more conventionally, in a dark gray three-piece suit, white shirt, and light blue tie. It was unusually warm for October, so we sat around a wrought-iron table on uncomfortable wrought-iron chairs in the shade of a weeping willow that partially overhung the patio. At the bar in the library, he poured himself a red wine and brought one out to the patio for me.

"I feel responsible for what's happened," he said, handing me my glass and taking a seat opposite me. "I mean, getting us together after all these years."

"It was a good thing," I said. "I'm glad you did it."

"I don't understand how all this could happen. Ray seemed contented with his life here. Why would he just up and leave?"

"Why do you assume he left?"

"What other reason could there be? Kidnapping? There is no conceivable purpose for that. Ray's not a wealthy man."

"There are several possibilities," I said, "all ugly. I'll make a list if you want."

"I don't care to think along those lines."

"I have to," I said, "if we want to find Ray."

He nodded understandingly and sipped his wine.

"Well, it's unfortunate this had to happen now," he said, "just when we were getting reacquainted. Time has taken a lot away from us."

Like you took Sherilyn away from me, I almost said aloud.

I thought I'd lost *that* memory forever, but seeing Drew again brought it back to the forefront of my consciousness. The animosity I'd held for him lay dormant inside me all these years, and to my surprise, resurrected itself upon my seeing him again.

It's funny how revisiting good memories can rekindle bad ones as well.

By the end of our graduating year, it was no secret things were fizzling out between Sherilyn Fasano and me. Throughout our two years of steady dating, we had had our occasional break-ups but had always managed to rekindle our romance. It had become routine with us; at least it had with me. I never believed we would permanently split. I guess Sherilyn began to think differently. It was during our alleged final break-up that Drew started dating Sherilyn behind my back, even before the paint was dried, so to speak. I suppose I could have blamed Sherilyn as well. I'll never know what convinced her to hook up with Drew. I even hated her for a while, but got over that quickly. I guess when you have fond feelings for someone, you're inclined to overlook their transgressions. Besides, who thought shy, unobtrusive Drew Flannery could steal anyone's girl away? And it was how he'd tried to hide it from me that compounded my anger. He had been seeing her clandestinely for more than a month and never spoke a word about it. I suppose he could have been honest and confronted me with it, but he chose to be ignoble and secretive. I felt betrayed and humiliated and hated him for it when I found out.

It was of little comfort to me when Sherilyn split with Drew soon after graduation and moved—for whatever reason—with her new boyfriend to Wisconsin. She had been out of my life and mind since then, and I had no desire to resurrect her memory.

I sat back and sipped my wine, telling myself I was being stupid for even thinking about Sherilyn. I had been through a nineteen-year marriage, two kids and a divorce, and in all those years never gave Sherilyn a thought. I wouldn't let it bother me now.

"I feel better that you're involved," Drew said. "Otherwise, this would have fallen into the hands of the police alone, probably wind up unsolved. Have you discovered anything helpful?"

"Not much."

"Have you officially reported him missing?"

"No."

"Why not?"

"I think he'll show up on his own."

I lied.

"Why would you think that?"

"He's probably on a binge. We both know how much he likes to drink."

"How can you be sure? We don't know if he's done this before. We haven't seen him in years."

I had to keep Drew at ease. I didn't want him to think I was suspicious of him or that I knew about his wife's affair with Ray. Sandy was right. I would see guilt in him if there were any. So far, I hadn't. He seemed as concerned for Ray as he had been, and my hypothesis of the situation hadn't changed. I still didn't buy the fact that he would kill Ray over a woman, but I'd learned a long time ago how good he was at being deceitful.

"Why are you so complacent?" he said. "Ray was a good friend to both of us."

"I'm on it," I said. "And as far as we know, no crime's been committed."

He thought about that, and then asked, "Have you got anything to go on?"

"Not a thing."

I lied again.

He stood up and began pacing the patio, drawing his eyebrows together and stroking his mustache while mulling over what I'd just said. I tried to read his face. He looked truly concerned, but there was that trickery he possessed and I wouldn't fall for it again. Maybe I was being overly cautious, but as far as I was concerned, it was the right thing to do. I wouldn't let my guard down. When he was ready, he stopped pacing and turned to me. "You could be looking in the wrong places," he said.

"What does that mean?" I said.

"Try looking in the most unlikely places, places that are *'excessively obvious'*. That's Poe's theory."

I hoped I wouldn't be sorry when I asked, "What is Poe's theory?" I knew Drew could go off on a tangent when it came to discussing Poe, giving long and boring recitations on his favorite subject. But to my surprise, he finished his drink, placed his glass on the table and answered quickly. "For example...who would look for something of value placed in a wastebasket? Most people wouldn't look there because they wouldn't expect it to be there, therefore that would be the safest place for it."

"Right under their noses," I said.

"Exactly. *Excessively obvious.*"

"But I didn't find any clues in Ray's wastebasket."

"Did you look in every place; every place that you thought was not worth looking into?"

"I was thorough," I said. "Have you searched Ray's car?"

He raised his eyebrows. "I never gave it a thought."

"Ray's 'wastebasket' has been parked outside your door all this time, and you never thought to look in it?"

"I suppose Poe's theory is correct," he said. "Let's look."

He walked hurriedly into the library and removed a set of keys from the top drawer of a desk. As I followed him out to the parking area where Ray had left his Nissan, I wondered how Drew had gotten Ray's keys. I didn't remember Ray handing them over, and if he had, how was he able to get into his apartment after I'd left him off? I suppose he could have had a spare, or borrowed Mrs. Kellerman's master key, or left his door unlocked. Or maybe I hadn't seen Drew coax the keys from Ray to prevent him from driving home in his liquid state. All reasonable possibilities. I made a mental note.

Drew unlocked the driver's door, then reached across and unlocked the passenger side for me. While he checked behind the visors, I opened the glove box and most of its contents spilled out onto the floor.

"Not like Ray," I said.

I gathered up the items and spread them on the seat between us. I saw nothing that didn't belong in a glove box. As we rummaged through the items, Drew picked up a small spiral-bound notepad, flipped it open and read the penciled notes inside. "This could be something," he said, handing it to me. On the first page had been written the date, time and number of an American Airlines flight to Los Angeles.

"I knew it," Drew said. "He's running away."

"From what?"

"He's getting help for his drinking problem. They've got some good clinics out there."

"We've got good ones here," I said. "I'll check the validity of this information later."

He looked at me, surprised. "What do you mean? We found it in Ray's car, didn't we?"

"Circumstantial."

"On his notepad."

"Doesn't prove he wrote it."

I tore the page from the pad and put it in my wallet. "You haven't learned much from those Poe mysteries," I said.

Chapter 6

"He was a goodly spirit—he who fell."
Edgar Allan Poe—Al Aaraaf

Mike Briggs was chief of detectives. He stood six feet-four and cultivated a gray handlebar mustache that rested symmetrically beneath his beak-like nose and matching head of gray hair. His biceps were bigger than his thighs, and in the twelve years that I'd worked for him, I'd seen him kick more than a few asses when necessary. Briggs took his profession seriously and ran the detective bureau by his own set of rules. He was as hard as nails and strictly by the book, yet he maintained a degree of compassion and understanding few in his position possessed. Because of his hard-nosed approach to criminal justice, opinions of him varied greatly but were typically more favorable among the men that worked for him than his superiors. Despite his tough reputation, any cop that was a part of his team was glad he was. Through the years, I found him to be a friend when I needed one. This morning he was wearing a dark blue three-piece suit over a gray shirt and a pastel patterned tie, loose at the collar.

Briggs's office was the largest one in the homicide bureau and the most lavishly furnished. *Rank has its privileges.* Three large windows let in light from 35th street, so he seldom had to use the overhead fixtures. A large mahogany desk sat in front of the windows with an upholstered high-back chair behind it for Briggs to park his huge frame into comfortably. Two visitor chairs sat obliquely in front of the desk. The desk itself was functional but neat, a computer monitor and keyboard were in easy reach and several framed photographs of his daughter and his grandchildren were placed strategically on one corner. On a far wall hung framed documents attesting to

Briggs's academic achievements in police work, and the numerous awards he had received over his long career. Several metal filing cabinets were to the right of the desk, over which hung a large black-and-white photograph of the New York City skyline. A large potted plant stood in the opposite corner. All this sat atop a thick beige carpet.

As I stood in front of his desk, he dropped a manila file folder in front of me. When I opened it and read the first page, I felt the blood drain from my face. I placed the folder back on his desk and sat down. I took a deep breath to prepare myself for what was to come. That first page had hit me like an uppercut. I knew the knockout would come from Briggs.

"Imagine my surprise," he said, "when we dusted this guy's apartment and found your fingerprints all over the place."

He eased himself into his desk chair, leaned back and waited for my explanation.

"He's an old friend," I said.

He leaned forward again and rested his forearms on his desk.

Here it comes, I thought.

"Your old friend is a drug peddler," he said. Briggs didn't sugar coat anything when it came to police work. I sat for a moment staggered by his accusation until I was finally able to ask, "How sure?"

"Enough to get an indictment."

I took out my handkerchief and wiped the perspiration from my face and forehead.

"We're keeping it quiet for now. Upstairs wants it that way until we know how big this thing is. You know these things can get ugly, sometimes bringing down some pretty important people."

He leaned closer and looked at me with sudden concern. "Christ, Max, you look like you're about to have a heart attack," he said.

He unlocked a side drawer of his desk, removed a pint of Jack D and a shot glass, and poured one. "That's a working dossier of your friend's criminal activities," he said, sliding the drink across the desk to me.

"This doesn't make sense."

"It doesn't have to," he said. "You've been around long enough to know there are no surprises on this job."

Maybe a few, I thought, like seeing Ray Deverol's name on the first page of that dossier. It was like getting a piece of steak caught in your throat and not being able to cough it up before the panic hits.

"Your friend is choirboy clean," Briggs said.

"Ray's no criminal."

"He is now," Briggs said. "Tell me something I don't know about this guy, Max."

I downed the shot, waited for the burn to subside than said, "We were buddies in college. I haven't seen him in more than twenty years until I ran into him a couple of weeks ago. Ray's unmarried. He lost his father when we were at school. I don't know if his mother is still living. He has one brother, at least he did. Today he's a sales rep for a pharmaceutical firm."

"Hoffman-Weir Pharmaceutical, across the Hudson," Briggs offered.

I made a mental note.

"It was their suspicions that brought your friend to the surface," he continued. "The local police filled us in. We had a meeting with their company bigwigs. Somebody's skimming off the top of certain inventories. Our investigation led us to your boy. He works with an insider. We got him on the hook, too."

His enthusiasm reminded me of the unbridled eagerness I'd had during my rookie years.

"I figure since you're a cop, you have access to channels I don't have, and I just might come up with some info on your friend."

I downed the rest of my drink, turned on the stool and rested my elbows on the bar. I looked out through the plate-glass windows onto the busy sidewalks of 7th Avenue, at the people scurrying by and the bumper-to-bumper traffic in the street beyond them. I certainly didn't need another partner. I had Danny Nolan and a corral full back at the precinct at my disposal. But anything or anybody that would help me find Ray was welcome, especially with Briggs eyeballing me.

"My caseload keeps me busy," I said, "so any bit helps. I don't need another partner, but if you come up with something tangible, give me a call. If I think it's worth something, I'll trade you something back. Okay?"

"Fair enough," he said.

I turned back to the bar, wrote my cell phone number on a napkin and gave it to him. "Use this number," I said. "Don't call the precinct."

"Sure," he said.

"Do you have anything you want to tell me now?"

"The doc is squeaky clean," he said. "Leaves for the hospital at the same time each morning, comes home the same time each night. His surgical staff and the people at the hospital love him. His reputation is impeccable. Is there anything more you can tell me about your friend?" he added.

"Monica Flannery can update you more about Ray than I can," I said. "I haven't seen him in a long while. That's what makes this tough for me. I only have his past to go on."

"She hasn't told me much," Montgomery said, "only that he's an old friend of her husband whom she's become fond of.

and is concerned for his safety. It may go deeper than that. It's obvious her marriage is on the rocks."

"See if you can come up with anything recent on Ray Deverol," I said. "You may find a loose tie to Dr. Flannery."

"Any suggestions?"

I got up and dropped a ten on the bar.

"Ray Deverol is a missing person, a dead person, and a secret lover," I said. "Take your pick and follow one or all of those leads."

I left Montgomery with his White Russian and drove out to Hoffman-Weir Pharmaceutical. Despite Briggs's admonishment, I was determined to find out just how much trouble Ray might be in and establish in my mind if he was running from the law, which, as far as I was concerned, was the preferred alternative. Knowing Drew, the jealous husband theory wasn't sitting right with me. There are other ways of dealing with an unfaithful wife other than murder—although murder is certainly one.

I'd phoned the drug company earlier and spoke to Mr. Fisk, the distribution manager, who told me he had spoken to the police more than enough times but was happy to answer any questions I had and would be available this afternoon. With Briggs's hand-off policy, I'd have to be cautious. I didn't want anything I did to get back to him.

Hoffman-Weir was a huge two-building complex in Secaucus, New Jersey. One building was used for manufacturing, the other for distribution. I'd learned from the Internet that they manufactured nearly every drug known to medical science and distributed them worldwide.

I pulled up to the main gate and showed my shield to the security guard at the gatehouse.

"Detective Graham," I said, "for Mr. Fisk."

He checked his clipboard. "Building number two," he said as he pointed across an expansive parking lot. I thanked him, waited for him to raise the iron bar in front of me, and then drove through to the parking area.

I parked in a visitor's space and walked toward a large brick building with an enormous red H/W on its facade. As I opened the door to the lobby entrance, a uniformed guard sitting behind a desk looked up at me as I approached, "Detective Graham?"

"For Mr. Fisk," I said.

He asked to see my ID.

After I showed it to him, he picked up a phone, spoke into it briefly, and then hung up. "Are you carrying a gun?" he said.

I nodded.

"You'll have to leave it with me."

I took my Colt from my holster, removed the magazine and cleared the chamber. I gave him the gun and the magazine and he locked it in a side drawer of his desk, scribbled out a receipt and handed it to me, then pointed to an elevator across the lobby. "Third floor, then take a left," he said.

When the elevator doors opened, Fisk was waiting for me. He was a short, balding man with dark rim glasses and a wrinkled gray suit. He weighed more than he should and stood with an unbalanced posture, as if he were about to tumble forward over his own feet.

"Detective Graham," he said, "Bill Fisk." He extended his hand without a smile. I took it. It felt like a damp washcloth. We started down a tiled hallway toward a double door entrance.

"On the phone, you expressed interest in our distribution process," he said. "We're one of the largest in the world," he added, proudly. He pushed back the double doors. and I found myself in a maze of machinery, boxes and wall-to-wall employees. The tableau resembled the floor of the New York Stock Exchange. A Roller coaster type setup carried various size boxes on rollers from one side of the large room and back. One long table stood against a wall beneath a row of barred windows where a regiment of employees diligently filled orders. Each wore a white lab coat and a pair of clear plastic gloves. Reading from a list of invoices from a computer screen hanging on the wall in front of them, each took what resembled a plastic shopping cart and rolled through shelves of medical stock set up in rows like in a library; the place was as noisy as Times Square. I wondered if those carts had horns and turn signals. We stood watching the activity for nearly a full minute until Fisk leaned close to my ear and spoke above the noise: "As chaotic as all this looks, Detective, it is all very well co-coordinated. It's a system that has worked well for us for years."

He motioned for me to follow him to a small cafeteria just off the main room where it was quieter. The room was painted a relaxing green. There was a sofa against one wall and a table and chairs beneath a large glass window that separated it from the main room so one could watch the constant activity without the noise. A small sink and counter with a coffee machine on it filled one corner. I sat at the table.

"I don't know what else you need to know," Fisk said. "Your people have been here more than once. Coffee?" He brought two Styrofoam cups from the counter to the table.

"I'm here to do a follow-up," I said.

He filled both cups from a carafe which had already been filled with coffee. He sat down with his and placed my cup in front of me. The coffee smelled burned.

"Does each packager work with one salesperson?" I said.

"Oh no," Fisk said. "Each works with several. We have over one hundred salespeople in the metro area alone."

He grabbed three packets of Sweet 'n' Low from the container on the table and consecutively tore each one open and dumped its contents into his coffee cup, then slid the remaining packets toward me.

"Black," I said. "Do they always work with the same salesperson?"

"As a rule, unless there is a vacation scheduled or an illness, it's easier to maintain quality control," he said.

There were no coffee stirrers available, so he gave his coffee a quick stir with his forefinger. "We pride ourselves on quality control," he said.

"Who handles Mr. Deverol's orders?" I said.

"I believe your office has that information," he said.

"I'll need it for my records. My superior wants assurances I was here."

He took a drink from his cup, then got up and walked to a wall phone. He punched up a few numbers, spoke in a low voice, then hung up and came back to the table. "You can pick up a folder of that employee's name and work record at the lobby desk on your way out," he said.

"Thanks," I said.

I gulped some coffee and screwed up my face at its bitterness. Fisk looked at me quizzically.

"Quality control," I said.

***

The name in the employee folder was: Michael Dean Hamlin. He lived just ten minutes from Hoffman-Weir. I turned off the main highway and drove the secondary roads looking for Durant Street. After twenty minutes, I realized I'd passed the same Exxon station three times. When I pulled in and asked directions, the attendant told me Durant was a dead end just two blocks on the left. I thanked him and headed that way.

Number forty-two was in the middle of a row of two-story brick buildings that looked pretty run down. I parked at the curb in front and walked up the stairs. The name on the mailbox told me Mike Hamlin lived on the first floor, 1B. I opened the inner door and stepped into the hallway. There was a bicycle with two flat tires against a wall and a shopping cart filled with newspapers under the stairs. I wrinkled my nose at the armpit smell as I walked toward 1B at the end of the hall. I knocked and waited.

It seemed like a full minute passed before the door opened a few inches and a shadowed face appeared. Before I got a word out, the door slammed shut and a commotion erupted behind it. I turned the knob and swung the door back. As I did, something flew passed my head and shattered against the doorframe. When I looked up, a skinny kid was swinging a table lamp like a club as he rushed me. He looked about twenty, with short-cropped blonde hair and a clean-shaven face. He was wearing black sweatpants, a black pullover shirt, and black socks, but no shoes.

I got low and met him head-on, knocking him and the lamp to the ground. He kicked free, scrambled to the other side of the room on all fours and came back at me. He was tough for his size and weight, and when he hit me; I landed on the carpet with him on top of me. I caught his arm in mid swing when he tried to throw a punch at my face and brought my right around to his jaw. I saw him grimace and felt his body relax. I got to my feet thinking it was over, but he jumped up and charged me again. I feinted to one side and watched his head crack against a windowsill. In a stupor, he struggled to his feet, picked up a metal wastebasket and held it in front of him like a shield. His offense quickly turned to defense.

"Back off, dude, or I'll kill you," he said.

I put my arms in the air in a non-threatening way. Experience has taught me to avoid violence, if possible, even though it's part of the job. I'm comfortable with my ability to handle most confrontations. Years of working out at the police gym have kept me in good enough shape to defend myself, although occasionally I lose my Italian temper and go too far. I'm still working on the temper thing.

"Take it easy," I said, "I just want to talk to you." He was breathing heavily and I could see he was terrified of something far worse than me.

"I told those cops all I know," he said.

"I'm not the cops," I said.

He moved toward me with the wastebasket out in front of him, and I wasn't sure if he intended to get a closer look at me or bash in my head. I prepared for the latter.

"Who are you?"

"I'm a friend of Ray Deverol's."

"How do I know that?"

"Why would I lie? If I was a cop, I'd say so."

He looked at me intently, taking his time deciding whether to believe me. When he was satisfied that I might be telling the truth, he put the wastebasket down. I lowered my arms.

"I just need to ask you some questions," I said.

He pulled a handkerchief from his back pocket and pressed it against the bleeding cut on the right side of his forehead> Then he walked to the door, glancing back at me several times to assure himself he was doing the right thing. He turned the deadbolt and hooked the security chain. "I gotta be careful," he said, stuffing the bloody handkerchief back into his pocket.

He sat on the sofa, took a cigarette from a pack on the coffee table and tried to light it with trembling fingers. The match danced like a firefly on a diving board. This guy was either scared stiff, or he had a bad habit. After playing "catch me if you can" with the end of the cigarette, he finally managed to light it, took a long draw and settled back. I sat in an armchair opposite him.

"Why should I help you?" he said.

"I'm trying to find Ray."

He took another long drag, letting the smoke out slowly and studying it as it encircled his head and dissipated into the ceiling. I waited while he decided whether he wanted to be cooperative. When the smoke cleared he said, "I should've never got hooked up with that dude."

"Why did you?"

"I need the cash."

"Yeah, there's never enough. How deep you in?"

"Ray told me it would be a cinch, easy money for both of us, he said, and now, cops are all over me and Ray's nowhere to be found."

"Do you know where he might be?"

He took another drag on the cigarette and shook his head.

"I'd appreciate anything you can tell me."

"I told them cops everything. They said if I helped 'em, they'd go easy on me. Now they want me to sit back until they're ready to send me to jail."

"Why didn't you split?"

"I know better."

"Why'd you slam the door?"

"I'm scared, man. Somebody might be trying to keep me quiet. I don't know who else is hooked up."

He'd just answered my next question: *Who else is involved?*

"How does it work?"

"I went over this with the cops."

"I told you, I'm not the cops. I'm trying to find Ray."

He snuffed out his cigarette in what looked like the top of a mayonnaise jar, and after another short flame dance, lit a second one. I waited while he removed the handkerchief from his pocket again and pressed it against his wound. When he was satisfied he had survived the onslaught, he dropped the handkerchief onto the coffee table and decided to talk to me.

"I was a packager for Ray for almost a year," he said. "We got to know each other pretty good. One day he tells me we can make some fast, bucks. All I got to do is pad up his order with more than it says on the invoice."

"How'd you know what to pad and how much?"

"It made no difference. As long as there was a surplus, Ray said anything more than the invoice order was money in our pockets."

"Was there something in particular that you packaged more of?"

"You name it, cocaine to cough syrup."

"How's the stuff get to the street?"

"My job was to make up the package, what Ray did at his end was on him."

"What was your payoff?"

"Fifty-fifty."

"Regularly?"

"Sometimes I waited a month, sometimes less. From the time the invoice is submitted to the time of delivery can sometimes take as long as a week. Ray slipped me the cash when he came to the distribution center."

I almost felt sorry for this kid. He had done something stupid and gotten in way over his head, thinking he could make an easy buck.

74

"Anything else?"

"That's all I know, man."

I walked to the door and unlocked it. When I pulled the door open, I paused with my hand on the knob and looked back at him. "Didn't you think you might get caught?" I said.

"Ray said he could doctor the papers so no one would ever get wise," he said. "It was a sweet setup."

"Not sweet enough," I said and closed the door behind me.

Chapter 8

"Romance, who loves to nod and sing,
With drowsy head and folded wing."
Edgar Allan Poe—Romance

I met Sandy for lunch at Branigan's on 54th Street, which was our favorite haunt. It offered a theme of historic Americana and catered to a diversity of age groups from college students to the elderly. Sandy and I felt comfortable somewhere in the middle. Its walls were covered in knotty pine, varnished to a soft gloss and decorated with framed posters of historic U.S. headlines from magazine covers and newspapers that had long ago ceased publication. The stuffed and mounted head of a seven-point buck, which hung over the main entrance, seemed a bit out of place with the present motif. It had been displayed there by the elder Branigan, who had been an avid hunter and maintained over the years by Pete as a token of his father's memory. A well-kept mahogany bar ran along the entire length of one wall, with a brass foot rail and brass bar stools with red vinyl seats. Opposite the bar, the dining room offered patrons their choice of round tables covered with linen tablecloths, or dimly lit booths at the perimeter. The kitchen served lunch and dinner seven days a week, touting the best Clam chowder in Manhattan.

Joe Branigan opened the bar back in the forties and ran it as a local watering hole. After his passing, his son Pete inherited the place, added the dining room and kitchen and turned it into a popular neighborhood eatery. Pete Branigan was around my age, but with the addition of an overextended belly, cultivated by years of over sampling his culinary offerings from his kitchen. His hair was gray and coarse, with a part on the left side that could no longer be defined due to the sparseness of hair at the top. His gray beard was closely cropped and ran from temple to temple and around his chin, but with no mustache. Pete and I had gotten to know each other fairly well over the years and I was regarded as a regular, a distinction that carried with it several perks, like the occasional free drink and Pete's attention to one's dining comforts. His amiable personality was one trait that helped make his business successful. Whenever he spotted me, he'd saunter over to my table to say hello. I think he liked the idea of having a cop eat in his place regularly and hoped I would convince other members of the city's finest to do the same. I never bothered.

The place wasn't crowded this afternoon, which was unusual for a Friday. In the twenty minutes I'd been waiting for Sandy, I'd place our lunch order with a young waitress, then sat with a watchful eye on the kitchen door, expecting Pete to appear at any minute. He didn't.

I was beginning to get fidgety when Sandy finally appeared through the front door. She looked excitingly attractive as I watched her approach the booth where I was sitting. She was wearing a dark gray pantsuit with light gray pinstripes and a white blouse with an open collar. A pair of patent leather heels defined the classy lady she was.

"Sorry I'm late," she said.

"Always worth the wait," I said.

She slid into the booth across from me.

"I ordered club sandwiches and a Zinfandel for you," I said.

She leaned over and kissed my cheek.

A young waitress brought Sandy's wine and a beer for me. She set the drinks down with a smile, turned and shimmied away. She had a great face and a body that wouldn't quit. I tried not to look, but Sandy caught me and I thought I was in for it until she took a sip of wine and said, "Have you heard from your friend, Ray?"

"No," I said, "but I found his brother on the Internet. When I phoned, he was more than willing to talk to me. He lives in North Jersey. I'm driving up after lunch. Wanna come?"

"Can't. Court reconvenes at two."

I told her about my meeting with Briggs and Ray's alleged infringement with the law and updated her on how things had gotten more complicated. She looked at me sympathetically and reached over and rubbed my cheek with the back of her hand. "That must have been a shock," she said.

"One hundred K," I said, "and Briggs tripped the switch."

"Why would Ray get involved in such a thing?"

"Don't know."

"People can change in twenty years."

"I guess he needed money, or just wanted *more*."

My beer had a high head on it, but I found my way through it and took a good drink.

"Would you like me to talk to the DA," she said, "find out what his intentions are?"

"Thanks, but I need to keep this low-key. Briggs doesn't want me snooping. Besides, I don't even know if Ray's breathing."

She reached across the table, picked up my napkin and handed it to me. "Your upper lip," she said. I liked it when she showed those little concerns for me, although sometimes it made me feel like she was being too maternal. I took the napkin and wiped my mouth.

There was a lull in our conversation while we waited for our lunch. I fixed my eyes on Sandy as she brought her glass to her lips and sipped, delicately. She looked radiant and nearly perfect, almost like an advertisement in a gourmet wine magazine. Although I had genuinely loved Marlene, I kept thinking about how I was able to love Sandy, who was, in many ways, the antithesis of Marlene. I don't mean that unfavorably. Marlene was unpretentious, understanding, warm and easy in temperament. Sandy possessed those same attributes but chose to display them more selectively. She could be steadfastly autonomous when she needed to be, but as helpless as a kitten when she wanted to be. I was trying hard to make our relationship work. Seeing her now made me feel warm and tender and glad she was a part of my life.

"When was the last time I told you I love you?" I said.

"I'll check my calendar."

"You look beautiful sitting there with the pale red of the Zinfandel reflecting in your eyes."

"Thanks," she said, "but you're beginning to sound like a soap opera."

"I'm just saying what I feel."

"You mean you're looking for a feel."

I brought my hand up over my heart. "Oh, that hurt," I said. "An enchanted moment destroyed by incredulity."

She smiled and reached over and rubbed my cheek again. "You should have been a romance novelist," she said.

Our waitress came back with our lunch dishes balanced on one arm. Before she could set them on the table, one of her ample breasts disrupted the delicate stability, and a dish slid forward and was about to make a crash dive onto the table. I reached out, and with a quick balancing act, managed to catch it. "Saved!" I said.

"That was quick," the waitress said.

"I used to be a juggler in college," I joked.

She laughed as Sandy took her plate from her and I set mine in front of me.

"You look more like a wrestler," the waitress said, "with those big arms."

I glanced at Sandy. There was a hint of jealous indignation on her face, and I could see she was about to intervene on her own behalf.

"He ran," Sandy said.

The girl gave Sandy a bewildered look.

"He didn't wrestle in college," Sandy continued, "he ran."

The girl's brow wrinkled with confusion. "He ran?" she repeated.

"He was fast," Sandy said. "They even called him, 'Jet'."

She started in on her sandwich without offering any more information. I knew where she was taking this.

The waitress looked at me. "You mean…like, you ran away?"

I couldn't help smiling, and at the risk of evoking Sandy's wrath, I said, "I ran track at college," then looked cautiously at Sandy for her reaction. There was none.

The waitress leaned her head to one side and clicked her tongue. "Duh…" she said, "I feel so stupid."

"It's a bit confusing," Sandy said, and then gave me a furtive smile.

I took a bite of my sandwich and knew enough to say no more.

We spent an easy thirty minutes enjoying our lunch. Just before we were about to leave, Pete Branigan walked through the swinging doors of the kitchen. He spotted us immediately and walked toward our booth. He was wearing jeans, a sweatshirt and work boots, which wasn't his usual attire when he was working in the dining room. A ball cap was cocked precariously on his head.

"My favorite regular couple," he said.

"I'll bet you say that to all the girls," Sandy said.

He leaned down and kissed her cheek, then reached over and shook my hand.

"You two look like newlyweds," he said.

"Yeah, right," Sandy said.

"You say that with trepidation," Pete remarked.

"With caution," Sandy said.

Pete had cast caution to the wind when it came to matrimony. He had been married and divorced three times to women almost half his age and scratched his head each time, trying to figure out why the marriages failed. At the risk of being a *buttinsky*, I once suggested, if he had a penchant for younger women, he could be with them without having to marry them, but he said he liked being married, and to younger women, and he'd keep trying until he got it right. I shook my head and offered no more about it.

"How was lunch?" Pete said.

"The salad was limp, but the croutons were good," Sandy joked.

"That's the last straw," Pete said, "that chef's out of here."

He straightened his cap and slid into the booth beside me.

"Easing up on the dress code around here?" I said.

He looked down at himself as if to be sure he understood my reference.

"Problem in the kitchen. Just can't get a good plumber when you need one. They're too damn independent. Make too much money, if you ask me."

"Like city detectives," Sandy said.

"Without the money part," I added.

"Any luck finding your friend?" Peter said.

I shook my head.

"Hell of a thing," he said, "somebody just disappearing like that. Reminds me of that kid that went missing a few years ago in Connecticut. They searched Statewide for weeks, helicopters, dogs; you name it, only to find her in a shallow grave not more than a hundred yards from where she lived. Sometimes you got to look close to home," he said, "It's easy to miss the obvious."

"I've heard that theory before," I said.

"I'm sure Ray will show up safe and sound," Sandy said, in an attempt to change the subject and offer me solace.

"Sure," Pete said, "Although it's different from adults. Sometimes they don't want to be found."

I was hoping Ray wanted to be found.

After we left Branigan's, I walked Sandy to the steps of the courthouse, kissed her and told her I'd call her when I got home, then I walked to my Chevy and drove out of the city. I made my way onto Route 78 and headed toward the town of Clinton; a quaint New Jersey community situated off Route 31. I remember Ray talking about his younger brother, Allan, who had been in the Navy while Ray and I were at college. I'd never met Allan, but I'd seen the photograph Ray carried of him in his military uniform and remembered Ray's proud smile each time he passed the photo around. I was sure Briggs had informed Allan Deverol of the situation and detectives, McClusky and Nolan, had questioned him extensively. Now it was my turn.

I estimated the drive would take a couple of hours, but it would be worth it if I could get an insight into Ray's recent years. I slid a Brubeck CD into the player and listened to *Take Five*. Joe Morello was working his sticks to the unusual time signature, and I tapped my fingers on the steering wheel to try to duplicate it. I couldn't.

An hour later, I exited Route 78 and drove US highway 31 until I saw the sign for Clinton. On Main Street, I passed the Red Mill Museum, a 200-year-old Clinton landmark. With its shimmering lake and cascading waterfall, its beauty and serenity reminded me of a Currier and Ives lithograph, particularly since the leaves were turning their fall colors.

I continued through quiet tree-lined streets in an area that looked more rural than suburban; until I arrived at the address I wanted. I pulled to the curb in front of one of those small colonial houses that seems to have been built more than a hundred years ago, and although the house looked sound, it appeared to have been neglected in recent years. The graying paint around the windows was stained and peeling, and several of the green shudders were askew. I walked up the walkway to the front door and pressed the doorbell. The door opened almost immediately, and I found myself looking at a man about my age with a striking resemblance to Ray. His hair was silver gray, and he cultivated a pencil-thin mustache situated more above his upper lip than under his nose. He wore a maroon sweater vest over a brown shirt, khaki pants, and tan suede-hiking boots. "Detective, Graham," he said with a cordial smile and an extended hand.

"Mr. Deverol, thanks for seeing me."

We shook hands. I showed him my shield and ID. He glanced at them indifferently and said, "Allan will do."

"Call me Max," I said.

He led me to a front dining room and indicated for me to take a seat at the table. What appeared to be a white bed sheet had been spread over the table to serve as a tablecloth. From where I sat, I could see a modestly furnished living room, a sun porch and a hallway leading to a kitchen at the back of the house. Allan Deverol pulled a chair out and sat opposite me. "I'm glad you called," he said. "I was hoping to talk to someone about Ray without having to look at guns and badges."

"As I mentioned on the phone, I'm not on the case. I'm just trying to do what I can for Ray."

"That's appreciated," he said. "Brandy?" Without waiting for my reply, he walked to a liquor cabinet, removed a bottle and two glasses and brought them back to the table.

"Quiet neighborhood," I said.

"We've been here fifteen years," he said as he filled both glasses. "But I'm afraid I haven't kept the place up as I should." He looked around the room, embarrassed by its condition.

I took a sip of brandy and changed the subject.

"What have the police done so far?"

"A few weeks ago, Chief Briggs phoned and explained the situation to me. The following day two detectives came out and questioned me and recorded everything I said. They were all business and matter-of-fact. That's why I was glad you called. I thought I might learn something about the situation from a different perspective."

"Then we're on the same page," I said. "I'm looking for an update on Ray. How he's been living in recent years, his daily routine, acquaintances, anything that might be helpful."

He took a drink of brandy and gazed into his glass contemplatively before saying, "Ray lives a sedentary life, content and quiet. Not having a family of his own, he devotes himself to my daughter and me. The feeling, of course, is mutual. Together, we fulfill each other's needs."

"If your daughter's at home, I'd like to speak to her. She might have something to say that's helpful."

"My daughter is always home," he said. "She's an invalid."

"I'm sorry," I said.

He took a large swallow from his glass before he continued. "Melissa was the victim of a hit-and-run driver five years ago. She was seven then and has been wheelchair bound ever since. Losing her mother two years ago to cancer has put an even greater strain on me." He took another swallow. "I had to give up full-time employment after that to be home with Melissa. I substitute at the High school now, but the money's not enough and they don't offer paid medical coverage to part-timers. Without Ray's help, I couldn't make it."

"How exactly does Ray help?"

"I'm a proud man, Mr. Graham," he said.

"Max," I said.

"Max," he repeated.

"But when it comes to Melissa, I do what I have to."

"Of course," I said.

"The doctors said there was a surgical procedure that could allow Melissa to walk again. At first, I refused to take Ray's money, but he persisted and his arguments made sense. He said it was a family thing and together we would save the money for Melissa's surgery. The operation would never happen if it weren't for Ray's help." He stopped and considered the present circumstance. "Of course, now things are different."

"When did Ray begin giving you this money?"

"It's been nearly a year now."

"Cash?"

"Yes. I assumed with his modest lifestyle and good job it wouldn't be a problem, but now with these allegations, I wonder if I should have been more prudent in accepting the cash."

He paused in a moment of thought, and then said, "Truthfully, it didn't matter to me how Ray got the money as long as he was helping my daughter."

"Did you have any reason to think Ray was doing anything illegal?"

"No. Ray's life has always been transparent. He's been a giving person as far back as his days with the Peace Corps and a loving brother and—as you well know, a good friend."

"Sure," I said.

"What can you tell me about Ray's lifestyle in Los Angeles?"

"Not much, I'm afraid. We've kept in contact over the years, but our lives are different, being on opposite sides of the country. Ray was happy living the bachelor's life."

"Do you have any idea where Ray might be?"

"None. We have no relatives and Ray doesn't have a circle of friends."

"What about girlfriends?"

"He had a steady about a year ago, but I'm not sure if they still see each other. I may still have her address around somewhere. Ray's car broke down one evening after work and he phoned and asked me to pick her up at her apartment and bring her here to meet him."

"That'd be great," I said. "Do you have a recent photo of Ray?"

"I'm sure there's one from last summer," he said.

He walked into another room and when he returned, handed me a 4x6 photo of Ray in shorts and sandals, stretched out in a lawn chair in the shade of a giant Sycamore, his niece beside him in her wheelchair. Both were smiling into the camera. *Happy times,* I thought. He also handed me a scrap of paper on which he had written the address of Ray's former girlfriend.

We left the table and walked toward the front door. As I was putting the address and photo in my wallet, my eye caught the glimmer of metallic coming from the hallway. When I looked, Allan Deverol's daughter was moving gingerly toward us, her frail arms rotating the black rubber rims on the sides of her chrome wheelchair. She was a pretty kid with strawberry blond hair cut to her shoulders. Her pale face was sprinkled with pink freckles and despite her condition and what she'd been through; her bright blue eyes hadn't lost their luster.

"My daughter, Melissa," Allan Deverol said. He leaned down and kissed her forehead. "This is Uncle Raymond's friend."

She looked up at me and smiled, the kind of smile that makes you want to take someone like that into your arms and squeeze as hard as you can. I thought of my daughters and gave her a big smile back.

"Are you going to find Uncle Ray?" she said.

"I'll do my best," I said.

"We miss him very much."

"I know," I said.

I left with a lump in my throat.

Chapter 9

*"Some of these, as he detailed them,
interested and bewildered me."*
Edgar Allan Poe—The Fall of the House of Usher

I got out of bed earlier than I usually do on Saturday, out of necessity to clean my apartment. I spent two hours with the vacuum, duster and glass cleaner working my arms and legs to the rhythms of *Doo Wop Gold*. I'd pulled the CD from my collection, which I kept on shelves on my living room wall. Sandy gave me the CD last year for my birthday. It contained my favorite songs and although I had nearly a hundred Doo-Wop recordings, including box sets, this was the one I played most often. Doo-Wop was the greatest. At my age, the nostalgia meant more to me than the music. The upbeat tunes made me feel good, and the romantic harmonies brought back memories that made me moody. As far as I was concerned, it was the only music to listen to, although I'd had a hard time convincing Christie and Justine to agree with me.

Whenever I cleaned the apartment, I skipped my weekly workout at the police gym. The rigors of cleaning far surpassed the meager results I could obtain there. I tried to convince Sandy to help me with my once-a-month cleaning, but she said I was on my own. I even offered to help her clean her apartment in return, but she wasn't having it. I guess I'm doomed to the drudgery of ammonia, alcohol, and pine cleaner.

It was nine-thirty by the time I finished cleaning. I shut the CD changer. Then I loaded the coffee machine with grounds and water, pushed the start button and took a shower. After I dressed, I made myself some eggs and toast, poured a cup of coffee and sat down at the table to a well-deserved breakfast.

While I ate, I thought about Ray's niece confined to that wheelchair. My daughters had been the innocent victims of a contentious divorce battle but had emerged unscathed and healthy. I also thought about how big-hearted Ray had tried to do the right thing but in the wrong way and became a victim himself. I was still finding it hard to believe he would involve himself in a crime. Sometimes circumstances in life cause people to do strange and desperate things. But I was making excuses for him. The end doesn't always justify the means. What he'd done was wrong, plain and simple, regardless of his intentions.

The door buzzer rang. I walked to the door and peered through the peephole. Ross Montgomery was standing in my hallway, looking eager. I wondered how he knew where to find me.

"I know, I should have called first," he said, as he stepped through the doorway, "but I was close enough to stop by."

"How did you know where to find me?"

"I'm a detective," he said.

I closed and locked the door and let it go.

As he walked further into the living room, he wrinkled his nose, grimaced, and then looked back at me.

"Pine cleaner," I said.

"You have help?"

"I work alone."

"Do you hire out?"

"No, but you can have a cup of coffee."

We walked into the kitchen. I pointed to a mug tree and sat down to my eggs again. He chose one of the pretty flowered mugs Sandy had given me, filled it with coffee, and sat at the table.

"There's a tin of chocolate chip cookies in the cabinet," I said.

"Chips Delights?"

"Homemade."

"It's not the same," he said.

My eggs were getting cold, and I began to eat them hurriedly.

"Deverol is a salesman for a drug firm in Secaucus," Montgomery said. "He's been with them for about a year. The people at Hoffman-Weir are very tight-lipped about him, only admitting he hasn't been to work in weeks. That's all I could get."

"Not much more to get," I said. "I told you, I've been out of touch with him for a long time."

"Maybe Monica Flannery is right. If Deverol is nowhere to be found, maybe her old man did snuff him and ditched the body."

"Maybes don't count," I said. "You've got to do better than that."

He smiled, then took a sip of coffee. "I have," he said.

He leaned over the table closer to me and spoke in a soft voice, as if he suspected someone might be listening.

"I've been sticking close to the good doctor, and let me tell ya, no one could be more ordinary, that is, until yesterday when he did something out of the ordinary.

"I was sitting in the hospital lot watching his Mercedes, which is part of my routine. When he left the hospital at his usual time on Friday, in addition to his briefcase, he was carrying a flat cardboard box under his arm. It looked like a mailer box, but with no printing or labels on it, and it was secured with masking tape on all sides. He placed it in the trunk of his car and then got in behind the wheel, but instead of heading east to the Island, he drove uptown. I followed him.

until he pulled into an underground parking garage on 34th Street. I parked across the street and hoofed it to the garage just in time to see him push the elevator button for the fourth floor. I sprinted the stairs to the fourth floor and caught him exiting the elevator."

"Youth has its advantages," I said.

"I stood behind a large planter by the elevator," he continued, "and watched him walk to a door at the end of the corridor. He held the box cradled in his left hand. He knew exactly where he was going and didn't have to look at any door numbers. He stopped at a door at the end of the corridor. When he rapped on it a few times, the door opened right away. He handed someone the box, which was exchanged for a legal-size envelope. I saw him put the envelope in his inside jacket pocket. The door closed as quickly as it had opened, and he headed back toward the elevator. The whole thing took less than twenty seconds.

"Could you ID anyone?"

"Not from my position."

"Was anything said?"

"No. After he got into the elevator, I walked to the door and got the number. I ran back to my car and waited for him to leave the parking garage and followed him back to the Island without incident."

He removed a scrap of paper from his shirt pocket but kept it in his hand. "Here's the building address and apartment number," he said. "I haven't checked it out yet. Is it worth anything to you?"

I took a sip of coffee to allow time for my brain to process the info Montgomery had given me, before I said, "How does this information help me find my friend?"

"You have to admit that's pretty bizarre behavior for a man of Dr. Flannery's position," he said, "playing delivery boy in an out of the way neighborhood. It could mean something."

"Or nothing," I said.

"Or everything," he said.

He was right. I was inquisitive enough to want the information. I sopped up the last of my eggs with a half piece of toast and downed the rest of my coffee.

"Here's one for you. Ray Deverol is under investigation by NYPD."

Montgomery's eyes widened with eager anticipation.

"They believe he's trafficking drugs."

"Then he's alive?"

"As far as they're concerned, he's on the run."

"So there's a possibility that Flannery didn't snuff him as his wife believes. He may have just split to avoid jail."

"Maybe."

He slid the paper across the table. I put it in my pocket. He followed me to the sink where I began washing my dish. "What do you think was in the box?" he said.

I shrugged. "Maybe Flannery delivers girl scout cookies part-time," I said.

My sarcasm was lost in his moment of thought. "Well, one thing's for sure," he said, "your doctor friend is involved in more than a possible murder."

Montgomery left feeling more enthusiastic about his prospects. He was determined to find Ray or prove Drew killed him. The information he gave me was important enough to check out, and Drew's behavior did seem odd, but did it have anything to do with Ray's disappearance?

I was cleaning up my breakfast dishes when my cell phone rang. I rushed into the bedroom and answered it.

"Is this Detective Graham?" a soft voice said.

"Who is this?" I said.

I never confirm my identity over the phone without first determining who is calling, a habit I acquired based on a sense of self-preservation and my own cynicism.

"Addie Kellerman," the voice said.

"Do I know you, Mrs. Kellerman?"

"You were here the other day. Mr. Deverol is my tenant."

"Oh, yes, Mrs. Kellerman."

"You said if I remembered something, I should call."

I waited through a short silence. Addie needed prompting.

"I'm here," I said.

"I was cleaning the kitchen drawer when I found the card. It reminded me."

"And what card is that, Mrs. Kellerman?"

"The one he left for me to give to Mr. Deverol," she said.

"Who?"

"The man who was here looking for him."

"When was that?"

"About a week before Mr. Deverol disappeared."

"What did he want?"

"He said he was Mr. Deverol's friend from California."

There was another short silence.

"What else did he say?"

"He said he worked for the same company as Mr. Deverol and was out here on a business trip. He wanted to visit with Mr. Deverol."

"Did he see Mr. Deverol that day?"

"I told him Mr. Deverol was at work but he left his card anyway and said he'd be back."

"Can you give me the information on the card?"

"Yes, but I need to get my glasses."

I heard her set the receiver down and walk away from the phone. While I waited, I opened the top drawer of my night table and found a sheet of paper and a pen. When she came back, she read me the info off the card. I wrote it down.

"Has this fella been back since that day?"

"I wouldn't know, Mr. Graham. I don't spy on my tenants."

"Of course you don't," I said. "Is there anything else you'd like to tell me?"

I waited again, through another short silence, before she said, "Have you found Mr. Deverol, yet?"

"No," I said.

"Will you let me know when you find him?"

"You'll be the first to know," I said.

"Thank you," she said and hung up.

Was she truly concerned, or was Ray was behind with his rent.

From the open drawer, I got out Ray's address book. The name Tony Evangelista was written in under business associates. Ray had him categorized as "sales personnel". On the back of his business card, Evangelista had written the name of the motel where he was staying and Mrs. Kellerman had read it off to me. The place was on the main highway in Secaucus, not far from Hoffman-Weir. I thought about calling but decided to drive out. I get more out of a person if I can see their face. Telephone interviews rarely work. They're the lazy man's way of doing things, and invariably, something goes wrong and a personal interview becomes necessary, anyway. It's a tenet of good detective work.

***

It was almost noon when I reached the Regal Motel on Route 3. It was what you'd expect from a motel, a low flat roof building with a paved parking lot in front, nothing fancy, maybe twenty units and an office, all on the ground level. I was surprised Hoffman-Weir hadn't sprung for better accommodations for its salespeople. Maybe Evangelista wasn't high enough on the ladder yet.

I found unit number 14 and parked the Chevy between the white lines directly in front of it. I got out and knocked on the door. No answer. I knocked again and waited. The curtain behind the big front window was pushed slightly to one side, and I cupped my hands around my face to shield out the sun so I could look in. The room was dark, and there was no movement. I knocked one more time, then turned back to my car. As I did, a silver Subaru pulled into the space next to my Chevy. A guy got out carrying a briefcase and looked at me suspiciously. He walked toward me aggressively but with caution. He was wearing a black suit with a white shirt and red tie loose at the collar. His tanned face was clean-shaven and his straight black hair glistened from an overabundance of hair gel.

"Can I help you?"

I showed him my shield as quickly as I could to ease his concern. "Detective, Graham," I said. "NYPD."

"What's the problem?" he said.

"Are you Tony Evangelista?"

"Yes."

"I'm here about Ray Deverol."

"Is Ray okay?"

"Let's talk inside?"

He removed a key from his pocket and unlocked the door. The room smelled musty but looked clean enough. He tossed his briefcase onto the king-size bed and removed his jacket and dropped it next to it. "Has something happened to Ray? His landlady told me she's not sure where he is." He clicked on a lamp beside the bed.

"Nobody has seen Ray for a while," I said.

"Why are the police involved?"

"I'm doing this on my own time. Ray and I go back a long way, to our college days."

"But if he's missing, the police should know."

"They do know."

"Is foul play suspected?"

"Maybe."

"It should be reported."

"It has been."

I could see he was becoming impatient.

"Well, what's this all about?"

"Ray's disappeared."

"Just like that?"

"Just like that."

"How could that happen?"

"I was hoping you'd help me make some sense of it. You and Ray were pretty good friends, right?"

He opened his briefcase, removed a pint of J&B, took a short pull, and then held the bottle out for me. I held up my hand. He capped the bottle and put it back in the briefcase.

"Sure, Ray and I were close," he said. "But what do you expect me to tell you about him?"

Although he had seemed initially concerned about finding Ray, it irritated me that he suddenly came at me with an arrogant attitude. *Was this guy stubborn or stupid?*

"Oh, just the important stuff," I said, sarcastically, "like what his favorite movie is, does he wear boxers or briefs, does he go to church regularly, does he masturbate?"

He closed his briefcase and sat on the edge of the bed, looking annoyed and embarrassed. "Okay," he said. "I get it."

I sat in a chair at a small desk and waited.

"Ray and I were in sales together," he said, "until he got transferred here. When they sent me on this business trip, I thought I'd look him up, you know, surprise him."

"You haven't heard from him since his transfer?"

"He said he'd keep in touch, but it's been a year. That's why I wanted to look him up."

"When did you arrive here?"

"Two weeks ago, Monday," he said.

"That would be the 5th," I said. I was sure of the date because we'd spent that previous Saturday at Drew's mansion.

He nodded.

"How were you able to find Ray?"

"Company records. They told me he'd been on vacation, but I see now there's more to it. Apparently, they don't know where he is either."

"Tell me about Ray's life on the coast."

"He was in good standing with the company, never any problem. We hung out, on and off, double dated and such."

"Did he have a steady?"

He shook his head. "Just a few girls he took out occasionally."

"What about business associates or male friends? Were there any problems with anyone?"

"That's not Ray's nature. He gets along with everybody. He's a natural-born bullshitter Like they say: 'He could sell ice to Eskimos.' That's why they made him top salesman and transferred him here."

"What about financial problems? Did he owe money?"

"Who doesn't? But if you're asking me if he was in serious debt, I'd have to guess, no."

"How long will you be here?"

"I'm scheduled to leave on Friday."

"What else can you tell me? Any little thing could be important."

"Ray is a good guy. In Los Angeles, he led a happy, sedentary life—almost boring."

I tore a sheet of paper from a note pad on the desk and wrote down my cell number. "Keep this conversation to yourself," I said. I handed him the paper, got up and pushed the chair back under the desk. "If you think of anything else, call me."

"Sure," he said as he followed me to the door. "What do you think your odds are of finding Ray?"

"I don't play odds," I said.

As he opened the door, and I stepped outside, I heard him say, "Boxers."

I turned back to face him.

"Ray wears boxers," he said, with a snide smile.

I wasn't impressed by his attempt to be clever at Ray's expense and said, with a stern expression, "Thanks for the info." He lost his smile and closed the door.

Driving back to my apartment, I felt empty. I hadn't gained a thing from that interview except to corroborate what Allan Deverol had told me that Ray's life on the West Coast was happy and content. Evangelista had added, "almost boring". He seemed to be telling me the truth, but I'd check out his story, anyway. Ray's address book was chock full of his West Coast associates and if I needed to dig further, I could. Right now, I was convinced the circumstances involving Ray's disappearance began with his arrival on the East Coast.

Chapter 10

*"Upon the first discovery of the corpse, it was not
supposed that the murderer would be able to
elude for more than a very brief period..."*
Edgar Allan Poe—The Mystery of Marie Roget

I was locking my desk and about to leave for the day when
Monica Flannery showed up at the DB. She looked good, as
usual, but I could see dark circles under her eyes despite the
amount of make-up she wore. This lady was definitely losing
sleep. Today she was wearing designer jeans, her white
Reeboks, and a tight-fitting pink V-neck sweater. Her hair was
pulled back against her scalp and held with a matching pink
flowered headband.

"Montgomery phoned me," she said.

I waited.

"He wants to meet with me at a Chinese restaurant."

I waited some more.

"He said he had information, and it was a safe place to
talk."

"What kind of information?"

"He didn't say."

"Why are you telling me this?"

"He asked me to call him back to confirm, but I've been
unable to reach him."

"Was he calling from the restaurant?"

"His cell phone. Why wouldn't he answer his phone if he
expected me to call him back?"

"Maybe his battery died."

"Something's wrong," she said.

"What do you want me to do?"

"I'd feel a lot better if you'd come to the restaurant with me." And then, as if to entice me, "He might have information about Ray."

I looked at the wall clock. It was 5:10. I had decided to have dinner at my mother's house at seven. She had promised me Linguini and meatballs and a fresh loaf of garlic bread. Since the passing of my father three years ago, she hadn't had the desire to cook much, but on occasion, I could convince her to cook for me and that made us both happy. My mother lived with my aunt Theresa, her sister, in the same house where I grew up. When Uncle Carlo passed last year, Aunt Theresa moved in with my mother. Since Marlene moved the grandkids to South Jersey and my younger brother Vinnie left for Arizona to sell real estate, I tried to alleviate my mother's loneliness by visiting her as much as I could.

My mother could never understand why Vinnie wanted to leave. He'd been living at home at the time, rent free, with a "come and go" lifestyle. But his meager real estate following was taking him nowhere, and his dream of bigger and better things had been eating away at him for a long time. After my father died, the idea of being the man of the house was too much for him and that pushed him into leaving. It wasn't that he didn't love my mother, but rather, he'd hung on to a selfish priority and felt the time for a career change was now or never. When the opportunity arose for him to sell land in Arizona, he jumped on it. I couldn't blame him. He'd always hated living in the northeast. He detested the bitter winters and the hustle-bustle of the Metro area and preferred the laid-back sunshine of the Southwest. The day he left, he told me he would probably never come back to Jersey, not even in a box, and if I ever wanted to see him again, I'd have to travel west. I believed him.

Inhaling the smoke from three packs of cigarettes a day for sixty years, finally took my father away from us. After he died, his doctor told me his lungs looked like a piece of burned toast, a difficult analogy to accept about one's own father's medical condition, but true. An uneducated man who rarely touched alcohol, he did his best to keep his family happy, but sometimes the constraints of ignorance made it difficult for him to make the right choices. He worked hard to support his family, earning a meager income, which left no time or money for vacations away from home. I can't recall one trip we took as a family that included a car ride or a flight on a plane. While our schoolmates were enjoying trips with their families to Disneyland and Magic Mountain, my brother Vinnie and I were consigned to fishing trips with our father to the muddy banks of the Passaic River, less than two miles from our home. Although most times we enjoyed ourselves, it wasn't Disneyland.

My father had verbally abused my mother, although I never saw him raise a threatening hand to her. Nevertheless, she loved him in the only way she knew how, as he had loved her in his own genuine but meager way. He treated my brother and me with as much understanding and love that he knew how to give, and that's the way I've chosen to remember him.

I left Monica Flannery waiting for an answer while I slipped into my jacket. I was not incline to help her personally, but if Montgomery had any info about Ray, I wanted it. With a little luck, I'd be twirling spaghetti onto my fork in time.

"What time did he say?"

"Six o'clock, Chen's Garden. Do you know the place?"

"Uptown."

"At this time of the day, we won't make it on time."

"He'll wait," I said.

She insisted on taking her Jag, which was okay with me, we'd make better time. I left the Chevy in my usual parking spot and let her drive. Thirty minutes later, we pulled into the restaurant parking lot. It was still early for dinner and there were only a few cars in spaces closest to the building. She pulled into a spot near the front door. "That's his car, she said." She pointed to a red BMW parked in a space away from the building at the end of the lot. We got out and walked into the restaurant. The interior had a typical Asian motif. A large dining room was on the right, segregated from the main entrance by a wall of white wooden lattice. A long cherry wood bar stood directly opposite the main door, with red paper lanterns strung above it on a length of gold chain. There were brass and chrome figurines and a huge fire-breathing dragon mounted on one wall. A maitre'd station sat in the middle of it all. A few servers walked casually in and out of the dining room carrying trays of food. Several young couples were the only patrons at the bar. I peeked through the lattice into the dining room, where just a few tables were occupied. I didn't see Montgomery. I walked back to Monica Flannery, who had been waiting at the door.

"I don't see him anywhere," she said.

"I'll check the men's room," I said.

When I returned, she was pacing by the front door. I walked out to the parking lot and headed for the BMW. She followed me without a word. The convertible top was down and I could see a key ring with a single key in the ignition switch. I took my handkerchief out of my pocket and wrapped it loosely around my finger. I leaned in and pushed the button to the glove box. Inside, I found what I'd hoped to find, Montgomery's vehicle registration. I read it and tossed it back into the glove box. I started back toward the Jag with her following close behind.

"What did you find?" she said.

"Montgomery's address. We're going to visit him."

I got in behind the wheel. "I'll drive," I said. She handed me the keys without protest as she slid in beside me.

I turned the key, and out of habit waited for the Jag to cough and hesitate. It didn't. The engine purred as I drove out of the parking lot and made a left onto the main road. With all of its precision engineering, it still lacked the character of my Chevy Nova.

"Why would Montgomery leave his car here with the key in it?" she said.

"Maybe he's just forgetful," I said.

She was getting used to my sarcasm. I could tell.

***

Montgomery was doing better than I thought. His address was a two-story townhouse situated on a quiet, tree-lined street on the upper west side. Most of the cars parked at the curb were upper-end. Maybe papa was paying the rent.

We walked up the stairs of number 620 and I rang the bell. No one answered. I turned the knob and the front door opened.

"Is it okay to go in?" Monica Flannery said.

"I'm the police—remember?"

She walked close behind me and put her hand on my shoulder as we entered the foyer. It was the first time she'd showed sincere confidence in me. I let her keep it there. The inner door of the foyer was also unlocked. When I pushed the door back and stepped into the living room, my first thought was: *Goodbye Linguini dinner*.

Ross Montgomery was lying on the floor on his back, his sightless eyes staring wide-eyed at the ceiling. A pool of blood had saturated his white shirt and dripped down his sides onto the beige carpet. Monica Flannery saw it too. She turned away and buried her face in my shoulder.

"Is he—dead?" she said.

She was visibly shaken. I closed the door behind us and brought her to a dining area in the adjoining room. I sat her at a table and told her not to touch anything. Then I walked back to Montgomery and crouched beside him. He was wearing the same suit he wore the day I met him at Moran's bar, except his jacket and tie were lying over the arm of a nearby sofa. Some blood had dried dark on his white shirt, which told me he had been lying there for a while. There were two bullet holes in his chest. Someone had fired at close range; I could see powder marks on his shirt beside the bloodstains. It looked like a medium caliber, possibly a .38 or 9mm. When I looked around, I saw no indication there had been a struggle. There were no spent casings near the body, but that didn't mean there were none. They could have bounced anywhere in the room, or the murder weapon could have been a revolver, or the shooter might have cleaned up after himself. I'd leave the details to forensics. I checked the other rooms. Everything was in its place, windows were closed and locked, drawers were undisturbed and closet doors shut tight. Although the front and inner doors were unlocked, it was safe to rule out burglary. Somebody had highjacked Ross Montgomery, brought him back to his place and killed him. Why?

When I walked back to the living room, Monica Flannery came out to meet me. She was trying not to look at Montgomery.

"Shouldn't we get out of here?" she said.

"We need to call the police."

"The police? I don't want to get mixed up in this."

"You already are," I said. "You're his client. A police investigation will turn up your name sooner or later. Do you have a lawyer?"

"Of course."

"Call him now."

"What shall I say?"

"Tell him what happened, you're being detained for questioning. When they take us—"

"Us?"

"You don't think they'll let me walk, do you?"

"But I thought you were—"

"That's a dead man on the floor. The police will want to know why we're here with him."

"But if we leave now, they won't know we were here."

"I can't do that," I said. "Tell your lawyer to meet you at their precinct. And don't answer any questions until he gets there."

She took a cell phone from her purse and began pacing the floor.

"What will I tell Drew when he finds out?"

"Tell him you hired a PI to help find Ray Deverol, and he got himself killed."

"There'll be a scandal," she said, "because of Drew's reputation."

"Maybe not, your husband knows a lot of people."

"What do I tell the police?"

"Tell the truth. If you lie, they'll find out, and that'll make things worse. Do you understand everything I told you?"

She nodded and began punching numbers into her cell phone.

It didn't take long for the troops to descend on the townhouse. Four uniforms arrived first. They checked our IDs, frisked me and took my gun, asked me if I'd touched anything.

and stood around writing in their note pads until their homicide got there. The room got crowded when Forensics arrived. A photographer and two guys from the medical examiner's office showed up. The commander of the homicide bureau was Lieutenant Sean McCaffrey. He was one of those big Irish cops like you see in the movies, but without the familiar accent. He had red hair parted neatly to one side and a red complexion to match. He had red freckles on his cheeks, and the tip of his nose was red. Everything about this guy looked red and paralleled patriotically with the blue sports jacket and white shirt he wore.

I'd worked with McCaffrey for a number of years until he made rank and was transferred uptown. He'd embroiled himself in a rivalry with me for rank that I'd never been a part of. Although he'd gotten what he'd wanted, he held on to an inherent dislike for me. There was never any love lost between us and we had butt heads more than once in the past.

McCaffrey was the last to arrive. When he saw me, I could see a look of disdain pushing through those freckles. I was sitting at the dining table in the other room with Monica Flannery. He walked into the room and stood between us. One of his minions approached and handed him my gun; a young detective with a physique like a bodybuilder. His tar-black hair was plastered down against his scalp and around his neck hung too many gold chains, which sparkled obtrusively behind his open collar. He wore a gold watch on his left wrist and I noticed a gold pinky ring on his left hand, obvious accouterments inappropriate for police work. He was, no doubt, a new DB assignee sucking up to McCaffrey to get ahead. I'd seen the type before.

McCaffrey dropped my gun into his jacket pocket and then looked at me. "A little out of your territory, aren't you, Graham?"

"I get around," I said.

"Talk to me," he said.

"We came in here and found this guy," I said.

"What's your connection with him?"

"None, he's a PI hired by the lady."

"Then why are you here?"

"She asked me to accompany her here."

"She a friend of yours?"

"No."

"Then why are you here?"

"You already asked me that."

The guys from the ME's office had zipped Montgomery into a body bag and were rolling him out the door. Monica Flannery looked away.

"I'm Lieutenant McCaffrey," McCaffrey said to her. "What's your connection with these two men?"

She looked at me, then at him. "I'm…we…He told me not to say anything until I spoke to my lawyer."

"No one is under arrest," McCaffrey said. "I'm just trying to get a preliminary of what happened here."

She looked at me again. I hoped she could read my face. After a second, she said, "I want to call my lawyer."

McCaffrey looked at me. "Okay, Graham, you know the drill," he said. "We all go downtown now for statements. You wanna call your lawyer too?"

I didn't answer.

"These gentlemen will escort you," he said to Monica Flannery. "Tell your lawyer to meet you at police headquarters."

"Her car is parked out front," I said.

"We'll get her a ride back."

Two detectives escorted Monica Flannery through the foyer. I followed behind with McCaffrey.

"Do I get my gun back?" I said.

"If you're a good boy."

"Should I call my lawyer or Briggs?"

"I can't wait 'til Briggs hears about this," McCaffrey said, through a broad smile.

"Don't bust a nut," I said.

I got into an unmarked car with McCaffrey and Golden Boy. The uniforms put Monica Flannery in a cruiser and drove to their precinct. In less than ten minutes we pulled into a parking lot next to a four-story brick building. The police cruiser parked beside us, and we all got out and went in through the side door. We took the elevator to the homicide bureau on the third floor and stepped out into a large open room. Several glass-enclosed cubicles stood along the perimeter walls. In the center of the room was an array of metal filing cabinets and small desks, all occupied by the four to twelve shift. The place smelled like cigar smoke and burned coffee. A guy in jeans, wearing a corduroy sport jacket and holding a briefcase was waiting by McCaffrey's cubicle. As we approached, he removed a card from his breast pocket and shoved it in McCaffrey's face. "I'd like to speak with my client," he said.

McCaffrey turned to me. "You'll need more than one lawyer before this is over, Graham."

"Not mine," I said, then added a deliberate smile.

"He's my attorney," Monica Flannery said.

I got that look of disdain from McCaffrey again. I knew he wanted to slap the smile off my face, but instead, he pointed to an empty cubicle, "In there," he said.

Monica Flannery and her lawyer went in behind the glass. I followed McCaffrey and Golden Boy into McCaffrey's cubicle. McCaffrey sat behind his desk while Golden Boy stood by the door with his arms folded over his chest like a sentry. Through the glass partition, I saw a detective walk in and sit at the desk between Monica Flannery and her lawyer.

"You're in deep shit, Graham," McCaffrey said.

"I've been in deep before," I said.

"Not so deep that it might cost you your shield."

"In your dreams," I said.

"You sure you don't want a lawyer?"

"If things get too hot, I'll call Briggs."

A detective came in and handed McCaffrey a sheet of paper and walked out. McCaffrey sat in his chair and took his time reading it, then looked up at me. "What's your connection with Dr. Drew Flannery," he said.

"We were friends at college."

"Are you a friend of his wife too?"

"I already told you—no."

He leaned forward and wiggled his way out of his jacket and hung it on the back of his chair. From the look on his face, I could tell he didn't believe me. "Look, Graham," he said. "It's your business if you're banging your friend's wife, but when a dead man comes between you and her, it becomes my business."

I felt myself stiffen. "You piece o' crap!" I said. "You wouldn't know how to solve a murder if the killer confessed. You're only sitting in that chair because you kissed ass for ten years." Right then I could have reached across the desk and tore McCaffrey's head off.

Golden Boy dropped his arms and started toward me.

"Back off, rookie," I said. "Your boss can handle it."

McCaffrey gestured with his hand. Golden boy relaxed.

"Take it easy, Graham," he said.

He got up and walked to a water cooler in the corner of the room and began filling a paper cup. Without turning, he said, "I've got a homicide on my hands, Graham, and you're in the middle of it. Let's put our differences aside. Help me out here."

"Not while you're trying to hang me." I said.

He took a drink, crushed the cup and tossed it into a wastebasket. When he came back to his chair, he said, "Okay. I'll play fair, tell me what you know and we'll sort this out."

He opened his desk drawer and took out a handheld recorder, stood it on the desk and pushed the record button. I scowled at the machine. McCaffrey knew what I was thinking.

"It's the electronic age, Graham," he said. "We don't use pads and push pencils anymore."

Golden Boy slid a chair over to me. I sat in it. I knew McCaffrey would eventually find out the entire story, but I had no intention of letting him hear more than he had to from my lips. I could see Monica Flannery in the next cubicle wiping her eyes with her handkerchief and spilling her guts about everything, including her affair with Ray. I knew what I told McCaffrey would have to be as close to the truth as possible. I proceeded with caution.

"What's your connection with Dr. Drew Flannery?" McCaffrey asked again for the record.

"We were friends at college," I repeated.

"Did you know Flannery's wife is having an affair with Ray Deverol?"

"That's the story she gave me."

"And now he's missing?"

"She came to me and asked me to help find him. I agreed to do what I could on my own time."

"And what'd you find?"

"Nothing."

McCaffrey would learn from Briggs there was a case being built against Ray, so I didn't offer any information. No favors today.

"So she hired—" he referred to the paper—"Ross Montgomery, a PI, our recently deceased."

"He told her he had information. She asked me to accompany her to meet him. I went because I thought he might have information about Ray Deverol. When we got there he was stiffed."

"Do you know why anybody would want to kill this guy?"

"I don't even know him."

"Where do you think your friend is?"

"That's all I'm trying to find out. I have no interest in this woman's indiscretions."

"You said Flannery was a friend of yours."

"Flannery, Deverol, and I went to college together. We were close then, but we haven't seen each other in twenty years until Ray reappeared and Drew Flannery took it upon himself to get us together for an afternoon of old times. It was Drew who alerted me he hadn't been able to contact Ray."

"Since that time you were all together?"

"That's right. I confirmed that Ray hadn't been seen by anyone for at least a week after that."

"Is Flannery wise that his wife's cheating on him?"

"She says he knows."

"Has he discussed it with you?"

"No."

"You said he was your friend."

"If he wants to tell me, I'm here."

"Do you think Flannery snuffed this Deverol? According to his wife's statement, she believes it's highly probable."

"Maybe," I said.

"Is he the kind of person that could commit murder?"

"What kind of person is that?"

"Don't be a wiseass, Graham. You know what I mean."

He'd interpreted my candor as sarcasm. It was a legitimate question. People from all walks of life commit murder. I wasn't sure how he wanted me to answer.

"He wasn't when I knew him," I said.

"Twenty years ago?"

"That's right."

"What happened after you arrived at the townhouse?"

"We found Montgomery."

"After that?"

"Mrs. Flannery became upset. I comforted her, then called the police."

"How long after you discovered the body was that?"

"A matter of minutes."

McCaffrey pushed the off button on the recorder, got up and walked out of the office, leaving me alone with Golden Boy, who remained steadfastly at his post. After a long minute of awkward silence, I gave him a short smile. He didn't return it. I got the idea he didn't like me.

McCaffrey came back carrying several sheets of paper. He sat down and read through them quickly, then opened his top desk drawer and slid the papers inside. He picked up the recorder, put it in the drawer with the papers and shut and locked the drawer.

"Your story checks with Mrs. Flannery's," he said, "but you're not off the hook. Don't take any vacations."

He reached into his pocket, took out my gun and slid it across the desk. "I don't want to have to put the hounds out for you."

I got up and put my gun back in my belt holster. "Now I'll have to cancel my trip to Bangladesh," I said.

"The only trip you'll be taking is to Briggs's office tomorrow morning, wise guy."

McCaffery was right. Briggs wouldn't be happy, and I'd have to explain everything to him. I knew McCaffrey would phone him as soon as we left and fax him a full report.

Monica Flannery came in behind me with one of McCaffrey's men. She was still dabbing her eyes with her handkerchief. Although they were red, they looked dry to me.

"Detective Hartman will drive you back to your car," McCaffrey said.

As we started out the door, he added, "Thanks for your co-operation, *De-tec-tive.*"

He'd pronounced the title deliberately and with just a hint of disdain. I shot back at him by emphasizing each syllable of his rank. "Anytime, *Lieu-ten-ant.*" I had lowered myself to his juvenile antics, but it made me feel good, just the same.

Chapter 11

"We must endeavor to satisfy ourselves by personal inquiry."
Edgar Allan Poe—The Mystery of Marie Roget

I only got four hours of sleep. I need at least six or I feel crappy for the rest of the day. I got up and was about to make some coffee when the kitchen phone rang. It was Detective Nolan.

Danny Nolan had become a member of the bureau a little more than a year earlier. He recently became a regular partner of mine. There wasn't much to Danny: tall, handsome and a graduate of NYU, thirty-one, unmarried and living a happy bachelor life in a rented apartment in Queens. When he was working, he was the epitome of professionalism, always impeccably dressed in a tailored suit and never without a tie. Unless a special assignment required casual clothing. He kept his shoes polished like mirrors and his black hair neatly trimmed and combed to perfection. Danny's parents retired to Florida's West Coast to start a small fishing business, but Danny chose to stay behind, search for a wife and pursue his police career. Although he was considerably younger than me, we got along well. I think it was out of mutual respect, he for my age and experience and me for his youthful exuberance and dedication to his profession. Socially, I was a Jazz, Doo Wop guy while his musical preferences ranged from Heavy metal to Country. Nonetheless, under my auspices, he had become a competent detective I knew I could trust.

"Briggs wants you in his office as soon as you get in," he said.

"How pissed is he?"

"Off the wall. How'd you screw up now?"

"I took too much vacation time," I said and hung up.

I skipped the coffee and eggs I had planned and ate a bowl of Cheerios instead. I took a cold shower and shaved, got dressed and drove to work. I wondered how upset Briggs would be and how much McCaffrey had spun the truth to discredit me. I hadn't told Briggs about Monica Flannery's involvement with Ray and knew I'd have to face his wrath now.

I arrived at the DB at my usual time. I checked my mailbox, then headed straight for Briggs's office. It was eight-thirty, and I hoped he had at least had his morning coffee. His office door was open and I could see him at his desk with his head down, no doubt reading the report McCaffrey had faxed to him. He looked up and waved me in before I had a chance to knock.

"Sit down, Graham," he said. Whenever he was unhappy with me, he called me by my last name. His face was hard and his voice stern. I wondered if he had lost as much sleep over this as I had. At least he was sipping a coffee.

He stood up and tossed the papers on the desk in front of me. "What've you got to say?"

"I'm sure McCaffrey said it all," I said.

"He did, including the part about Deverol banging Flannery's wife. Did you forget to mention that to me the last time we talked?" His face was turning a harsh pink.

"I didn't think it pertinent at the time," I said.

"Didn't think it pertinent. She believes her husband killed Deverol. If he did, I've had a third of my squad looking for a dead man for the past two weeks. How do you think that makes me look to City Hall?"

"And if he didn't kill Ray, you've still got a case," I said. "She's an unhappily married, confused woman caught with her hand in the cookie jar. I found absolutely no evidence that points to Mrs. Flannery killing anybody."

"*You found*?" he repeated.

"On my own time," I said.

"I don't want that."

"It's personal."

"I don't give a damned how personal it is," he said. "I ordered you to lay off."

He sat down and rubbed his temples with the heels of his hands, took a sip of his coffee and read more of the report. When he was through, he tilted his chair back and looked at me soberly. "We've got a situation here, Max," he said. At least we were on a first name basis again. "You're too close to this thing. I can't run the risk of having you inadvertently make the department look bad by making a foolish mistake that you normally wouldn't make." I saw his face harden and knew he was about to do something he didn't want to do. "I'm putting you on administrative leave," he said.

That was a volley I didn't expect.

"When did doing my job become grounds for punishment?" I said.

"It's not a punishment," he said. "It's for your own good, and the department's. I don't know where this thing with McCaffrey is going." And then he added, almost consolingly, "I'll keep it out of your file."

I wasn't worried about McCaffrey. He had nothing on Monica Flannery or me, and he knew it. Ross Montgomery's murder was his problem.

Briggs could be fair or hard, depending on the circumstance, and what he believed was right. Today he was being hard. He held out his hand without saying a word. I knew what he wanted. I put my ID and shield on the desk.

"And your piece," he said.

My gun had been in and out of my holster more times in the past twenty-four hours than in the past two years.

Reluctantly, I unclipped the holster from my belt and set it on the desk. He took it and my ID and locked them in his top drawer.

"Let's not give McCaffrey any more fodder," he said. "Take some time for yourself until this thing is solved. If your friend can be found, we'll find him."

"And you expect me to sit home and do nothing until this thing is over?"

He came around the desk, put his hand on my shoulder and walked me to the door.

"I'm expecting you to keep a low profile. Let things play out on their own." He opened the door to the main room.

"Thanks for the advice," I said.

As I started walking away, he called my name. I turned.

"Be careful," he said.

I went downstairs to the gym and worked out for an hour. The release of endorphins helps me think and sleep better. I was beat, but I knew I'd be able to catch up on my sleep that afternoon. Driving back to my apartment, I realized Briggs had done me a favor. I'd have more time now to devote to finding Ray. Briggs knew I wouldn't sit idle, no matter what order he gave me. Maybe he knew exactly what he was doing.

***

I had set my alarm for 4:00 p.m. and it jolted me awake. I'd slept a solid six hours but felt like I had jet lag. My eyes hurt and my mouth felt like I had been chewing chalk. I walked to the window and looked out. It was raining, and the streets were shiny. I stood there listening to the rhythm of the rain pelting the windowpane as I waited for the grogginess to leave my head. My stomach began to rumble, and I wondered if Sandy had gotten home yet. Hunger often triggered thoughts of Sandy in me. It's a Freudian thing, I suppose; probably stemming from the comfort and security she brings me. I called her apartment but got her answering machine. I hung up and took a shower. The shower felt good and brought me back to life. I brushed the chalk out of my mouth, dried off, got into my worn jeans and fuzzy slippers and put on my T-shirt with the NYPD logo on it. It would feel good to stay out of a suit of clothes for a while. I tried Sandy again. No answer. I took out my George Foreman grill and plugged it into the wall outlet. While it heated up, I gather the necessary ingredients to construct two cheeseburgers the way I liked them, an inch and a half high, with lettuce, tomato, ketchup, two slices of yellow American and a couple of rings of raw onion. When the beef patties were well done, I slid them onto a pair of sesame seed buns and carefully constructed my culinary masterpiece. I grabbed a beer from the fridge and sat down at the kitchen table.

While I ate, I used my cell phone to call the airlines. Ray's name was not on the passenger list for the flight number and times that were written on the notepad Drew had found in Ray's car. His name wasn't on any flights or cancelations, leaving any metro airport with any carrier on any day that entire week. Why was that information in Ray's glove box, how did it get there, and if he hadn't written it—who did?

As I cleaned up the dishes, I rethought the info Ross Montgomery had given me about Drew. A dark picture was focusing in my mind that I didn't want to come to light. I'd use my newfound time to check things out more thoroughly before I came to any reasonable conclusions. I'd start by finding out who occupied the suite at 417 Tower Park West.

I called Danny Nolan at the DB. He was working the four to twelve.

"I'm not getting involved with this, Max," he said. "If Briggs finds out, I'll be the next one on suspension."

"Administrative leave," I said.

"Whatever."

"I need you to make an official inquiry for me." I said, "a quick phone call."

There was a silence on the line, as if he had to think it over. The truth was, I'd bailed Danny out of more jams than he cared to count, and he knew it.

"You owe me from that night at Hooter's," I said. "Remember, I had to bring you—"

"All right, all right," he interrupted, "but if I get busted, I swear I'll kill you."

He'd have been really upset if he could see me smiling. "Write this down," I said. "Tower Park West on 34th Street, suite 417. Got it?"

"Yeah, yeah,"

"Find out who the renter is and call me back. Now is that so hard—booby?"

"Real funny," he said and hung up.

Still smiling, I walked into my bedroom and dug out my snub-nose .38 from the top drawer of my night table. It was a Smith & Wesson "chief's special" I used to carry off duty but hadn't used in years. I brought it back to the kitchen table and gave it a good cleaning. I was loading it with .38 hollow points when Danny called back.

Anton Denali was the owner, operator of a chain of beauty salons in the city. He had been living at the Tower Park West for almost two years. I wasn't familiar with the man or the corporation, so I thanked Danny and phoned Sandy. She said she'd make a couple of calls and get back to me. While I waited, I got Ray's address book from my night table and brought it back to the kitchen table. I opened it to the first page and began to read the names Ray had entered. Most of the listings were people on the west coast, but there were some from right here in the metro area. I began flipping pages, looking for something that would stand out, something Ray might have written that would indicate a special interest to him, an asterisk, an underlined name, something written in bold letters, a note in the margin, anything that might give me a hint of what was going on in Ray's life at the time. But after a while, it all became a blur, a useless brigade of names and addresses, just pages of black letters on yellow paper. I slammed the book closed just as my cell phone rang.

"Talk to me," I said.

"Not even a hello?" Sandy said.

Oops!

"Oh, sorry," I said. "Hello, Dear."

There was a short silence before she continued, "Anton Denali is a small-time operator with big dreams," she said. "He's been mixed up in several criminal schemes over the years, but never arrested. His beauty salons are fairly well known around Manhattan, legit but probably fronts for other questionable activities."

"How many locations?"

"Four of five."

"A success story."

"He's trying hard. Turn over any rock and you'll find him under it. Despite his Latin name, he's an American citizen, born in the Bronx. When his father died at an early age, he was left to care for his mother and two sisters. As a young man with little education, his means of income was obtained from the streets. In time, he graduated from street gangs to building a small criminal organization, but by criminal standards, he's small potatoes. Why the interest in beauty salons?"

"I'm thinking of changing my look."

"You'll have to change your whole wardrobe."

"Not a problem after today," I said.

"What does that mean?"

"I'll explain over lunch tomorrow," I said. "Thanks. You're beautiful *and* helpful."

"You better not have shaved your head," she said.

Chapter 12

"It might have been half an hour after the altercation when,
as I was deeply absorbed in the heavenly scenery beneath me,
I was startled by something very cold..."
Edgar Allan Poe—A Predicament

By Saturday morning the rain had stopped, and the sun had dried everything to a clean brightness. I don't mind the city on weekends, ; traffic is always lighter making it easier to get around and although the sidewalks are less crowded, that enduring hustle and bustle that is Manhattan is still present.

I was driving down Ninth Avenue, on my way to one of Denali's beauty salons. I figured I'd stick my nose in and see what I could find out about the guy and how he or someone in his employ was connected to Drew. I was resisting confronting Drew about any of this until the time was right. He had no idea I knew about his wife's involvement with Ray or that Ray was wanted by the law. As far as he was concerned, he was keeping his marital problems to himself and we had a mutual concern in finding our friend. For now, I wanted to keep it that way.

I spotted the sign for the beauty salon and parked at the corner. The place was an older building, painted red, and sandwiched between a bakery and a shoemaker. When I pushed open the front door, the pungent odor of hairsprays and gels hit me like a fist. I wondered how one worked in that environment all day. The place was typically what you would expect from a beauty salon: rows of chrome chairs upholstered in red vinyl, a wall of mirrors, bright lights and cross-legged woman sitting under hairdryers looking like alien creatures reading "Woman's Day" and "Cosmo."

Sitting behind a desk by the front door, a good-looking redhead was smoking a cigarette and hawking me as I walked in. "Need a haircut, sweetie?" she said. She crushed out her cigarette and stood up. She had a curvy body, full breasts, and long red hair that complemented her seductive green eyes.

"Maybe," I said. "Who's the best?" I was winging it.

"I'm the best for whatever you need," she said. "My name's Carla, Carla Darling. What's yours?"

"Maxwell Graham," I said.

"Do they call you, Max?" she said.

"Some do," I said.

She moved closer to me and ran her long fingers through my hair, emitting a low moan of approval. I took out one of my business cards and handed it to her. She read it, then slipped it behind her blouse near her cleavage. "Cops need haircuts, too," she said.

She put her arm around my waist and led me across the room to her workstation. I let her guide me into her chair. She walked behind me and began massaging my shoulders. "Now, what can I do special for you?" she said.

"I'm looking for your boss," I said, "Mr. Denali."

She continued rubbing my shoulders, occasionally walking her fingers up the back of my neck to massage my scalp.

"He in trouble?" she said.

"I want to get some information from him about a mutual friend."

"I don't think anybody here can help you. We hardly see him. All I know is he owns the place."

Through the mirror in front of me, I watched a guy behind us at the far end of the room sitting behind a glass top desk, eyeing our conversation with inordinate interest. He'd been following me with his eyes since I came into the shop. "That your boyfriend?" I said to Carla, indicating the guy at the desk with a movement of my head.

Carla Darling looked toward the desk, then back to me. "Who, Bernie? Yuk! He comes in once in a while and checks on things."

Bernie was skinny with a ferret shaped face, probably mid-twenties. He had a thin neck with an Adam's apple the size of a walnut and sported a thin blonde mustache and blonde hair that hung straight to his shoulders. His skin was sallow and taut, as if there weren't enough of it to cover the bones of his face. His eyeballs bulged eerily from their sockets further than they should and his cheeks and forehead were pocked marked so much so, that they looked like a bas relief map of the western hemisphere. He wore a cream-colored three-piece suit over a white shirt, but no tie. He was leaning back in his chair, nervously twitching his head and pulling on his nostrils more times than he needed to while he kept an eye on us. It was easy to see Bernie was playing with the white rabbit.

"He works for Denali?"

"None of the girls like him," Carla Darling said. "Comes in and pushes people around like he cares, takes money from the register, then leaves."

I gave Bernie a friendly smile through the mirror. He pretended not to notice.

When I checked my watch, it was almost eleven. I had a lunch date with Sandy that I didn't want to miss. I pushed myself out of the chair with Carla's hands still on my shoulders. When I turned to face her, she brought her arms up quickly and dropped them back on my shoulders. "Leaving already? I haven't given you today's special," she said. She leaned in close to me. I could feel her thighs against mine. She was solid under the tight jeans she wore. She didn't make leaving easy. "I'll get the special next time," I said. I took a ten from my wallet and stuffed it inside her blouse next to my business card. Bernie was still watching us. I was pretty sure Carla Darling would get the third degree after I left.

I drove over to Eighth Avenue near 34th Street, where Greasy John kept his newsstand. Selling newspapers and magazines was a sideline for Greasy, his real source of income derived from illegal betting. He'd take a bet on almost anything that moved around a track on four legs or four wheels at higher than normal speeds. Having been arrested more than once for improprieties against the law, and having recently completed a two-year prison term, John Arden, which was his real name, made his way back into society dedicated to the proposition that he had become a new man, and would not break the law again. But old habits die-hard, and his penchant for illegal gambling soon overcame his declared intention.

Greasy knew I was well aware of his illicit activities and could take him down at any time, but he also knew I wouldn't. Not as long as he remained my reliable pipeline to the street, my source of underground information. In the two years I'd known Greasy, I'd tried to keep my association with him friendly but professional.

Before he retired, Greasy John had been a short-order cook for most of his life, flipping burgers and eggs in local diners throughout the city. But it wasn't his culinary skills that earned him his nickname, it was his dark leather-like complexion that glistened perpetually. He looked like he was in a constant sweat, regardless of the season. Some believed his condition derived from working over a hot griddle all those years, but I believed it to be genetic. Greasy never talked about it.

When he saw me crossing the street toward his newsstand, he became anxious, as he always did, snubbed out his cigarette, and quickly wiped his face and forehead with a balled-up handkerchief he pulled from a pocket behind his overalls. As I approached, he gave me a big smile showing cracked yellow teeth.

"Detective Graham," he said, touching the brim of his cap. "It's been too long."

"Since Hector was a kitten," I said.

Although it had been only months since I'd last seen him, he seemed to have aged faster than he should. At 78, his thin frame was already beginning to bend forward at the waist and the deep rivulets on his face stood out like coarse muslin. Short gray hairs protruded from the sides of his cap and gray stubble on his chin, of what might be perceived as a goatee, contrasted against his dark skin. His wet eyes glistened almost as much as his face, and his thick lips hung loose when he spoke. We both knew why I had come, but went through the usual preamble, anyway.

"How's business?"

"Lousy, man," he said. "Print and paper are finished. Damned internet's taking over everything."

"It's the electronic age," I said.

I took a pack of gum from a rack on the counter and slid a piece into my mouth. It felt stiffer than it should be, but I managed to make it soft after some hard chews.

"Electronics don't help my arthritis none," Greasy said, as he bent down behind the counter with a low moan. He brought up a tied bundle of magazines and began cutting the strings with his penknife while he waited for me to say what he knew I would.

When I felt the time was right, I said, "I need the word on an upper class."

He continued to work and spoke without looking at me. "How upper?" he said.

"Very," I said.

He pulled the strings out from beneath the bundle and dropped them into the trashcan while I leaned closer to him and whispered Drew's title and full name, which was the only information I needed to give him. If there were any buzz on the street connected to Drew, Greasy would eventually ascertain it and pass it to me. I never questioned his tactics or sources, since he had always been a reliable informant and almost always came through for me.

"Sounds way up, man," he said. "Take some time." He began separating magazines into small piles according to their titles.

"While you're at it, see what you can get on Raymond Deverol," I said.

He removed the stub of a pencil from behind his ear and then found a scrap of paper from the trashcan. He laid both on the counter in front of me and went back to his work. I wrote the names out carefully and slid the paper back toward him. He folded it and put it into a pocket behind his overalls.

"What's the connection?"

"Maybe none," I said.

"A few days," he said.

I nodded without thanking him. "Okay," I said.

As I turned to leave, he said, "Hey, man! Ain't you gonna buy a magazine? I got some new girlie ones, just come in."

I took a twenty-dollar bill from my wallet and slid it under a rock paperweight on the counter. He smiled at that and touched the brim of his cap again. "Keep your head down," he said.

"Yeah, watch your back," I said as I walked away.

If there were anything out there on Drew or Ray, Greasy would get it to me.

I kept my lunch date with Sandy and told her that Briggs had put me on administrative leave. She said Briggs was an asshole and couldn't make a judicial decision to save his stripes. I told her he was a cop, not a judge. She said she was glad I hadn't shaved my head.

It started to rain again on my way back to my apartment. It was almost three o'clock when I arrived. I slid my key into the deadbolt and found it unlocked. Mrs. Jankowski had forgotten to lock the front entrance again. I stepped into the alcove and started up the steps toward the second-floor hallway when I noticed pools of water on the stair treads. I hadn't been home since this morning and other than Sandy, no one else had my door key. My mailbox was in the alcove and I wasn't expecting any special deliveries. I continued up the steps cautiously. I rarely use the hall light during the day, the window at the far end lets in enough daylight for me to see my way, but now someone had pulled the shade down, leaving the hallway in complete darkness. I stopped before the top step and listened. *Did I hear heavy breathing or was my instinct for self-preservation playing tricks on me?* I took the top step and moved slowly toward my door, keeping close to the wall.

As I reached under my sweatshirt for the gun I had in my belt, the window shade flew up with a deafening flutter, letting in a torrent of light. At that moment, a hand clamped down on my shoulder from behind me. I spun around quickly, loosening the grip, but found myself facing a big guy who proceeded to slam me against the wall. He brought his forearm up under my chin and pinned me while his partner yanked my gun from my belt. The big guy held me against the wall with the force of a steamroller. This guy was so big he made Briggs look small. He wore a tight black muscle shirt and black jeans, and the shine on his shaved head was almost as brilliant as the gold earring he wore in each ear. His face was chiseled and hard and never changed expression. His keeper was small and thin, with dark skin and a full head of curly black hair. He wore a black pin-striped suit and black pointed patent leather shoes. One silver earring dangled from his left ear. When I struggled to get out from under Muscle boy, he leaned on me harder, choking off my air. "Let him up," Keeper said. Muscle boy lowered his arm. I massaged my throat to start the air flowing again.

"You boys are in the wrong neighborhood," I said, "the muggers work Wilson Avenue."

"Open it," Keeper said.

He kept my gun pointed at me. I reached into my pocket for my keys and unlocked the door. Inside, Muscle boy closed the door quickly and leaned against it. Keeper motioned with my gun for me to sit on the sofa. I did.

"What's this about?" I said.

"It's about Detective Max Graham, Manhattan South, and NYPD...currently suspended from duty. You've been a bad boy, Graham."

"Okay, you did your homework."

"What's your business with Anton Denali?"

"Never met him."

Keeper gave muscle boy a look, which I knew meant, "Teach this guy a lesson."

I figured I'd better throw him a bone before I got steamrollered again. "His name turned up during my investigation," I said quickly.

"What investigation?"

"I'm looking for a friend of mine."

"Gimme a name."

"Deverol, a friend from college."

"What's his connection with Mr. Denali?"

"None, as far as I know."

Keeper thought for a moment, then moved closer to me and made a threatening gesture with my gun. "Your investigation stops now," he said.

I sat unmoved.

"Somebody must have a lot to hide if they sent you and—" I looked over at Muscle boy— "Tarzan," I said.

"As of today, you're gonna forget you ever heard the name."

"Tarzan?" I said. My sarcasm might have gotten my head knocked off, but I couldn't resist.

"Denali," Keeper said.

"Never met him."

That was enough to piss off Keeper. He gave Muscle boy the look again. Muscle boy reacted to the command and started toward me. I was surprised he understood the order without verbal communication; but then, a good hunting dog reacts the same way. I jumped up and grabbed the table lamp next to the sofa, but the plug end got hung up in the wall outlet and Muscle boy was on me before I could yank it free. He drove his massive fist into my midsection, knocking the wind out of me and causing my knees to buckle. On my way down, he hit me with an uppercut and I thought my head came off. The room became a vortex of light and dark as I hit the floor in front of the sofa. Instinctively, I curled into a tight ball but not before Muscle boy slammed his size fourteen boot into my stomach and tried to field goal me across the room. I couldn't fight back. I could only hope he wouldn't beat me to death. I tried to protect myself as much as I could. I lay there barely able to cringe as his boot slammed into me a second time. My head felt like a water balloon, heavy and fluid; and it was getting harder for me to keep it on my shoulders. I inhaled one deep breath and exhaled long and slow as darkness wrapped itself around me.

***

I was lying on my back in the soft grass, looking up at the azure sky, surrounded by a profusion of brightly colored flowers and enjoying the sun's warmth on my face. At the base of a foothill where I lay, cool water from a sparkling falls trickled gently onto my forehead before spilling into a limpid pool. Bluebirds sang above me in harmonies that could have only been composed in Heaven, accompanied by the syncopated whispers of the gentle breeze.

The pain that put me out was the pain that woke me up. My head was pounding and the hollowness in my stomach felt like somebody tried to open me with a can opener. I forced my eyes open and waited. It was dark, very dark until I saw a fuzzy yellow light above me. Cool water was spilling over my head; it snapped me back to the real world. When I managed to get my eyes fully open, I found myself on my back on the floor. Sandy was leaning over me, squeezing water out of a towel and wiping it over my face and forehead. "Thank God," she said. "In a minute, I'd have—" She leaned closer and kissed my face. "Are you all right, Lovey?"

"I don't think so," I said.

"Can you sit?"

She helped me onto the sofa and sat me upright; the room went around one full spin then settled down. I tried to get comfortable, but every part of my body ached.

"What happen?" she said.

"I didn't see it coming."

"What?"

"The freight train."

"Not funny," she said. "It's a good thing I came by. When you didn't answer the door, I used my key. You were lying on the floor and I—"

"Right there when I need you," I said, with an appreciative smile.

"What time is it?"

"Almost six."

"I've only been gone a half hour," I said. "It was kinda nice. I was lying in the grass—"

She leaned against me and put her arms around my neck. I couldn't hold back an agonizing moan as my ribs gave under her weight.

"Oh, I'm, sorry," she said, jumping back quickly. She kissed my cheek to make up for the pain, then went to the kitchen, took down a bottle of rum from the cabinet above the stove and brought it back to me. I took a long draw. It hurt when I swallowed, but it felt good going down.

"Do you need to go to the ER?"

"I'll be okay," I said. "That punk punches like my Aunt Theresa."

She didn't think that was funny, either. "How'd this happen?"

"I paid a visit to our friend Denali's beauty shop this morning. Word got to him quicker than I thought. He sent two of his myrmidons to tell me to lay off."

"Couldn't they just tell you?"

"They tried."

"But you wouldn't listen."

"I should let them come in here and push me around?"

"Someday that hard Italian head of yours is going to get permanently broken," she said.

"What's Denali so afraid of?"

"Don't know," I said.

I told her what Ross Montgomery said about Drew delivering a box to Denali's apartment.

"What's the connection?"

"I'm not sure."

"What was in the box?"

"Don't know."

"Does it have anything to do with Ray's disappearance?"

"Maybe."

"How do you feel?"

I pushed on my ribs. "Nothing a little Krazy Glue won't fix."

She helped me to my feet and walked me to the bathroom.

"Are you hungry?"

"Very," I said.

"I'll make something. Will you be okay?"

"Sure, I got all this nice clean porcelain to hold on to."

She left me standing in front of the mirror. Fortunately, Muscle boy hadn't hit my face, although there was a bruise under my chin. I washed my face, neck, and arms with soap and cold water, combed my hair and brushed my teeth. A shower would have been better, but my body couldn't handle it. When I walked back to the kitchen, something was beginning to smell good. Hunger rumbled through my stomach, and when it did, it brought the pain back with it. As I eased into a chair at the table, Sandy came toward me from the living room carrying my gun. She had a pencil through the barrel like they do in the movies. The cylinder was open and empty. "I found it on the floor by the door," she said.

"It's mine. They took it from me."

"Have it dusted for prints."

"It doesn't matter."

She laid it on the table in front of me.

"I'll stay the night," she said.

"You don't have to."

"Yes, I do."

She walked back to the stove and began to stir a pot of soup she had over a low flame.

"What's bothering you?"

"My ribs."

"Something else, I think."

Sandy was getting perceptually better at reading my emotions. She was good—almost to the point of scary. If Marlene had had that talent, we might still be married. But I was being unfair. I could apply that fault to myself as well.

"I feel like I'm peddling in the same place," I said. "I've gathered a load of information but can't put it together."

"Maybe you don't want it to come together," she said.

I knew what she meant. I had been denying the idea that Drew had anything to do with Ray's disappearance, but now, I wasn't so sure Drew was as innocent as he would like me to believe. If I couldn't connect him directly to Ray's disappearance, then I'd have to continue my investigation on the assumption that Ray was dead. Working on that premise, I could move on to the next question. Who killed him and why?

Chapter 13

"When the hours flew brightly by, and not a
cloud obscured the sky,
My soul, lest it should be, thy grace did guide
to thine and thee."
Edgar Allan Poe—Hymn

I awoke the next morning with Sandy beside me. She was lying on her stomach with her arm draped over my chest. Her hair fell lightly across the bedsheet and over my shoulder. I could smell its fragrance without even trying. It was like waking up in a rose garden. I lifted her arm gently and placed it beside her, then sat up and was quickly reminded of the pain in my ribs.

I had slept well and was at least able to function. I got up and walked to the bathroom and stood in front of the full-length mirror behind the door. There was a bruise the size of a softball forming on my right side over my ribs and a small red blotch under my chin. Considering the bulk and power of Muscle boy, I considered myself lucky.

I took that long shower I so desperately craved, and despite the injury under my chin, I was able to shave without much difficulty. I was beginning to look better, even to myself. When I walked back to the bedroom, Sandy was out of bed. I could smell coffee, bacon, and toast. coming from the kitchen. I slipped into a pair of jeans, my sneakers, and a sweatshirt and walked into the kitchen. Sandy was at the stove. I came up behind her and kissed her on her neck.

"Feeling better?"

"Thanks to you," I said.

The rain had stopped and the morning sun threw a distorted square of yellow through the kitchen window and onto the breakfast table. Sandy was making a huge bacon, pepper and cheese omelet. She had set toast, coffee and orange juice on the table. I sat down behind my coffee mug and watched her scramble some eggs and add a variety of ingredients for a double omelet. When she was done, she set the steaming dish in front of me, then sat down with hers. We sat in the warm sunlight and ate, held hands and kissed once or twice. Despite my aches and pains, I felt better than I had in a long time. Sandy did that for me. After we finished breakfast, we teamed up to do the dishes, Sandy washed, I dried.

"It's a great day for a walk in the park," she suggested.

The idea sounded good to me. Right now, Monica Flannery, Drew, Ray, Briggs, Denali, and McCaffrey were a thousand miles away. We finished the dishes, locked the apartment, and walked the short distance to Oakwood Park.

The morning was exceptional. The air was crisp and clean, the sky a cloudless blue, and the grass and foliage sparkled from the previous night's rain. We strolled tree-lined paths, bought ice cream from a vendor, and sat on a bench by a duck pond. Sandy looked prettier than ever with the sunlight accenting the red highlights in her hair. Our time together was always good, and I felt lucky to have her. When she slipped her arm around my waist, I winced. She laughed, apologized, then bent over and kissed my ribs. I winced again. Although it wasn't as romantic, we agreed it would be safer to hold hands the rest of the way. We continued along the path, passed a running brook and up a grassy knoll to a large lake surrounded by trees. As we strolled around the lake, we talked of our past and our future, and sometimes we didn't talk at all. People jogged by and we dodged kids on skateboards and couples on rollerblades. Sandy stopped a dog walker to ask what breed an animal was and pet its head. It was nearly a perfect morning...until I spotted Bernie.

I didn't know how long he'd been following us or why, but I intended to find out. I continued walking, keeping Sandy at our normal pace while keeping an eye on Bernie. He moved furtively along the trees and walked cautiously on the path, keeping a good distance and stopping each time we stopped. He was wearing the same suit he wore when I saw him at the beauty shop and looked out of place here in the park with the spandex and sweatpants. Why was he following me? Denali had already sent me a message. I suppressed the anger that was seething inside me so Sandy wouldn't ask questions, but right then I could have snapped Bernie's skinny body in two.

I had to get Sandy out of harm's way and do it so she wouldn't get curious enough to make it obvious. I stopped on the path, took her arm and spun her to face me. Before she could say a word, I pressed my lips against hers, then said, "Give me a big hug, then walk away and wait for me at my apartment."

"What?" she said.

She tried to pull back, but I kept her lips near mine.

"Do as I ask," I whispered.

"What's the problem?"

"Nothing I can't handle."

"But, I—"

"Wait at the apartment. I'll explain when I get there."

She had been cool enough to handle situations like this before, and I knew I could count on her. She gave me a squeeze and a smile and walked away with a big wave. *Nice touch*, I thought. I waved back as I watched her disappear up the path, and then I turned and walked back toward Bernie.

When Bernie saw me walking in his direction, he turned his back, leaned against a tree and lit a cigarette. I took my gun out and held it behind my back. I waited for the path to clear, then moved in on him. The cigarette dropped from his

137

lips when he felt my gun on the back of his neck. "Into the shrubs," I said. We moved off the path and walked about twenty feet into the foliage, then stopped at a small clearing.

I spun him around to face me and pushed my gun into his belly. "Why are you following me?" I said.

He looked at me, more terrified than he had to be. "D-Don't shoot me," he said. He began to twitch his head.

"I want an answer," I said.

He held his hands out in front of him, palms open, to let me know he wasn't a threat. I reached out with my left hand and gave him a quick pat down. He wasn't carrying. I shoved my gun hard into his bony ribs. He offered a quick response. "Denali sent me."

"Not much loyalty to your boss when your life's threatened," I said.

"I-I had to do it," he said, *twitch, twitch.*

"I already got Denali's calling card. What's he want?"

"For me to follow you," he said, *twitch.*

"Why?"

"To keep you from snoopin'."

"What's he afraid I might find out?"

With my question, fear exploded over his face as his eyes locked onto mine and begged for mercy. His lips began to tremble and his breathing came in short, heavy bursts.

"What's he afraid of?" I said again.

"Don't make me tell you. If I do, I'm a dead man," he said, *twitch.*

I put my gun up against his forehead, between his eyes, and held it there. Beads of sweat formed on his forehead and rolled down his temples. His eyes began darting from side to side as if he expected someone to jump out of the shrub and waste him. He seemed more afraid of what Denali might do to him than my gun against his forehead.

And then I saw his face soften, and his shoulders droop. His entire body relaxed in a posture of defeat. I guessed the muzzle of my gun pressed tightly against his forehead, gradually annulled any loyalty this weasel might have had for Denali. "I'm a dead man either way," he said. "Can I smoke?"

"Easy," I said. I let him reach into his pocket. I lowered the .38 but kept it pointed at him.

He took a crumpled pack of cigarettes from his inside jacket pocket, removed one and lit it. He pulled on his nostrils a few times, then drew on the cigarette long and slow. I let him take his time.

"Denali's dealing," he said.

Big surprise!

"Keep going," I said.

"His shops are losing money and he owes a bundle."

"How does he get the stuff?"

"Through a hospital, it gets delivered to his apartment then distributed to the street through his shops."

"What hospital?"

"Don't know."

"How often?"

"Once a month, sometimes sooner."

"Who drops it off?"

"Don't know."

I brought my gun up between his eyes again and tapped the barrel a few times on his forehead.

"I swear. I don't know," he said.

I watched the fear well up behind his eyes as I let him sweat a few seconds before I lowered the gun.

"Sloppy setup," I said.

"It's all worked out. Everybody gets a piece and nobody says nothin'. There's a ton of money in that junk," he said. "You'd be surprised what people will pay for a thimble full."

139

"Is that how he pays you?"

He didn't answer.

"Where's Ray Deverol?"

"Who?"

He thought I was going to bring the gun up again and said, quickly. "I don't know names. I swear, I never heard of the guy. Everybody does his part and don't know nothin' about the other guy."

"What's your job?"

"I watch the shops, collect the legit money and make sure nobody gets wise."

"Nobody like me," I said.

"I saw you talking to Carla, knew you were asking questions."

"I'm naturally inquisitive," I said, "especially when somebody's trying to put me in a hospital."

"Carla gave me your card."

"You rough her up?"

"No. She knows where her bread gets buttered."

"So, like a good soldier, you brought the info to Denali."

He nodded with the contriteness of a schoolboy caught with his hand in a cookie jar.

"And he sent Superman and Lois Lane to my apartment."

He nodded again.

"Why are you tailing me?"

"I told you, he wants me to keep an eye on you."

"Why?"

"To make sure you lay off."

"What else?"

"That's all," he said. "What happens now?"

"I call Denali and tell him you spilled your guts to me."

"Cut me a break, Graham," he said.

There wasn't much I wanted to do with Bernie just then. I could have arrested him on a number of charges, but I thought he might be more valuable to me if I sent him back to the pack.

He stood there looking around nervously and sucking on his cigarette while he waited for me to say something.

"If I see you again," I said, "Denali's going to know you and I are buddies."

I lowered my gun to my side. "Get lost," I said.

"Thanks, Graham," he said. "I swear I was only—"

"Get lost!" I repeated.

He looked around, stamped out his cigarette, and then scurried through the foliage like a frightened rabbit.

Chapter 14

"Oh, lady dear, hast thou no fear?
Why and what art thou dreaming here?"
Edgar Allan Poe—The Sleeper

Another week passed, and I was no closer to finding Ray than I had been. I was beginning to believe he would never be found or didn't want to be.

Where are you, Ray? What have you done? Or what has someone done to you?

NYPD continued building its case against him and his alleged collaborators. From the standpoint of the law, Ray's existence made little difference. There would be arrests, indictments, and punishments just the same. Ray had become irrelevant to everyone—but me.

Fortunately, I had another stone to look under. It was one of those things that might turn out to be nothing but couldn't be left unattended. Experience has taught me that the stone left unturned is where the treasure is. I wanted to talk to Ray's former girlfriend. It might be a dead end but, sometimes, in police work, dead ends take you to the right place.

The address Allan Deverol had given me was in Queens.

Sunday traffic on the Queensboro Bridge was unusually heavy. After more than thirty minutes, I found myself on Northern Blvd where I exited onto Ashton Street. The map I'd printed off the Internet took me through several neighborhoods populated by neatly kept row houses. After another ten minutes, I found Carlyle Place and made a right.

Number 17 was in the middle of a row of two-story structures. Each building had a porch beneath the front windows and a second-floor balcony just above that. Other than the house numbers and paint colors, structurally, they were identical. I parked at the curb and walked up the wooden steps. Two mailboxes were mounted on the wall beside the front door, but neither had a name on it. A small alcove with an inner door connected the upper and lower apartments. I pushed open the door and stepped into the hallway. From behind the door to my left, I heard the sounds of a children's program on television and kids laughing. I looked up the shadowed staircase in front of me. Despite the quietness, I followed my instincts and started up. The second-floor hallway was dark. Light from a side window told me there was one door in the center of the hall. I walked up to it and listened. There was no sound from the other side. I had no idea who I was looking for, what I hoped to find, or if I was wasting my time, but that "dead end" theory told me I was doing the right thing. I knocked and waited.

A voice that seemed vaguely familiar came from behind the door.

"Who is it?"

"I'm looking for a friend of a friend," I said.

There were a few moments of silence, then, "Who's your friend?"

"Ray Deverol," I said.

I heard the security chain rattle and the deadbolt click. When the door opened, I found myself looking into the seductive green eyes of Carla Darling. A cigarette was dangling from her lips and although her hair had fallen partially over her face, it didn't hide the bruise on her left cheek. She squinted through a veil of smoke and took her time recognizing me.

"I've got nothing to say to you," she said. She tried to close the door, but I leaned on it.

"I need to talk to you," I said. "It's important."

"We talked enough," she said. Self-consciously she brought her hand up and touched her bruised cheek.

Bernie had lied to me. He had come down on this girl harder than he'd had to. I should have busted his nose before I let him go.

"I'm sorry about that," I said. "Can I come in?"

"No," she said.

"I need your help. Ray's missing."

She didn't move and kept the door in the same position.

"I think he's in trouble," I said.

She thought about that for a moment and then let go of the door. I followed her in and closed the door behind us.

The apartment was what you'd expect from a single woman living alone, modestly furnished but neat, a large living room up front, a kitchen and one bedroom at the rear. A collection of ceramic dogs sat on a coffee table by the sofa between several ashtrays and a couple of crumpled cigarette packs. The place smelled of stale cigarette smoke. This girl definitely needed a nicotine break.

Carla dropped onto the sofa and tucked her legs under herself. She was wearing an oversized sweatshirt and sweatpants. Her feet were bare. Although she wasn't wearing make-up and the bruise on her cheek had turned a purple-black, she was still inherently attractive. She took a drag on her cigarette, then crushed it out in an ashtray. I stood in front of her.

"Why'd he hit you?"

"He gets his rocks off."

"Does he do it to all the girls?"

"Just the ones he likes."

She removed another cigarette from a pack of Marlboro on the table and fired it up.

"I don't have to talk to you, you know."

"True," I said.

"I wouldn't have let you in, except I like looking at you." She said it seriously and without a smile.

"You should be more careful," I said. "What you see isn't always what you get."

"No fun in being careful," she said.

"Maybe," I said.

"How'd you know where to find me?"

"I wasn't looking for you. I was looking for Ray's ex-girlfriend."

"Small world."

"Ray's brother gave me your address."

"I'm surprised he remembers me. What kinda trouble is Ray in?"

"He's missing. I was hoping you could tell me where he might be."

She got up and walked to the front window and looked out over the balcony at the street below. She took a long drag on her cigarette and let the smoke out slowly.

"What kind of missing?" she said, without turning.

"He disappeared."

"Did he run away?"

"I don't know."

She turned and looked at me. "Is he hiding from something? Was he kidnapped? Missing can mean a lot of things."

"He might be dead," I said.

Her expression went from indifference to concern. She walked back to the sofa, sat down and snuffed out her second cigarette. "If Denali finds out I'm talking to you, *I'll* be dead," she said.

Denali must rule like a tyrant. This girl was as much afraid of Denali as Bernie had been.

"This is between us," I said. "What can you tell me about Ray?"

"What's there to tell?" she said. "He came into the shop one day for a haircut. We became fuck buddies for a few months, then broke up—end of story."

"Tell me about the deal."

"You said you wanted to know about Ray. I don't want to get mixed up with the cops."

"I'm here as Ray's friend, nothing official."

She leaned her head back on the sofa, closed her eyes for several seconds, then opened them again. "Ray told me about the deal, said he needed a way to get the stuff to the streets. I suggested Denali might be interested, that he was low on cash and had street connections. Ray got excited about that, asked me if I'd talk to him. I saw it as a way to make points with Denali, so I agreed."

"You got involved in a criminal enterprise just to make points with Denali? Pretty stupid."

"What was I thinking?"

"Not about the consequences," I said.

"The truth is…I fell hard for Ray and would do almost anything for him. Guess he didn't feel the same."

"Did he tell you why he was doing this?"

"Just that he needed the money."

"When did Denali go for it?"

"Not right away. He checked things out, as he always does. Guess the idea appealed to him because he met with Ray to work out the details. That's all I can tell you. By the end of that month, Ray and I broke up. I haven't seen him since."

"How does Denali buy your loyalty?"

"He gives me something every month for the rent."

"Small recompense for some brownie points and possible jail time," I said.

146

She became suddenly anxious. "You said the cops wouldn't be involved."

"Just me and you," I said. "Did Ray explain the operation to you?"

"Only that the stuff would go out through the shops."

"How…exactly?"

"Bernie meets people at the shop and they go into the back room. The deals are probably made there."

"Have you seen it, first hand? It's important."

"I know a deal when I see one. That's all I know," she said.

I took a card from my pocket, wrote my cell phone number on the back and dropped it on the coffee table. "If you think of anything else, call me," I said.

"Sure," she said. "Come identify me at the morgue."

As I started for the door, she stood and blocked my way. "Do you have to leave already?" she said. She slid her arms around my waist and pulled herself into me. I could feel those solid thighs again, and her small rounded belly, and firm breasts pressing against me. Her body felt exciting against mine and I let her keep it there. Suddenly she was the old Carla I'd met at the beauty salon. When she pushed up on her toes and tried to kiss me, I turned my face.

"Don't you like me?" she said.

"What's not to like?" I said.

"Then why don't you—?"

I pushed away from her and said, "If you hear from Ray, let me know." I walked to the door and opened it, leaving her alone in the middle of the room.

"Sure," she said. "Be careful, handsome."

"Thanks," I said, and closed the door.

***

I left Carla with her pack of Marlboro and drove to Drew's mansion. I wanted to hear his reaction when I updated him on my progress and I wanted to allow him to talk, maybe say something that would reinforce or abate my suspicions of him.

I'd promised Sandy we'd spend the evening together at her apartment, and I was sure I'd have enough time to get to Drew's and back. We didn't have anything special planned, just some quiet downtime we both deserved. We were good for each other that way.

Weekend traffic was slow but treacherous on the way, and it was almost 4:00 pm when I finally arrived. I turned off the main street and headed up the road toward the house. The sun was beginning to set and the myriad trees and foliage kept the grounds in the usual gray shadows. In the distance, I could see a dim yellow light coming from inside the mansion.

As I took the last turn toward the parking area, I saw something I didn't expect, something that didn't fit the picture, something that caused me to brake the Chevy and pull off the road beside a stand of trees. Evangelista's Subaru was parked opposite the portico, and he was just getting out of it. I turned off my engine and watched him walk across the parking area to the front entrance. I got out, closed the car door gently and stood behind a tree as he approached the front doors. He pressed the chime button and waited. In less than a minute, Drew opened a door, and the two disappeared inside. No words were exchanged.

I walked around the Chevy and moved through a grouping of Evergreens trees closer to the house. From my position, I could see through the barred front windows as Drew and Evangelista walked along the front corridor and turned into the library. I knew if I could get to the house unnoticed, I could see into the library through the wall of windows at the rear. I stayed in the long shadows of the Evergreens as I worked myself closer and then ran across an open stretch of lawn to the stone chimney. Keeping close to the building, I moved toward the back of the house until I turned the rear corner. I could see the lights from the library spilling out onto the rear patio as I inched along the building, keeping in the shadows. When I reached the rear windows, I leaned my head in just enough to see inside. In the center of the room, Drew and Evangelista were engaged in conversation. Although I couldn't hear what they were saying, their body language told me enough. Drew shook his head from side to side in a "no" expression more than once, while Evangelista poked his forefinger in the air near Drew's face. Drew turned and walked back to the double doors of the library. Evangelista stayed with him, spewing words that seemed to fall on deaf ears, and waving his arms vehemently in the air while trying to make his point. Then, in a sudden display of aggression I had never seen in Drew, he grabbed Evangelista by his shirtfront and shoved him against the doorframe. Evangelista pushed Drew away and grabbed him at the front of his neck. Drew reached up to free himself from Evangelist's grip, but Evangelist had the advantage. A short struggle ensued until the two men separated. There was a tense moment of silence between them until Drew let loose a barrage of words and phrases I only wished I could have heard. Evangelista gave no response, but turned and hurried out of the library.

With the show over, I moved back along the house, peered around the corner, and then jogged across the lawn and back to the stand of trees. As I ran, I heard the Subaru's engine start. Through the Evergreen branches, I watched Evangelista turn the Subaru around with a squeal of tires and start down the road away from the house. I made my way back to the

Chevy and crouched behind the rear bumper just as he passed. He didn't look happy.

I got back into the Chevy and started the engine. My visit with Drew could wait. This unexpected revelation brought a new set of questions to light. I sat and thought about what I'd just seen. My mind was reeling. What business could Evangelista have with Drew Flannery? From the conversation I'd witnessed, he certainly wasn't soliciting medical advice. Having just arrived here from the West Coast, how would he have known Drew Flannery even existed? As I drove down the road away from the house, I racked my brain trying to find any feasible answer. By the time I arrived at the front gate, I'd concluded the only logical link between Tony Evangelista and Drew Flannery was Ray Deverol.

I followed Evangelista back to the Regal Motel and waited for him to park the Subaru and go inside. I found a parking space not far from his cabin, then walked to his door and knocked. The curtain behind the big window slid back and a wary Evangelista peered out. After recognizing me, he released the curtain and opened the door.

"Have you found Ray?" he said.

"No," I said, "but we need to talk."

He closed the door, and we stepped into the center of the room.

"What's your connection with Dr. Flannery?" I said before he had a chance to say any more.

He looked surprised and thought about what he wanted to say before he answered, "I thought he might know where to find Ray."

"Why would you think that?"

"Ray talked about Flannery and you more than once. Said you were close friends, that you hadn't seen each other in a lot of years. He said he was glad he was being transferred and hoped he could locate one or both of you."

"You didn't mention that the last time we talked."

"I thought it better not to say anything. I thought I could find Ray myself."

It got me more than angry to think this guy was arrogant enough to believe he could find Ray on his own and disparage the hard work of a lot of professional people who would do a better job than he ever could, myself included. Maybe he was reading too much Sherlock Holmes. I let him have it.

"I spend most of my conscious time trying to find Ray, and what I've come up with so far couldn't fill a thimble. There are also at least three full-time detectives working on this case who aren't making much headway either. What makes you think you can do better?"

He looked genuinely contrite when he said, "I just wanted to help."

I let the rest of it go, and said, "What did Flannery tell you?"

"Just that he was as much in the dark about Ray's disappearance as anyone."

I didn't buy that. The exhibition I'd witnessed through the rear windows at the mansion told me more than Evangelista was telling me. Their conversation was more than just about Ray. He was lying through his teeth and getting my temper up. I don't like being lied to.

I took a deep breath instead of grabbing him by his throat and removed Ray's notebook from my pocket. "This belongs to Ray," I said. "Do you recognize any names that might ring a bell—for any reason?"

He took the book and sat on the bed by the table lamp. He turned on the lamp and took his time turning the pages and running his index finger down the list of names and addresses.

"Most of these are business associates," he said. "People that work for the company in one capacity or another. Some names I don't recognize."

I watched him turn a few more pages until he stopped at a page that generated more interest than the others. He brought the book back to me and held the opened page up for me to see. He pointed with his finger and said, "This one—maybe."

I took the book from him and read the name, Aaron Matetski.

"He's a veteran salesman," Evangelista said, "a real asshole. I remember him because he and Ray were in contention for salesperson on the year. The guy was spiraling down fast, drank too much, lost his wife over it, and needed the money award to get himself up again. When Ray took the award, he held it against Ray personally, antagonized Ray for weeks after, even threatened him, as if Ray didn't deserve the award."

"How did Ray react?"

"He handled it the right way. Tried to avoid Metetski whenever he could, but there was always bad blood between them—until Metetski got transferred here."

"To the east coast?"

"Secaucus. A few months before Ray. Ray was glad to see him go."

"Would Metetski know Ray got transferred after him?"

"Sure, they both work out of Secaucus. And there's the employee newsletter and email."

"Why would you think he has something to do with Ray's disappearance?"

"I don't. But you said anything that rings a bell."

Evangelista might be trying to throw me off the scent for whatever his reasons were. But he had given me a lead I'd check out, just the same.

As I put the notebook back into my pocket I said, "I'll keep you informed on a need to know basis. Otherwise, take my advice...stop playing detective."

***

Aaron Metetski lived in North Bergen, which wasn't far from Secaucus and the Regal Motel. I decided to make the trip while I was close and hoped I could still make it to Sandy's on time.

I pushed the Chevy hard along I-95 more than a bit beyond the speed limit and found myself where I wanted to be in less than thirty minutes. Once she was on the open road and running at higher speeds, the old gal seemed to get her second wind and keep up easily with competing traffic. I kissed her steering wheel and patted her dashboard as a gesture of appreciation. She showed her gratitude by emitting flatulence from her tailpipe.

Negotiating my way through a district of short residential blocks, I finally turned onto Blair Road. Number 630 was a single-story home situated on a lot of overgrown grass and surrounded by a rusted chain-link fence. The house was small and sorrowfully neglected. It needed fresh paint and its roof, although intact, was stained dark in several areas due to the overhanging tree branches, which needed to be trimmed back from the gable ends. I parked across the street and walked toward the house. Before I could unlatch the front gate, a dog began to bark furiously at the back of the house. I looked around the building cautiously and spotted a Rottweiler the size of a small buffalo jumping onto the part of the fence that enclosed the rear yard and crossed the blacktop driveway. The fence rattled and gave under the dog's enormous mass and looked as if it would fall over at any moment. My instinct for self-preservation told me to stop and reconsider how badly I wanted to talk to Metetski, but a delusory belief that I could run as fast as "Jet" Graham, won out, and I opened the gate and went in.

As I walked up the wooden stairs, the barking grew louder and more ferocious. I had an image of this brute toppling the fence, rounding the front corner of the house and tearing a chunk out of my ass before I could make it inside, its red eyes glaring, its mouth froth with white. I put my hand on my gun and hoped I wouldn't have to use it. I hurried to the door and pushed the doorbell. It was difficult to hear over the barking, and I wondered if the bell even worked. I began knocking rapidly on the pane of glass in the center of the door when I heard a voice from behind the front windows scream over the barking, "Quiet, General! Quiet, dammit!" The barking continued until I heard what sounded like a screen door slam at the rear of the house and the command was given again. After a quick yelp from the animal, there was silence. I stood in the quiet on the front porch and was about to press the doorbell again when Aaron Metetski appeared around the corner of the house and glared at me suspiciously.

"What do you want?" he said, almost angrily.

Metetski was well over six feet, but with a slender build. He was wearing jeans and a white tee-shirt and sneakers. His hair was almost as white as his shirt and fell onto his forehead and covered most of his ears. His face was redder than it should be. He studied me through glassy eyes as he walked toward me swinging a dog leash, almost threateningly, in his right hand.

"Aaron Metetski?"

"Who wants to know?"

He was close enough now for me to detect the aroma of whiskey, although he didn't seem drunk. I removed my business card from my wallet and handed it to him. He looked down at it without taking it from me.

"I'm trying to locate a friend of mine," I said. "I was hoping you could help."

"I'm busy," he said. "Try the lost and found."

"Ray Deverol," I said, ignoring his remark. "I understand you work with him."

Metetski looked at me with an expression that told me he was trying to decide if he wanted to say anything more to me. When he thought enough about it, he said, "I heard what happened to Deveral. Personally, I hope I never see him again."

"Why do you say that?"

Instead of answering my question, he looked at me suspiciously again and said, "How did you know where to find me?"

"Company records," I said. "Your name's on the roster."

He seemed to accept that and said, "Well, you picked the wrong name, I have no connection with that weasel and don't want any."

"I'm not interested in your conflict with Ray," I said.

"What do you know about that?" he said.

Before I could answer, he answered for me. "His buddy, Evangelista," he said. "Another weasel. Hangs out with Deverol—birds of a feather."

"I'm just looking for information that might help me find Ray," I said.

"I don't care if you ever find him," he said and meant it. "I don't owe Ray Deverol a thing. If anything, he owes me."

"How so?"

He drew his eyebrows together in an expression of sudden concern.

"I don't want to get mixed up with the police," he said. "I've got nothing to say."

He turned away from me and started back around the house, but I stopped him with,

"This stays between us. Ray's a personal friend of mine. I'd appreciate it if you'd help me."

He took a second to think about that, and then walked back, put his foot on the bottom step and leaned against the newel post. I waited while he assessed the circumstance. When he was ready, he said, "I saved Ray's ass, big time, and he screwed me for it."

"Salesperson of the year?"

"Evangelista leave *anything* out?"

I didn't answer.

"I'll give ya the real story," he said. "I don't want to look like a jerk to anybody." He pushed away from the newel post and stood straight when he spoke, making sure I understood every word.

"Ray and I were drinking buddies," he said. "When you drink with a guy, you get to know what he's really like. We hung out off the job, got drunk, got laid, the usual buddy stuff. There was never any problem between us until I accidentally stumbled on to what he was up to."

"Up to?" I said.

"Criminal," Metetski said. "I saved his job and kept him out of jail."

"And how did you accomplish that?"

"By keeping my mouth shut."

"I'm listening."

"When Ray took a week's vacation, I was assigned to cover his sales. I wasn't happy about it, but it's part of the job. It meant doing my paperwork and Ray's as well, twice the usual amount. By the end of the second day, I began getting calls from some of Ray's buyers, complaining their orders were incorrect, orders too large, items arriving in duplicate even triplicate. When I checked my order invoices against the shipping invoices, they checked out identically. I couldn't see the problem. I spent the rest of that week making phone calls, rechecking invoices, and pulling my hair out. By the time Ray came back to work, I was pissed. When I confronted him about it, he tried to come up with a half-ass story, but finally spilled the truth."

"Which was?"

"He was padding inventories to put money in his own pocket. It was a pretty elaborate scheme. He admitted to having used it on occasion whenever money was tight, but this time, something went wrong, he screwed up and almost got caught."

"But you said Ray was on vacation."

"He couldn't or wouldn't let downtime interfere with the continuity of the scheme."

"Did he do all this alone?"

"I don't know, and I didn't want to know. I'd stumbled onto too much already. He tried to give me a feeble excuse to justify what he was doing, but I told him I didn't want to hear it. Whatever he was into was on him. I didn't want any part of it."

"Did Evangelista know what Ray was doing?"

"Maybe. He was closer to Ray than I was, but I can't say."

"Go on."

"Ray was more than worried, begged me not to say anything. I told him I'd keep quiet if he stopped the bullshit. He said he would. I thought he'd learned a lesson."

"And you remained friends?"

"More or less."

"Until salesperson of the year came up," I said.

"Ray and I were both in contention for the thousand dollar prize, Ray being the favorite. At the time, I was having personal problems and the winning spot would have helped me financially as well as professionally. You know, help turn my life around. All Ray had to do was remove his name from the running, and the prize was mine."

"But he didn't."

"He said he needed the money himself, which was a lie. I almost suggested he continue stealing from the company if he needed money, but I didn't. Instead, I kept my mouth shut and Ray took the prize from me. I hated him after that, but never said a word to anyone about what he'd been doing...until now. A month later I got transferred here."

The barking at the rear of the house started up again. Meteski turned away and started to walk back around the house. He stopped before he turned the corner and looked back at me.

"This stays between us," he said, looking for reassurance.

"Between us," I said.

"I hate that shitbird, but I don't want him to go to prison."

Chapter 15

"And what means are ours for attaining the truth?
We shall find these means multiplying and gathering
distinction as we proceed."
Edgar Allan Poe—The Mystery of Marie Roget

Sandy lived on the top floor of a three-story garden apartment on Lindsey Street, not far from where I lived. Her rooms were more contemporary than mine but situated almost in the same way: A large living room, a small kitchenette, a bathroom, a long hallway, and one-bedroom at the rear.

I was in her living room, watching TV from her sofa, while she waited in the kitchen for the buttered popcorn to finish in the microwave.

"Ray is mixed up in bad business," I said, "and Drew Flannery is in just as deep."

"You'll have to prove it," she said.

"Briggs will have to prove it. I'm just trying to just find, Ray."

I was watching Bogey in *The Treasure of The Sierra Madre* and Fred C. Dobbs had just gotten his head bashed in with a rock by a Mexican bandit. Sandy carried in a bowl of popcorn and two beers on a tray and set it on the coffee table, then sat beside me. We watched as Dobbs fell to the ground and a second bandit gave him a couple of whacks with a machete, finishing him off.

"The consequence of greed," Sandy said.

"Huh?" I said, reaching for a handful of popcorn, without taking my eyes off the screen.

"Greed," she repeated. "Dobbs had plenty of gold for himself, but still wanted more."

"It's one of the seven deadly sins," I reminded.

The bandits were slicing open bags of gold dust, letting their contents dissipate in the wind. I cringed at their ignorance. As I stuffed some popcorn into my mouth, a few pieces slipped between my fingers and fell to the carpet.

"You'll clean that up," Sandy said.

"Sure, soon as the movie's over," I said.

She put her feet up on the coffee table and sat back with the bowl of popcorn on her lap.

As she scooped a handful for herself, several pieces fell onto the sofa cushion and bounced to the floor next to mine. She looked at me quickly, but I pretended not to notice.

"Why would Drew get mixed up in trafficking?" she said. "He's got plenty of money."

"And Dobbs had plenty of gold," I said.

She gave that a thought and then said, "I guess that rules out Monica Flannery's theory that her husband killed Ray out of jealousy. If he kills Ray, the operation stops."

"Maybe he had another motive," I said.

"For killing Ray?"

"It's possible."

"I guess," she said. "And it's also possible he's on the run like Briggs said."

I took a sip of beer, wiped my fingers on a napkin and went to the kitchen.

"Where are you going?" Sandy said.

"Recapping," I said.

I took a pad and pencil from a drawer by the stove and sat at the table. I made a list of things I was sure of so far and numbered them consecutively. Then I made a list beside that of the things that were possibilities, but I couldn't corroborate. My third list was of things I didn't know yet but wanted to know. It was considerably shorter than my first two lists, which told me I was making progress.

Sandy picked up the remote and clicked off the TV.

"Wait," I said. "Let's record the rest of that."

"You've seen the movie before."

"Twice," I said.

"How can you watch the same movie again and again?"

"I can if it's one of my favorites. Besides, each time you watch a movie, you see something you missed the time before."

"That's not true."

"How many times have you seen *Gone with the Wind*?"

"That's different," she said. "It's a love story with meaning."

"A four hour movie and I'll bet you know every line of dialogue."

She gave up the argument even though I was only partially right; she probably knew only half the dialogue.

Resignedly, she pushed a couple of buttons on the remote, then came to the kitchen table and sat beside me. She leaned over my shoulder with intense curiosity.

I referred to my lists and said: "Ray turns in a legal sales order. The Hamlin kid pads it up as much as he can get away with. It's boxed and shipped to the respective hospitals, only Hamlin's padded order always goes to Andover Medical, where Drew resides. Ray makes sure of that. The surplus from the order is repacked and delivered to Denali's apartment where it's disseminated to the street from Denali's shops."

"And if the sales order is checked," Sandy said, "it would agree with the shipment since the surplus wasn't on the list. Everything would seem in order."

"Right," I said. "All someone had to do was go to receiving, find the order, transfer the surplus to another package and reseal the original box."

"Would Drew risk doing that?"

"More likely, Ray. A salesman wouldn't look out of place in a receiving room. Ray probably left the package in a pre-designated location for Drew to pick up when the opportunity was right. Drew then took the package with him at the end of the day and made the delivery to Denali's apartment."

"Why wouldn't Ray make the delivery?"

"Because Drew collects the payment on delivery."

"Guess he doesn't trust Ray."

"Guess not."

"Like Dobbs didn't trust his partners," Sandy said.

"Exactly," I said. "Having too much money can distort a man's mind just as easily as not having enough."

"If you let it," Sandy said. "Where does Evangelista fit in?"

"I haven't figured that out yet. But I'm sure he's lying about his relationship with Drew. There's more than he's admitting."

I went back to the living room to retrieve my beer.

"Why would a man like Drew get mixed up with these kinds of people?" Sandy said.

"Tomorrow I'll see Monica Flannery. Maybe she can tell me."

"Don't forget to clean up that popcorn," Sandy said.

***

The next morning I phoned Monica Flannery but got no answer. I decided to take a chance and drive out to the mansion. It was mid-morning. The sky was a dull gray and rain fell intermittently on my windshield, but not enough for me to use my wipers. As I drove through the opened gate and started toward the mansion, I spotted the silver Jaguar coming down the road toward me. I put the Chevy into reverse and backed down onto the main street. I parked across the street just as the Jag appeared at the gate. Monica Flannery was behind the wheel. I slouched down and watched her make a right turn and drive down the block. I decided to follow her. She might only be going to her hairdressers, but I had that "stone left unturned" feeling.

I trailed her into Manhattan, being careful not to lose her in midtown traffic. When she got to 5th Avenue, she parked the Jag and disappeared into a department store. I guessed being estranged from her husband didn't preclude her from spending his money. I parked and waited. It was almost forty minutes before she came back to the Jag; she tossed several shopping bags into the back seat and drove to the Williamsburg Bridge.

I followed her into a Brooklyn neighborhood, which was beginning to look familiar, and my guess was she was heading for Ray's apartment. I was right. She parked near a corner and walked the half block to Ray's building. I parked at the opposite corner across the street. I watched her walk briskly up the front walk, climb the stairs, remove a key from her raincoat pocket and go inside, just as easily as if she had lived there herself. I checked my dashboard clock, which was one of the few things that still worked like new in the Chevy. It was just past noon. Twenty minutes later, she came out and headed back to her car. She wasn't carrying anything. What was in Ray's apartment that she felt was important enough to warrant her drive all the way here?

After Monica Flannery drove away, I walked up the front steps and pressed the button for Mrs. Kellerman's apartment. She opened the door wearing a white housecoat and a white kerchief wrapped tightly atop her head. She stood for a moment wiping her hands on a dishtowel, looking like she didn't remember me.

"Mrs. Kellerman," I said. "I'm Detective, Graham. Ray Deverol's friend."

"I remember," she said. "I still ain't seen, Ray."

"I'd like to see his apartment again if you don't mind? It's important."

She gave me what I perceived to be an annoyed look as she opened the front door to let me in. I followed her to Ray's apartment, where she unlocked the door for me.

"If Ray don't show up, soon I got to rent this place," she said. I got a right to do that, you know. I got bills to pay."

"I understand," I said.

Her sudden indifference to Ray's disappearance surprised me, given the genuine concern she'd shown and the favorable opinion she'd had of Ray when I'd first met her. I supposed money take precedence over friendship, as far as she was concerned.

"Close the doors when you leave," she said and disappeared down the hallway.

I didn't see anything different in Ray's apartment from the first time I'd been there. I walked around the living room but found nothing disturbed or missing. I gave the bedroom a quick check and was satisfied everything there was the same as well. Ray's cell phone was still on the night table where I'd left it, and nothing in the closets had been disturbed. In the kitchen, everything was still spotless. As I turned to leave, I instinctively pulled back the kitchen door to look behind it, as if I'd expected to find Ray there. Ray's calendar was still hanging behind the door with the days marked out, as he had left it. But now, I saw the addition of a handful of words scrawled across the days in bold black letters. Monica Flannery had left a message for Ray on his calendar.

I drove back to the Island and parked across the street from Drew's mansion. The sky was beginning to brighten, and I was starting to feel warm. I opened the windows to let out the stuffiness, then took out my cell phone and dialed the mansion. Monica Flannery answered on the third ring. I told her I needed to discuss some important things with her and asked her when I could see her. She said anytime this afternoon was okay. I told her I wasn't far away, and I'd be there in a few minutes. After I ended the call, I waited a while, and then I drove up the road.

When she opened the door, she looked haggard and worn, hardly the woman who came to my office almost a month ago to vent her concerns for Ray. No amount of eyeliner could help her listless eyes, and the foundation and color she wore did little to enhance her natural beauty as it once had. In the short time that I'd known her, the ravages of worry and guilt had exiled her to the land of aging beauties.

She led me into the living room, which was bigger than the library and distastefully ornate. There was a stone fireplace here too, and several framed oil paintings on the walls. I recognized a *Dali* and maybe a *Pollock*. I was sure they were the real things. Behind a large desk in a corner of the room hung a framed pencil drawing of E. A. Poe, I wondered why it wasn't in the library with the other Poe memorabilia. I guessed Monica Flannery was the collector, since I'd never known Drew to be interested in framed art. The room was homier than the library and furnished with upholstered armchairs and sofas and lots of antique brass. There were brass lamps on cherry wood end tables and a brass chandelier and several brass statuettes on a coffee table. A brass coat of arms above crossed swords hung on the wall above the mantle, and a vast collection of brass plates sat precariously on several shelves on the rear wall.

We stopped in front of a flowered sofa.

"Does your husband own a gun?" I said.

"He did," she said, without offering me a seat.

"What kind?"

"A silver one."

"I mean, what make? What caliber?"

"I don't know anything about guns," she said, "He used to keep one beside the bed."

"Does he still have it?"

"I'm not sure," she said. "If you like, I'll see if it's still there."

"Thank you," I said.

She walked out of the room and returned a few minutes later carrying a big shiny handgun. She held it in both hands in front of her as though she thought she might contract a disease from it. The barrel was pointing directly at my crotch as she walked across the room toward me. I could see it was loaded. I stepped aside quickly and eased the gun from her hand as delicately as I could. I opened the cylinder and let the rounds drop into my palm, then closed the cylinder. I recognized the gun as a .357 magnum, Colt Python, nickel-plated with a six-inch barrel and diamond-cut wood grips.

"Drew used to belong to a club," she said. "He shot at targets, now he keeps it by the bed."

"Does he have any more guns?"

"I don't think so," she said. "It's the only one I've seen in the house."

There was a strong probability that Montgomery's murder was connected to Ray's disappearance, so I'd called Danny Nolan earlier and asked him to check with ballistics to find out what kind of round had killed Montgomery. The bullets the coroner dug out of Montgomery's chest were identified as .32 caliber wadcutters, a bullet which is suited more for a revolver than a semi-automatic and used primarily for target shooting but will make a clean hole in human flesh just as effectively, not usually the bullet of choice to commit murder. I'd established the fact that Drew had access to guns, knew how to handle them and was probably a pretty good shot; although one doesn't need to be a good shot to hit a target six inches away. I was hoping Drew wasn't crazy enough to want Montgomery out of the way so badly that he would resort to killing him. Even though, right now, I had no valid reason to think he would. His wife's claim that the Python was the only gun he owned was, of course, unreliable. As a member of a gun club, he would have access to a variety of handguns.

I had to check myself from guessing at possibilities rather than working from facts. Homicide cases are supposed to be worked objectively and without emotional attachment. But this was different—homicide, suicide or sunny side, dead or alive, Ray was nowhere to be found.

Not only was I feeling more afraid for him, but I was also beginning to feel anxious, frustrated and impatient. Nonetheless, I had to maintain some semblance of logic in my thoughts and actions if I expected to get anywhere. Sandy and Briggs were right. My personal feelings were muddying up my thinking, no matter how much I tried not to let it happen. I'd try harder.

"You'd better return this to the drawer," I said.

I handed her the gun, grip first, barrel toward the floor.

She eyed the rounds in my hand.

"Can you put the bullets back in?" she said.

"I think it'd be safer if we didn't."

"He'll know I took it," she said.

I took the gun back, reloaded the cylinder and handed it to her again.

"Keep your fingers away from the trigger," I said, "with the barrel pointing to the floor."

"What is the barrel?" she said.

"The hole where the bullet comes out," I said.

She did exactly as I'd instructed and walked gingerly out of the room with the gun. When she returned she said, "Since I'd been questioned by the police, Drew and I have been further apart and I don't want to give him another reason to get angry. I'm afraid of him. He's been moody and detached, spends his nights in the library until passed midnight engrossed in his books."

"Has his daily routine changed his work at the hospital?"

"Not noticeably. He spends more time away from his office these days but always fulfills his obligations. There have been no problems with his practice, as far as I know. Professionally, he's the medical demigod he has always been. Personally, he's becoming a monster."

I took this last assessment as a gross exaggeration and let it go.

"I won't take another day of it," she said. "Tomorrow I'm going to stay with my sister in Westchester."

"Did Drew agree to that?"

"He protested at first, but didn't give him a choice."

"I'll need that address."

"I understand," she said.

She walked to a small table nearby and wrote the address on a piece of pad paper.

"I told Drew what you suggested," she said, handing me the paper, "that I'd hired Mr. Montgomery to help find Ray."

"What was his reaction?"

"Anger."

I put the address into my wallet.

"Does he know I was involved?"

"It never came up."

She walked to a serving table and began to make herself a martini. She held up the bottle.

I shook my head.

"Now that the police are in this, it'll be difficult to separate yourself from Ray," I said.

"Why would I want to separate myself from Ray?" she said. "I want to find him."

"I don't mean personally. I mean, legally. The police told you Ray is a wanted man. Weren't you aware of that?"

"Ray never told me. Why would he involve me in that?"

Up until now, she had been helpful and co-operative, but suddenly, I was beginning to feel she was being evasive. It was time for me to try a different approach, push her a little.

"I think you *are* involved," I said. "I think you're just as involved as Ray or Drew."

She began to drink her Martini with short, nervous sips. "That's a crazy notion," she said. "Why would you think that?"

I moved closer to her. "Because you haven't been completely truthful with me since the day you walked into my office and asked for my help."

"Everything I said is true. I don't know where Ray is."

I lost myself. "Ray could very well be dead!" I shouted. "Stop waiting for him. If he's not dead, help me find him."

She raised her hands to her face, letting her martini glass fall to the carpet. As I continued, she began to sob.

"You're so wrapped up in lies you can't see things clearly anymore. Well, let me bring things into focus for you."

"Ray told you about the gig he set up, but things weren't supposed to turn out like they did. The two of you weren't supposed to get involved. You thought you fell in love with Ray and saw a way out of your relationship with Drew."

She sat on the sofa and let me go on.

"I don't believe you love Ray anymore than he loves you. You were convenient for each other. Ray needed you to convince Drew to go in with his scheme, and you saw Ray as a ticket out. If he could amass enough quick money, he promised to take you away with him. When Ray presented the idea to Drew, Drew was hesitant, but it was in your best interest to convince him it was a good deal and eventually Drew saw it as easy money."

"There could never be enough money for Drew," she said.

She picked up her glass, went back to the serving table and mixed another Martini, fighting back her phony tears. She was good at that.

"I didn't want to get involved in this thing. I only wanted to help Ray."

"Is that why you went to his apartment this morning?"

She gave me her best "surprised" look.

"I-I just wanted to—"

"Be sure Ray hadn't left any incriminating evidence to involve you," I said.

She took a long drink, and then said, "It's true, it's all true, but I never meant for anything to happen to Ray."

"If you know where Ray is, you'd be smart to tell me, now."

"I don't," she said. "I swear. I just want to find him...alive."

"Why'd you leave him a message on his calendar?"

Another surprised look.

"If Ray showed up on his own, I wanted him to call me immediately."

"Why?"

"I was afraid," she said. "Not sure of what to do. I needed to talk to him about it."

"An odd juxtaposition of beliefs," I said. "You believe Ray is alive, yet, you tell me your husband killed him?"

"You're right," she said. "I don't know what to believe anymore. Drew is such a possessive monster. It's easy for me to believe he killed Ray."

I could see fear and resentment for her husband in her eyes.

"Drew needs to be in control at all times. The great Dr. Flannery, saving lives with a scalpel and his God-given talent."

She sat on the sofa and took a few rapid sips from her drink. After setting her glass down on an end table, she opened up to me.

"Our marriage was a mistake from the start. In the beginning, we believed we were in love, but as time went on, we grew apart. We knew we'd made a mistake. When we found out I couldn't have children, Drew blamed me for ruining his plans for our perfect life. He would never have the family he wanted, and now he was stuck with me."

"You'd think Drew would be glad if Ray took you away."

"One doesn't take from Drew," she said.

"Why not adopt?"

"It wasn't the real thing for him. Despite our mounting problems recently, we were trying to work things out, but it was futile."

"Until Ray came into the picture. You saw hope in Ray."

"Ray was the catalyst that pushed Drew over the top," she said.

"When he discovered you and Ray were involved? That's why you believe he killed Ray?"

"I told you, he said he would."

She brought her hands up to the sides of her head, squeezed her eyes shut and pressed hard against her temples as if she were trying to keep her head from exploding.

"I'm so confused," she said.

She buried her face in her hands and sat in silence. I waited. When she looked up at me, her eyes were swollen with tears, her eyeliner zigzagging down her checks.

"Am I going to be arrested?"

"I'll turn in my report when the time is right," I said. "The rest is up to the DA."

She stood up and threw her arms around my neck. "Help me, Max," she said. It was the first time she'd called me by my first name. "I don't want to go to jail."

"It makes no difference to me whether you go to jail or not," I said, pulling her arms off me. "I'm in this for Ray."

I left Monica Flannery with her counterfeit tears and drove out to the motel where Tony Evangelista was staying. When I checked with the Hoffman/Weir's West Coast office, they told me Evangelista had arrived here on the 31st, which would be the Wednesday before he said he'd arrived. It didn't seem very likely that he would have gotten his dates mixed up. I intended to find out just how good his memory was and how many more lies he thought he could tell me.

I pulled into the motel parking lot around noon and immediately spotted Evangelista's Subaru parked in front of his room. The lot was nearly, but I found a space next to a minivan, got out and walked across the lot toward number 14. As I approached the cabin, I could hear music coming from inside and saw that the door was ajar. I knocked and waited. When no one answered, I knocked again and called to Evangelista, this time pushing the door back slowly. As soon as my eyes adjusted to the room semi-darkness, I saw Evangelista lying on his stomach across the bed. He wasn't taking an afternoon nap. He was dressed in a sweatshirt, sweat pants and running shoes, and his shirt and bed covers were saturated with blood. I stepped in and closed the door. The door and deadbolt were intact, and I was able to lock it behind me, which immediately ruled out forced entry. The room was undisturbed other than the bed covers hanging half onto the floor with Evangelista lying on top of them. I didn't think anyone had seen me enter, but I pulled the curtain back carefully and looked out into the parking lot to be sure.

A Country song was blaring from a small radio on the night table. I pulled the electrical cord from the wall outlet, then turned in the silence to take a closer look at Evangelista. Someone had fired a bullet into his head behind his left ear. His hair was soaked and matted with blood. His arms were hanging off the bed above his head, and what had once been the right side of his face had become an exit wound of bone fragments and human tissue. His left eye was open and staring blankly at nothing across the room. This guy didn't know what hit him. I'd seen lots of dead men in my time, but for some reason, I felt sorry for him. He'd come here from the West Coast and wound up a corpse.

His car keys and wallet were on the desk next to his briefcase and his pint of booze. There was a hundred dollars in cash in his wallet and some traveler's checks. This wasn't a crime for profit. It looked more like a mob hit. Whatever Evangelista was into, he'd gotten in too deep and somebody wanted him out of the way. I opened the briefcase and searched through a pile of folders and business documents. I was looking for the piece of paper I had given him with my cell number on it. It was the only thing that could link the two of us. I didn't need that connection with everything else hanging over me. In a closet, I searched the pockets of a couple of suits and a few pairs of pants but found nothing. A Pullman bag was on the floor in a corner filled with folded shirts and underwear. I rummaged through it, then checked the drawers in the bureau and night tables. They were empty, not even a Bible. That meant I had to search his car.

I took his car keys from the desk, turned the deadbolt and opened the door and peered out into the parking lot. Although almost every space had been taken, there was little movement in the lot. I waited for an SUV to pull out before I stepped out onto the walkway, then made my way to the Subaru, trying to be as inconspicuous as possible. I pushed the "unlock" button on the remote, opened the driver door and slid in behind the wheel, closing the door as quietly as possible.

The interior of the car was the apotheosis of untidiness. The dashboard was carpeted with road maps, even though there was a GPS stuck to the windshield. The center console was cluttered with pencils, felt markers and notepads and a cup holder was filled with coins, tokens and filling-station receipts. There were empty coffee cups and an assortment of empty fast food bags on the passenger side floor. A few fries and dried pickles kept the interior smelling tangy.

I began by carefully pulling papers from behind the sun visors, one at a time, so they wouldn't avalanche onto the front seat. It would be easy to discern a piece of notepaper from the larger ones, but that wouldn't make searching through the mess any less painful. I took my time looking between each paper, holding them by their corners and being careful not to leave fingerprints. When I exhausted the pile behind the visors, I moved to the bundle I'd found in the glove box. I slid the bundle out and set it on the passenger seat. I sorted through it like a deck of cards but didn't find what I was looking for. I continued diligently for nearly thirty minutes with the doors closed and the windows up and the heat from the afternoon sun bringing the interior of the car to near boiling. After looking in every conceivable place, I had no choice but to give up. Feeling defeated, I wiped the interior and exterior door handles, locked the Subaru and went back to the room.

Inside, I returned the keys to the desk, wiped my fingerprints from the car remote and everything else I had touched and closed the cabin door, leaving it ajar, as it had been when I arrived. Then I walked along the walkway for a short distance and cut across the parking lot to my car. I drove away as quickly and quietly as the Chevy would let me.

When I was far enough away from the motel, I stopped at a roadside phone and got the number for the local police. Without identifying myself, I reported the situation at the motel, giving them the address and room number. I was feeling guilty for what I was doing, and at least making the call assuaged some of my guilt. If an investigation eventually connected me with Evangelista, I'd have no choice but to come clean with Briggs. Until then, I needed to stay focused on finding Ray.

Chapter 16

"Sweet creature! She too has sacrificed herself in my behalf."
Edgar Allan Poe—A Predicament

The ringing telephone jolted me out of the darkness of sleep and into the darkness of my bedroom. I reached for my cell phone and flipped it open before I realized the ringing was from my kitchen phone. When I ran to the kitchen and answered it, a whispered voice said, *"Your girlfriend needs you—tonight."* The adrenaline that surged through me knocked the grogginess out of my head and started my heart pounding. "Who is this?" I said. The line went dead. I looked at the clock. It was 1:40 a.m. I dialed Sandy's apartment. Her answering machine picked up. "Sandy, are you all right? Sandy, pick up!" When she didn't answer, I hung up and dialed her cell phone. No answer. For a split second, I thought of calling PD but decided against it. I hoped I wouldn't have to make the call later. I jumped into my sneakers, a pair of sweatpants and a t-shirt, grabbed my gun, wallet, and keys and rushed out of the apartment. For the first time, I was afraid, really afraid. I'd always tried not to involve Sandy in my work, but I had a feeling I had somehow drawn her into this bad business. I hoped I was wrong. The voice said she needed me. If she were involved in an accident, why wouldn't the caller identify himself? Why wouldn't the police have called? I knew this was something more. Something that kept the panic rippling through my body the entire time it took me to drive to her apartment.

I parked in front of her building and ran up the steps to the top floor, taking them two at a time. I jogged the long hallway toward her apartment, at the same time searching through my key ring for her door key. As I put the key in the lock, it suddenly occurred to me someone might be trying to get me here for an unhealthy reason. I took my gun out of my pocket and turned the key. The door was unlocked. *Not a good sign.* I pushed the door back slowly and stood behind the doorframe, squinting into the semidarkness. The apartment looked undisturbed. I reached around and flicked on the light switch and stepped into the living room. The only sounds I heard were the ticking of the wall clock in the kitchen and my heart hammering in my chest. I scanned the living room and kitchen, then rounded the corner into the hallway that led to Sandy's bedroom. At the end of the hall, the door to Sandy's room was ajar. I could see a yellow light coming from behind it. I moved closer to the door, slowly, listening for any sounds from inside the room. When I pushed the door back, my head exploded with a fusion of panic and rage at what I was seeing. Sandy was lying in her bed—naked. Her outstretched limbs had been tied to the headboard and footboard with short lengths of rope, her eyes were closed and there was a length of duct tape over her mouth. I rushed to her and gently pulled the tape away. Her eyes were closed, and her face was ashen under a glisten of perspiration. I slapped her cheeks gently and shook her by her shoulders, but she didn't respond. I propped her up on the pillow and slapped her again, this time a bit harder. She let out a low moan. "It's okay," I said. "I'm here." I went to work undoing the knots that held her wrists and ankles. I had a tough time of it. My hands were shaking, and I couldn't move fast enough. I could see light bruising and broken skin where the nylon rope had cinched her ankles each time she'd struggled to free herself.

When I untied the last knot, I sat on the bed and lifted her to a sitting position. I saw no blood or other marks on her body. I hoped she hadn't been drugged. Her eyes fluttered open. "Are you hurt?" I said. She muttered a few unintelligible words before her eyes closed again. I lowered her back to the pillow, pulled the blanket up to her neck and went to the kitchen to get her a cold drink. When I got back, she was sitting up with the blanket around her shoulders. As soon as she saw me, her bottom lip began to quiver and tears rolled down her cheeks. I sat beside her and pulled her close to me.

"It was awful," she said. "They tied me and—"

"Don't talk now," I said. "Drink this."

She took a long drink.

I set the empty glass on her night table, then wiped the tears from her cheeks with my thumbs and kissed her gently on her forehead. She put her arms around my neck and squeezed.

"It's okay now," I said.

She leaned back against the pillow again. "It was like a nightmare," she said. "I opened my eyes, and they were there."

"Who?"

"Two men. They had a gun and a rope."

"Did they hurt you?"

"They made me take off my clothes."

She closed her eyes tight to hold back more tears, but tears squeezed out from behind her lids and rolled down her cheeks. I hated to see it. With each tear that rolled down her cheeks, my anger increased.

"Take your time," I said, as I wiped her cheeks again. "Just tell me what you can."

"They made me lie down and tied me to the bed. When I asked them what they wanted, one of them put the tape over my mouth. I was sure I was in for a double rape."

"Did they touch you?"

"No. When they finished tying me—" She stopped and looked away. She was having a hard time telling me the rest. I took her chin gently and turned her head to face me. "What else?"

"The small one said, 'Tell your boyfriend things'll get worse if he doesn't back off '."

I felt myself grinding my teeth. Denali had sent these scumbags to scare me into backing off. If they wanted to hurt Sandy, they could have done so very easily. Somebody had squealed that I was still snooping. Bernie was too afraid to open his mouth, so it had to be Carla. She'd ratted me out—twice.

I kissed Sandy again. "You're doing fine," I said. "What happened next?"

"They left without another word. It seemed like I laid there for hours struggling to get free. I must have exhausted myself to the point of unconsciousness."

"Is there anything you can remember about them?"

"One was much bigger than the other," she said.

"What were they wearing?"

"They were both dressed in black. The smaller one wore a suit. They had on ski masks."

"Of course," I said.

I pulled her close to me again. "I'll stay with you the rest of the night," I said.

"I won't sleep now," she said.

"Then I'll make some coffee."

I stood up and looked back at her. "Are you okay?"

She nodded.

Sandy took a shower while I made coffee.

When the coffee was done, I filled two mugs and brought them to the coffee table by the sofa. Sandy came into the living room wearing her robe and slippers. Her head was wrapped in a towel. She sat on the sofa beside me. I handed her a mug. She took a sip from it, then put it down on the table and put her arms around me. As I moved closer to her, she nestled her face into my chest. I held her tight while thoughts of doing very bad things to Denali ran through my head.

Chapter 17

"At length, I would be avenged."
Edgar Allan Poe—The Cask of Amontillado

Chestnut wasn't mean. He just looked mean. His nose had been broken more than once, so that now it lay a bit out of kilter against his face. His brow protruded like an eagle's which accounted for his falsely malicious countenance. The only pristine commodity he owned was his set of perfectly placed teeth, which shone pearly white whenever he flashed his big smile. He stood six feet, four inches tall, solid and well defined with broad shoulders and a slim waist. I don't think he had an ounce of body fat on him. He always carried himself with a proper posture and displayed an aura of inner and outer strength, acquired from years of training and self-discipline in the Marshal art. Anyone who knew him gave him the recognition his presence commanded, not out of fear but out of deference.

Chestnut got his nickname because his skin color resembled the smooth reddish-brown color of a chestnut. He was born in Kingston, Jamaica, the accident of a dope addict mother and a father who ran out on him when he was eight. After a period of getting involved with the wrong crowd and the Kingston Police, his aunt, who raised him till he became of age, rescued him from the streets. Deciding to take advantage of his youth and physical attributes, he took an interest in martial arts. Karate became his passion. Years of study earned him the rating of a fifth-degree black belt. After closing his failed karate school on the island nearly a decade ago, he migrated to the U.S. and found work as a custodian in a midtown hotel. Our paths crossed a few years back when he mistakenly became a suspect in a case to which I had been assigned, involving the murder of a hotel security guard. In the course of my investigation, I'd discovered he was in this country illegally. However, his co-operation in helping me solve the case was invaluable, and I showed my appreciation by not reporting him to Homeland Security. His gratitude over the years never waned. I likened our relationship to that of *Ishmael* and *Queequeg* even though all I knew about him was that his birth name was, "Jordan Allen." I knew nothing of his recent personal life since our paths cross only occasionally whenever I request his service. It wasn't that Chestnut had anything to hide. I just didn't ask, and I believe he preferred the anonymity. Of course, at any time, I could have found out all I needed to know about him, but it would've served no purpose. Our friendship survived on confidentiality. He had helped me out of many tight spots over the years, and whenever I punched up the phone number he'd given me, he was there for me.

When I opened my apartment door, Chestnut was standing there smiling like a jack-o'-lantern, those teeth gleaming, full and straight and contrasting against his dark creamy complexion. He was wearing jeans, a sweatshirt that read: "*Happy in Jamaica*" on it, and open-toe sandals. He put his arms around me and gave me a big hug. "My mon," he said. "You call. I come." He liked to call me, "My mon."

We walked into the kitchen. He took a seat at the table while I brought out the ceremonious bottle of rum. I set two glasses on the table and filled both. The routine was the same each time Chestnut came to visit. Rum wasn't my favorite drink, but I always kept a bottle or two for him in the cabinet above the stove. It didn't matter to him that it was 10:00 in the morning; he drained his glass without taking a breath. He could drink rum like water. I poured him another.

"What you need, my mon?" he said.

"I got to see somebody," I said, sitting opposite him.

"You got trouble?"

"Yes."

"Rough stuff?"

"Maybe."

"Okay," he said.

That was all Chestnut needed to know, I'd never had to provide him with more information than was necessary. He trusted me completely. But now I found myself telling him the whole story, partly out of a sense of obligation and partly because this had become more of a personal issue for me than the usual police procedures Chestnut was accustomed to helping me with. I told him how I was looking for my friend and how he had gotten himself into trouble with the law, and how he might be running away or dead. How I'd gotten myself mixed up with a bunch of merciless criminals and what they had done to Sandy and how I feared for her safety more than anything.

"They hurt Sandra?" Chestnut said.

"No," I said, and waited for the anger to well behind his eyes. It didn't. He was a pillar of self-control, a virtue acquired from his years of training and self-discipline in the martial arts. But I knew how he felt.

I continued updating him on all the major details as candidly as I could while he sat quietly drinking his rum and listening. When I was through, his only question was—"When?" And I knew he understood the seriousness of what I was into and what I expected from him.

"Tomorrow," I said. "One o'clock."

He downed his second glass, wiped his mouth with the back of his hand, and then took his time looking around the apartment. I took a drink from my glass, as I knew he would expect me to, and waited to hear what he had to say next.

"Place looks good," he said. "It's got a woman's touch."

I nodded.

"You marry her yet?"

"No."

"Why do you wait?"

"Cause I've been there."

Sandy and Chestnut had met on several occasions and had engendered a fondness for each other based on their mutual interest...my welfare.

"Fine woman like Sandra will treat you good," he said.

"She already treats me good," I said.

"A wife treats you better."

I didn't know if Chestnut was a husband or a father, but I believed he had the attributes to fill both positions.

"Maybe." I said, "but I want to be sure she can cook, first."

Chestnut let out a roar of laughter, then reached across the table and put me in a headlock. I tried to wiggle out of it, but I was at the mercy of his huge biceps and stonework forearms. When he released his hold, he stood up, still laughing. I stood with him and threw a short jab at his midsection. He feinted to the left, but I caught him anyway, just above his waistline.

"You're losing your quick," I said.

"Quick enough," he said.

My door buzzer rang.

"I'll take you to the gym with me to help you get it back," I said, on my way to the door.

When I peered through the peephole, I saw Sandy standing in the hallway holding a bag of groceries. When I opened the door, she said, "Lunch is on me, Lovey."

I was glad to see she was handling the ordeal from the other night as best she could. She had taken the following day off from work and slept the entire day. She looked rested now and back to her usual self.

She walked passed me toward the kitchen and spotted Chestnut. "Holy crap," she said, "The one and only Chestnut." She set the bag down on the table, and she and Chestnut shared an affectionate embrace.

"A joy to see you again, Sandra," Chestnut said. *Big smile.*

She began taking items from the grocery bag and placing them on the table. I saw a couple of sandwiches wrapped in wax paper and a large bottle of Dr. Pepper. "Sloppy Joes, from Kartcher's Deli," she said to me. "I only bought two so you'll have to share with Chestnut."

"It's okay, Sandra," Chestnut said. "I'm not so hungry."

"Don't be foolish," she said, "there's plenty."

She cleared the bottle of rum and our glasses from the table and brought them to the kitchen counter. Then removed three dishes and glasses from the cabinet above the sink and brought them to the table. Chestnut and I sat down at the table again and waited. She unwrapped the sandwiches, then took half of my sandwich and placed it on Chestnut's dish. Chestnut smiled at me, but I didn't smile back. While I opened the bottle of soda, Sandy took a pile of napkins from the bag and placed them in the center of the table. Then she sat down between us.

"What are you boys up to?" she said.

I picked up my sandwich and took a bite. Chestnut did the same. Neither of us spoke.

Sandy looked at me, then back at Chestnut.

"I love you," she said to Chestnut, "but I know, when you hook up with Max, there could be trouble."

"No trouble, Sandra," he said, trying to reassure her.

"Chestnut's helping me with the investigation," I said. "You know I use him sometimes as a consulting partner."

She wasn't buying it.

"You mean tag team partner," she said. "Haven't you been banged up enough already?"

"It's no big thing," I said. "If you must know the particulars, I'll tell you."

"Forget it," she said. "I don't need to know. I'll worry whether you tell me or not. Keep the sordid details to yourself."

Her revelation that she would "worry" made me think of Marlene and the years she'd spent worrying. It was all part of the baggage that came with being a cop's wife, the uncertainty of impending violence and the inevitable worry. It had taken its toll on Marlene and our marriage, and I hoped it wouldn't affect Sandy the same way. I was trying not to let that happen.

"You're making something out of nothing," I said.

"*Nothing is* always *something* with you," she said.

"Your mon is safe with me," Chestnut offered. *Big smile again.*

"At least there's comfort in that," Sandy said. She took a bite of her sandwich and said no more about it. Chestnut and I knew enough to do the same.

When we finished lunch, Sandy gave Chestnut a short hug, and I walked him to the door. When we paused in the doorway, he took my hand in both of his and shook it.

"Tomorrow," he said. "One o'clock."

"Wear something nice," I said. "We're going to a high-class place. No sandals?"

He smiled, then turned and started down the hallway. "You better marry that lady, mon," he said, just before he disappeared around a corner. I knew he wouldn't let me down. He never had.

I closed and locked the door and went back to the kitchen. Sandy was on her way to the sink when I grabbed hold of her waist and pulled her close to me.

"You okay?" I said.

She nodded. "I'll turn in early and sleep with the light on."

"With the light on?" I said. "What does that mean?"

"I feel more comfortable with the light on, right now," she said.

I understood her feelings and let go of her.

I had offered to stay with Sandy at her apartment for a few days, but she insisted she wanted to get her life back to normal and my staying with her wouldn't help. Maybe she was right, but getting back to normal meant sleeping with the light *off*. We'd see.

I cuddled Sandy beside me on the sofa and we watched TV for about an hour. Before she left, I asked her to call when she got home so I'd be sure she'd arrived safely. She did. Feeling better, I stretched out on the sofa and thought about the mess I'd gotten her into. Denali had hit too close to home. He wanted me to stop digging for obvious reasons, but I still hadn't found Ray and I had a few more stones to turn over. I could handle myself, but I was concerned for Sandy. Even though I'd never met Denali, it was obvious he'd stop at nothing to save his own ass. I had to be sure Sandy would be safe before I continued. I'd decided Chestnut and I would pay Denali a visit. I wanted to talk to him face to face, establish an understanding that Sandy was off-limits. Maybe I was being naïve thinking he would cooperate, but I had no boundaries when it came to Sandy's safety. Besides, I couldn't stop now and walk away, I was too close, and I owed it to Ray.

Chestnut showed up the next day just before one. He looked spiffy in his dark brown suit over a white shirt, open at the collar and tan patent leather shoes. I wore khaki pants and my brown corduroy jacket. We took the Chevy to Tower Park West on 34th Street. On the way, Chestnut questioned the bruising under my chin. I knew he had to have noticed it during lunch the day before but hadn't mentioned it. Today he wanted answers. When I had explained things to him earlier, I had left out the episode of how Keeper and Muscle Boy had visited me, but now I gave him the details.

"Why?" he said.

"To get me to lay off," I said. "The big guy punched me around."

"You punch back?"

"Not fast enough. He put my lights out,"

"I'll teach you some fast moves."

"For next time?"

"For any time."

"We'll go to the gym," I said.

"Sure," he said.

"Right now, I need to talk to this guy Denali, ask him to keep Sandy off his list. This is over the top. It's like going after a man's wife or kids."

Before I could finish, Chestnut began shaking his head slowly from side to side.

"What's that mean?" I said.

"Won't work."

"Why not?"

"Bad mon like that got no conscience," he said. "Mon with no conscience can't reason."

I sat quietly for a while, thinking about that, and hoping Chestnut was wrong.

***

I parked across the street from Tower Park West and we rode the elevator to the fourth floor. When the elevator doors opened, we stepped into a long hallway. Room 417 was at the end of the hall and I immediately noticed a guy in a dark suit standing in front of the door, smoking a cigarette. I looked at Chestnut. He shrugged indifferently, and we started down the hallway. When the guy saw us, he snuffed the cigarette out under his shoe, dropped his arms to his sides and waited for us to get close. This guy was big, not hard big but soft big. The top of his head was bald and freckled, with ribbons of red hair matted down on the sides, just above his ears. A tuft of red hair hung from his chin. He had small beady eyes, small ears, and a small nose. The biggest thing about him was his waist. If it weren't for his height and weight, there would be nothing intimidating about him.

"You the Doorman?" I said.

"Who wants to know?"

"I want to see Denali."

"You got an appointment?"

"No."

"He ain't home."

"I need to see him."

"He don't wanna see you."

"Let him tell me that."

"He ain't home."

"I need to talk to him."

Doorman pushed hard on my shoulder. "I told ya, he ain't home. Get lost."

I looked at Chestnut. "Is this guy getting on your nerves too?"

Chestnut leaned in close to Doorman's face. "Be nice," he said.

"Beat it," Doorman said.

"You could get hurt," Chestnut said.

"Who's gonna hurt me?" Doorman said.

Even though this guy was bigger than Chestnut, I was already feeling sorry for him. He didn't know it, but he'd already gotten in over his head.

Chestnut moved fast. I almost missed it. He snatched Doorman's right arm, brought it up around Doorman's back and slammed him against the wall, pushing his face into the doorframe. Doorman's features distorted like a ball of soft clay.

"Who's inside?" Chestnut said.

"Nobody," Doorman said, through twisted lips.

Chestnut pulled up on Doorman's arm like he was trying to bring it up over his head.

"Man, you're breakin' my arm," Doorman yelled.

"You better tell him before you make him mad," I said.

"Just a couple o' guys in there," he said. "I swear."

"Open the door," I said.

"I can't. They gotta open it from inside."

Chestnut pulled up on Dorman's arm even higher. I was expecting to hear a bone snap at any moment.

"Okay! Okay!" Doorman said.

Chestnut released Doorman's arm. Doorman rubbed the side of his face, trying to bring his small features back to the places God had intended them to be. After he worked his arm a few times at the elbow trying to bring feeling back into it, he gave the door a couple of cryptic raps with the knuckles on the hand of his other arm. Within a few seconds, somebody inside turned the lock. Before the door opened, Chestnut shoved Doorman against it, causing him to tumble into the room on all fours. We followed him in, my gun drawn.

We found ourselves in an elegantly furnished suite: a floor to ceiling window offered a spectacular view of Central Park through a set of rose-colored vertical blinds. There were two white leather chairs, a big screen TV and a chrome and glass wet bar on one side of the room. A smoked glass coffee table and a curved white leather sofa took up most of the remaining space. On the sofa, sitting surprised and wide-eyed were my two buddies, Muscle boy, and his keeper, the guys Denali had sent to my apartment to work me over, and who had also put Sandy through a night of Hell.

"What the fuck?" Keeper said.

"Relax," I said.

Muscle boy jumped up and was about to steamroller me until he saw my gun. I motioned for him to sit. He obeyed. We all waited for Doorman to crawl from the plush carpet to the sofa. Chestnut closed and locked the door, then checked the adjoining bedroom. I heard him opening and closing closet doors. He moved the shower curtain back in the bathroom and eyeballed the kitchen area before he came back to the living room. "Nobody here, mon," he said.

I turned to my buddies on the sofa. "Give me your heat," I said.

Doorman and Keeper reluctantly removed their guns from their pockets and placed them on the coffee table. I looked at Muscle boy. "He don't carry," Keeper said. I bent over and gave Muscle boy a quick frisk. As I reached down in front of Keeper to pick up the guns from the table, I couldn't resist jamming my elbow into his chest. He grabbed his chest and fell back onto the sofa. It made me feel better. "These boys do Denali's dirty work," I said to Chestnut as I turned and walked toward the kitchen. "They teach lessons and scare women." There was a stainless steel garbage can by the kitchen entrance, the kind with a foot pedal that opens the lid. I pushed down on the pedal, dropped the guns into the can and let the lid slam shut. Then I walked back to the living room. "Where's Denali?" I said to Keeper.

"Kiss my ass," he said.

It didn't look like I was going to get my chance to face Denali. But I'd stumbled onto a treasure trove just the same. Vengeance wasn't in my playbook, but after what these guys had done to Sandy, I was going to enjoy this.

I walked over to Keeper and leaned down close to his face. "You good with rope?" I said.

He gave me a defiant look from the corners of his eyes. "You *wops* think you can get away with anything," he said.

Chestnut gave me an incredulous look. "Did he say *cops* or..."

I'd heard exactly what he'd said.

This was one of those times when I willfully abandoned my self-control. I slapped Keeper hard across his face with the back of my hand. He fell back against the sofa. The imprint of my knuckles came up red and swollen on his cheek. "I'll bet you don't use that word in front of your boss," I said. He sat there without a response. I could see sweat break out on his forehead and the anger in his eyes. He'd remember me for a while whenever he checked his mug in a mirror.

I moved closer to Muscle boy and put my face close to his. "Where did you learn how to tie knots?" I said. He just looked at me, his face hard and expressionless. I felt like I was talking to a manikin.

"Maybe he was a boy scout," Chestnut said, as he walked toward the picture window.

I watched him remove a folding knife from his pocket and reach up and cut the cord that worked the vertical blinds. He was smiling as he walked back toward the sofa, the cord hanging from his hands like a lynch rope. "I think they need a lesson," he said. "Maybe we can—" Before Chestnut could finish his sentence, Muscle boy got a sudden burst of stupidity and lunged for me. Chestnut saw him first. With a fierce uppercut, he sent Muscle boy tumbling to the carpet. Muscle boy sprang to his feet quickly. Chestnut waited for his next move. Muscle boy lowered his head; his massive shoulders arching forward and came at Chestnut like an angry bull. Chestnut sidestepped the advance with the gracefulness of a ballerina, which sent Muscle boy crashing into the bar amidst breaking glass and clanging metal. While Muscle Boy shook himself from his stupor, Chestnut put one knee into the small of his back and brought Muscle boy's hands up behind him. He wound the cord several times around his wrists and tied a double knot. He looked like a cowboy trussing a calf.

"He's big, but slow," Chestnut said, while he bound Muscle boy's ankles. When he was through, he lifted him to his feet and helped him hop back to the sofa. I watched as Chestnut bound Keeper the same way. He cut the excess cord from Keeper's ankles and tied Doorman's hands and feet. When he finished, he walked into the bathroom and brought back a roll of toilet tissue.

"Potty mouth needs a lesson," he said as he walked up to Keeper.

Chestnut pulled out several feet of tissue, crushed it into a tight ball, and began packing it into Keeper's mouth. Keeper gagged and tried to resist, but Chestnut's fingers were like a plunger. I almost retched as I watched, but I'll admit I was enjoying it. When Chestnut finished, he propped all three up on the sofa like throw pillows. It was the first time I'd seen such a morbid display of vengeance from Chestnut. These dirtbags deserved worse, but I took satisfaction in knowing they'd have to deal with Denali's wrath when he witnessed this folly.

I put my gun away as we walked back to the door. After Chestnut unlocked and opened the door, we looked back at the comic display and smiled.

As we started to walk out, Chestnut said, "Wait, mon." He walked back to Keeper, lifted him off the sofa and placed him sideways on Muscle boy's lap. They looked like a ventriloquist and his dummy. We were still laughing when we closed the door behind us.

***

I dropped Chestnut off at a coffee shop on 14th street and thanked him. I knew I couldn't offer him compensation. He wouldn't accept it and had told me rather vehemently more than once. He took my hand in both of his and shook it. As he climbed out of the Chevy, I slid a twenty-dollar bill into his jacket pocket. I hoped he checked his pockets before putting that jacket away.

Sandy's safety was of paramount concern to me. And after what had happened at Denali's place; I wasn't sure if I hadn't started a war. Maybe it was a dumb thing to do, go up against Denali, but there was the chance he'd ease off Sandy. He'd gotten his point across to me, and he knew it. My other concern, of course, was my mother. It wouldn't be difficult for Denali to find out where she lived and work on her to get to me. The thought terrified me. I was glad Marlene and the girls were living in south Jersey. At least they were out of harm's way.

Chapter 18

"I saw but them—they were the world to me.
I saw but them—saw only them for hours."
Edgar Allan Poe—To Helen

Meola Beach is a small community at the Jersey shore, just south of Asbury Park. It's populated by condos and bungalows and has one of the best beaches in the state. Marlene always loved the water and used her share of the profit from the sale of our home to buy a small house a few blocks from the ocean. I've never been a shore person; all that salt and sand gave me a gritty feeling whenever I visited, but spending time with my daughters far surpassed any minor discomforts I might have had to endure.

The one-story house had been painted white by its previous owner and still looked good. A white picket fence surrounded the front lawn, which was covered with white stone rather than green grass—a condition indigenous to the locale. A brick walkway wound its way up to the front porch and brightly painted front door, where a windmill/mailbox hung above the doorbell. Christie and I had built the mailbox as a Brownie project several years ago. She had removed it from our former home and displayed it proudly on the new house for all visitors to see.

I intended to visit for a few hours and then drive back before dark. I hadn't seen the girls in almost a month and was becoming overwhelmed with guilt. I also wanted to reassure myself they were safe. The bad business I was into was making me overprotective of the ones I loved, and I needed to feel satisfied they were okay. Since Tuesday wasn't my regular visitation day, I'd phoned Marlene and asked her if it would be okay. She said, "Of course."

Marlene had always had a natural knack for interior decorating. She had made our home together as comfortable and attractive as could be without unintentional gaudiness. As I sat on the sofa in the living room watching the girls play a video game on TV, I could see she had applied her talent here as well. The room was large but cozy with the contemporary motif she preferred. There was a large sofa and love seat in the center of the hardwood floor, surrounded by cherry wood tables and a glass shelved cabinet against one wall where Marlene displayed her ceramic dog collection. Draperies on the windows, corresponding with the fabric color on the sofa and loveseat, tied everything together nicely. The kitchen was small but efficient without being overcrowded. It had been updated with oak cabinets, stainless steel appliances, and a double stainless steel sink. The girls had their own bedrooms, each of which had been transformed into a wonderland of all the delights of what young girls love.

A forty-two inch, big screen TV (I wondered how Marlene could afford that) had been transformed into a colorful tennis court. The girls each held a plastic wand and were swinging it like a racket, which caused the ball on the screen to go in whichever direction one wanted it to go.

"It's easy, Daddy," Justine said. "If you know how to play tennis."

Her hair was as red as her mother's and her skin was fair, accenting the freckles on her nose and cheeks. She was tall for fifteen and seemed like she had grown a full inch since I'd seen her last. She was wearing a blue sweat suit and pink sneakers, and her mother had tied her hair into a ponytail using a pink ribbon.

"It looks pretty hard to me," I said.

"Not if you practice," Christie said. She still had that tomboy nature as I watched her crouch low and swing the game wand quickly several times to beat her older sister. The sweat suit she wore matched her sister's, but she was wearing tan boots and her dark hair was too short to keep a ponytail.

"How has your mother been?" Marlene shouted from the kitchen. She was setting out plastic cups and dishes in preparation for lunch.

"She misses the girls," I said.

"It's like homework," Justine continued. "If you keep at it, pretty soon you get it."

"I got a hundred on my spelling test last week," Christie said, without taking her eyes off the screen.

"That's very good," I said.

"I'll try to get up there next week," Marlene said.

"Maybe I can be there," I offered.

Not giving much credence to that statement, she walked to the fridge, removed a bottle of fruit juice and brought it back to the table. I got up and went to the kitchen.

Marlene looked good despite the divorce and all she'd been through. Her figure was still intact, and although her hair had lost some of its sheen, it was neatly kept as it had always been. She rarely wore makeup and seldom needed to. I waited for her to settle down in one spot by the table before I said, "How are things going?"

"Financially or in general?" she said.

"You know what I mean."

She began to fill the cups with juice. "Justine may need braces," she said. "We'll find out next week."

I didn't react to that but said, "Have things been okay? I mean normal."

"Normal? What are you talking about?"

"Are there any problems I should know about?"

"Come play, Daddy!" Christie shouted from the living room.

"Everything is as good as it can be, Max, but it would be nice if the girls got to see their father a bit more."

I was half expecting that zinger and had no comeback other than to say, "The job."

"I know," she said sarcastically as she walked to the sink and began to rinse her hands under the faucet. She'd heard those words from me a myriad of times over the years and wasn't surprised to hear them now. I followed her to the sink.

"What I mean is, are you and the girls safe living here?"

"Safe? What are you getting at?" She turned off the faucet and looked at me seriously. "Is something happening on the job? Something I should know about?"

"Not at all," I said.

"Are the girls in any danger?"

"No. I just want to be sure you're all safe."

"If I should know something, Max, tell me. I've spent too many years worrying and don't need to go through this again."

I had opened a can of worms, and now she was overreacting. I took her by her shoulders and turned her to face me. She looked surprised, and I felt her body stiffen. It was the first time I'd touched her since the divorce. I looked straight at her and said, "There is nothing wrong. I just want to be sure you and the girls are okay." She looked at me skeptically, but her only choice was to believe me. We stood for a moment, looking into each other eyes, trying to communicate without words, trying to say things to each other that we should have said a long time ago. I wanted to kiss her, pull her tight against me and hold her in my arms. I wanted to say: *Let's start over again. We can make it work. I still love you and I know you love me.* But the improbability of it becoming a reality made me feel silly. Thoughts of Sandy entered my mind suddenly and began to muddle my reasoning. My love for Sandy was fresh, new and genuine, but my love for Marlene was the kind of love that is built on a foundation of time and togetherness. Remarrying Marlene was something I believed would be the right thing for her and the girls and me. But I dreaded the day if it ever came when I'd have to choose between Marlene and Sandy.

My hands slid from Marlene's shoulders as she turned back to the sink without a word and ran the faucet again.

I felt a sudden tug on my shirtsleeve. It was Christie. "Try it, Daddy," she said, pulling me back into the living room. She handed me her game wand and pushed me back down onto the sofa.

"I'll play against you," Justine said.

In the kitchen, Marlene was back to setting the table. I could see that familiar look of concern on her face, a look I'd caused her to have many times before, but today I didn't mean to do that to her. I swung the wand and hit the ball over the net.

It wasn't long before the girls tired of the tennis match and dragged me through the kitchen toward the back door. Before they were allowed outside, Marlene had them put on their jackets. When Christie had trouble zipping hers, I tried to help, but after fumbling with it for too long, Marlene zipped it up easily and I followed the girls out the back door.

The backyard was bigger than one would expect for the size of the house. Although there were several areas of burned-out grass, what was still green had been neatly mowed. An above ground pool stood empty in one corner of the yard with a bright green garden hose hanging over its side that wound its way through the grass like an anaconda until it reached the faucet at the house. Justine put on her sunglasses and stretched out on one of the aluminum lounge chairs, looking like a movie starlet sunning by the pool, while Christie snatched up a beach ball, and without warning, threw it in my direction. I caught it, then tossed it back to her, but she missed the catch and the ball rolled along the grass until it stopped against the chain-link fence that enclosed the perimeter of the yard. Marlene had purchased a corner property at an intersection where a stop street lay just beyond the fence where Christie had chased after the ball. Beyond the fence, I watched a car approach the stop sign, slow to a stop, and then continue across the intersection. Anyone could easily look into the yard as they passed, since there were no trees or shrubbery against the fence to obscure the view. A few quick drives around the block and the house and yard could be sized up in a matter of minutes. It would be a cinch for someone to jump out of a car, snatch one of the girls and be gone before anyone knew it. I shuddered while that scenario played out in my mind until I was literarily knocked back to consciousness when Christie threw the ball to me and it smacked the side of my head.

Back at the kitchen table, Marlene updated me on the girls' progress at school while we ate lunch. Christie was in the school play, and Justine made me promise to attend her violin recital next month. I said I'd be there. Marlene gave me a look. I looked back at her and repeated, "I'll be there."

While Marlene cleaned up the table, I played three games of tennis with the girls, and began to get good at it; although, I wouldn't dare win a match. We laughed and had fun, and Marlene even sat in for one game. As usual, when you're having fun, time flies and before I knew it, the hours passed.

After hugs and kisses from the girls and a civil, "Take care," to Marlene, I was on the parkway heading north. I felt satisfied that they would be okay and told myself the backyard was safe enough. I hoped Denali's network didn't stretch into South Jersey. *I hoped.*

Two hours later, as I was parking the Chevy in front of my apartment, my cell phone rang. It was Briggs. He wanted me in his office ASAP. I wondered what kind of trouble I was in now. I checked my dash clock. It read, 4:35. I'd promised my mother I'd be at her house by seven for that spaghetti dinner she was keeping, and I hoped I wouldn't have to disappoint her or myself again. I pulled the Chevy away from the curb and headed for the city. When I got to the bureau, Danny Nolan was waiting outside Briggs's office.

"What's up?" I said.

He shrugged.

We opened the door and went inside. Briggs was at his computer. He stopped working and rubbed his eyes, then looked at me somberly. I waited.

"The 94th pulled a male floater out of the East River about an hour ago," he said. "I thought you might want to take a look."

Briggs was sending me to ID a drowning victim. I didn't know if he was doing me a favor or if it was all business. I like to think he was doing me a favor. The possibility that it could be Ray scared the Hell out of me, but I couldn't trust the ID to someone else and was glad I was going. I was anxious to find Ray, but not floating dead in a river, or curled up dead in a dumpster, or lying cold blue on a slab in a morgue. I'd have much preferred to find him lying in a hammock on a Caribbean island, accompanied by a hot blonde and sipping a margarita through a pink straw. Relief would quickly overcome my anger and frustration when Ray gave me his lengthy and reasonable explanation for what he had been doing. I'd smile understandingly and we would all live happily ever after.

"You're off the books, so take Nolan with you," Briggs said. "I'll tell them you're on your way."

"Thanks, chief," I said.

We took an unmarked to the 94th in Brooklyn. Danny drove. On the way, I kept thinking: *If it was Ray they fished out of those waters, how did he get in there? Was it an accident? Was it homicide? Had Ray taken his own life? Why? Why? Why?* The possibilities and scenarios were endless, and there was a good chance I'd never find the answers. But there I was, doing it again, guessing at possibilities rather than working from facts. I'd wait and see if it was Ray before I thought more about it.

"You must feel shitty," Danny said.

"Why?"

"I mean…this could be your buddy."

"I need to be sure," I said.

"I get it," he said. "But I hope I can handle it if something like this comes my way."

"Police work, Danny boy," I said. "You need to learn to separate your personal feelings from your professional obligations."

Who was I kidding?

It was beginning to get dark when we got to the river. The air smelled like mud, wet leaves and stagnant water. It reminded me of the times I'd gone fishing with my father as a boy; even the best fishing holes smelled that way. Our fishing trips to the banks of the Passaic River are one of the few pleasant memories I have of being with my father. He had purchased some cheap fishing rods for my brother Vinnie, and one for himself and me. With a well-stocked tackle box, we were off to catch the big ones. Although my father rarely spent quality time with us, Vinnie and I looked forward to the occasional fishing trip and enjoyed every minute of them. My father was a different person during those trips, teaching us the proper way to bait a hook and demonstrating his way to make a good cast. If one of us hooked a fish, he'd smile proudly and pat us on the back. It made us feel good. But in time, the fishing trips became less frequent until they stopped altogether. I still have that old fishing rod somewhere in my attic.

When we arrived at the scene, there was a medical examiner's van and a police cruiser parked beside a bridge. The on-scene investigation had been completed, and they were impatiently waiting for us to ID the victim. The area was covered with weeds and high grass, and there were no lights other than the headlights from the cruiser. The medical examiner's van was parked about a hundred feet from the bank on higher, dryer ground. A young girl and an older guy were standing at the rear of the van with the door open. They were wearing white jumpsuits, yellow rubber boots, and blue rubber gloves. The girl appeared to be in her mid-twenties. She had a pretty face, short blond hair, big eyes, and a hefty chest. I couldn't help noticing Danny as his eyes burned through that jumpsuit, trying to imagine what other "goodies" might be beneath it. To me, it seemed like the aliens had landed. Lying in the van behind them, I could see a black vinyl body bag.

Danny showed them his ID. "We're from the 14th," he said. "Nolan and Graham." Neither of them cared enough to look at it, but instead, stepped aside to allow us access to the victim.

"Any ID on the body?" I said.

"Nothing," the girl said, "not even clothes."

"Probably a jumper," the guy said.

He handed me a paper particle mask and a pair of blue rubber gloves. Danny, more than willing, stepped back and waited for me to climb in. I handed him the gloves, pulled the elastic around my head, adjusted the mask over my mouth and nose, and then hoisted myself into the back of the van.

At first look, the victim seemed shorter than Ray. I wasn't exactly sure how tall Ray was, but I knew he was at least my height, which is an even six feet. This guy looked to be a little more than five feet. A body soaking in a river for a good while will shrink and shrivel, but I doubt it would shrink almost a foot—unless it wasn't in one piece.

I kneeled beside the body and swung the interior light around so I could get a better look. Then I reached for the zipper and began to pull it down. My anxiety increased with each inch of movement as I was able to see more and more of the bag's contents. When I pulled the zipper down enough to expose the corpse's head and chest, my body jolted. I looked away for an instant, took a deep breath, then looked back again. The corpse was livid, bloated and partially decomposed, and for whatever time it had been in the river, it had been fish food. The features were grossly distorted and useless in identifying the victim without forensics, but I knew I could positively ID Ray by the scar on his right temple.

I held my breath and leaned over the body for a closer look. The temple was pale and swollen, but relatively unscathed. Other than a few dark hairs embedded in the skin, I could see no semblance of a scar. I leaned back and let out a long breath, relieved and satisfied it was not Ray.

***

My mother couldn't be more Italian if she tried, although she was one hundred percent natural-born American and proud of it. She strutted her Italian heritage, but being an American, she said, was something special, like living in a special place in the world. She liked to kid me for being half Italian. "Half Italian is better than none," she'd say.

Our family name, "Graham", was founded in the town of "Grantham" in the county of Lincolnshire, England, where my father's ancestry is. My mother told us, the name means: "Warlike child", which, she said, suited my brother and me since we were constantly scrapping with each other when we were youngsters.

At seventy-six, my mother kept herself in pretty good shape over the years, moderately overweight for her height but still spry on her feet. Her dyed black hair was always neatly kept and looked good against her olive complexion. Tonight she was wearing navy blue slacks and a matching blouse, light blue sneakers and a yellow apron around her waist.

I watched her balance a large bowl of Linguini and meatballs as she carried it to the kitchen table where Danny Nolan and I had been salivating while we waited for it to re-heat.

"It's leftover," she said, "but that's not my fault."

"I'm sorry, Ma...the job."

"It's okay, Mrs. G," Danny said. "It always tastes better the next day."

"Who told you that?" I said.

"I heard."

"That's only with pizza, I said."

"Eat," my mother said, "before it gets cold."

Danny put a small mountain of Linguini on his dish and speared two meatballs. I loaded my dish with a challenging amount, sprinkled the whole thing with Parmesan cheese, and then passed the shaker to Danny. My mother removed a loaf of garlic bread from the oven and brought it back to the table. She sat between us and placed the warm bread on a wooden cutting board.

"Why didn't you bring Sandra tonight?" she said, as she began to slice the bread. "Sandra loves my Linguini."

"We're working, Ma. We're on dinner break."

My mother wasn't aware I had been put on leave and I wanted to keep it that way, but I didn't want to disappoint her—or myself—by missing that Linguini again, so I'd asked Danny to pick me up with his squad car and drive me to my mother's house, ostensibly for our dinner break. A promise of Linguini and meatballs was more than enough incentive for him.

"You work too much," my mother said.

"I know," I said.

"You should see the kids more."

"I know," I said again, this time through a mouthful of Linguini.

She pushed a couple of pieces of bread toward Danny.

"When you going to get married, Danny?"

Danny was working on a mouthful but managed to get out, "I'm trying, Mrs.G."

"You got a girlfriend?"

"Nobody special."

"Someday you'll need somebody special," my mother said.

She was beginning to sound like Chestnut.

"Leave him alone, Ma. He's too young to get married."

"I was seventeen when I married your father."

"Things were different then. People don't rush into marriage today."

The wall phone by the refrigerator rang.

My mother slid her chair back, got up and answered it.

"Hello," she said. A pause. "Hello," she said again. She waited a few seconds, then put the receiver back gently and came back to the table.

"They hung up," she said.

"Who?" I said.

"I don't know. Happens every day. Nobody's there. They just hang up."

"Every day?"

"Sometimes I want to call the phone company."

"Every day?" I repeated.

"Almost," she said.

I got up and went to the phone to check the caller ID. When I scrolled through the list, I found more than a dozen calls from "unknown caller." *Was I being overprotective? Was I being paranoid? Wrong numbers happen every day.*

I brought the phone back to the table and showed my mother the screen.

"You can check to see who it is," I said. "See."

"I don't know how to use that thing."

"You should learn."

"Why? Who's important calls me?"

I cleared the numbers that were in storage to bring the phone up to date, then hung it back on the wall cradle and sat down again. I wanted to say something to my mother about being careful, but I didn't want to freak her out. I sopped up some gravy from my plate with a piece of bread and then looked at her seriously. "Ma, I want you and Aunt Theresa to be more careful around the house," I said.

"Careful of what?"

"Everything. Make sure the doors are locked and keep enough lights on at night."

"You're telling me how to live in this house after forty years? I raised you and your brother in this house."

"I just want to be sure you're safe."

"I'm safe. It's you that needs to be safe, out in those streets. You don't think I worry."

"I know, Ma. I'm just asking you to be more careful."

I poured a glass of Dr. Pepper for Danny and one for myself. Danny drank his down, wiped his mouth, then stood up and rubbed his belly. I looked at the clock on the stove.

"Thanks, Mrs. G," he said. "That was the best, as usual."

"Come anytime, Danny," my mother said. "Next time bring your girlfriend."

She reached for the salad bowl. "Have a salad before you go."

"We don't have time," I said. "Save it."

I got up, went to the kitchen door and checked the deadbolt and security chain. The door was locked, but the chain was hanging.

"Save it for who?" my mother said. She was already clearing the table.

"You'll eat it later," I said.

"I can't eat salad...my stomach. I'll throw it in the garbage."

I hooked the security chain, then walked back and gave her a hug and a kiss.

"Aunt Theresa will eat it when she gets home," I said.

"Aunt Theresa can't eat salad. It gives her gas. I'll throw it in the garbage."

She wiped her hands on her apron and followed us through the front parlor. I opened the front door and worked the deadbolt a few times and pulled on the security chain.

"Why do you keep doing that?"

"Just to be sure," I said.

"That my front door works?"

Danny walked out onto the porch. "Thanks again, Mrs. Graham," he said, and to me, "I'll wait in the car."

I leaned over and gave my mother another kiss on her cheek.

"Lock the door behind me," I said.

"Your Aunt Theresa will be home soon."

"She knows how to ring the bell."

"Be careful."

"I will."

After she closed the door, I waited until I heard her turned the deadbolt and hook the security chain, but it didn't make me feel any better.

Chapter 19

"By what miracle I escaped destruction,
it is impossible to say..."
Edgar Allan Poe—Ms. Found in a Bottle

The following morning dawned bright. I thought about going to the police gym but my ribs still ached so I decided to walk to Oakwood Park and jog the path around the lake one time. The run had become a routine of mine when weather permitted and helped me maintain my breathing and stamina. The air was crisp enough for me to see my breath as I ran, and it felt invigorating as always. My legs were still strong and my joints flexible enough to jog the mile and a half without a hitch. I set a good pace and monitored my breathing as I'd been taught during my running days at college.

When I got back to my apartment, I called Sandy. She said she was sleeping better—and with the light off—and felt nearly normal again. She was as tough as she was beautiful, and I knew she would overcome the emotional trauma I blamed myself for causing her. I blew a kiss through the phone and told her I loved her. To further satisfy my sense of concern, I hung up and dialed my mother. She said Aunt Theresa came home right after I left and ate some Linguini, but not the salad. I said that was good. She said she threw the rest of the salad in the garbage and that it was "sinfully wasteful." I told her I loved her and to be careful. She said I was being stupid but promised she would.

I took a shower, got into my sneakers, jeans and a sweatshirt, and decided I'd like some pastry with my coffee. I wanted to relax, watch the morning news and munch on a couple of biscotti. I drove down to Tortolla's Bakery, parked across the street, bought half dozen biscotti and walked back to my car. When I tossed the bag through the opened window onto the front seat, someone pressed a gun into my ribs. It hurt.

"Let's take a walk," a voice said.

The reflection in the side window told me Keeper and Muscle boy were behind me.

"Across the street," Keeper said.

"Can I take my Biscotti?"

"You're lucky you still got teeth to eat 'em with," Keeper said.

He prodded me toward a black Lincoln Crown Vic parked at the curb, pushing the gun into my ribs harder than he needed to. I slid into the back seat between Keeper and Muscle boy. Doorman was behind the wheel. "Doorman *and* chauffeur," I said to him. "You must get paid a lot more than these guys."

He gave me a contemptuous look through the rearview mirror while Keeper frisked me and took my gun. "You're not so tough when you don't have your animal friend with you," he said. "Couldn't he make it today?"

"He's busy cleaning his cage," I said.

Doorman put the car in gear and sped away from the curb. I was sure they were taking me to Denali.

More than an hour later, we pulled into the underground parking garage at Tower Park West and took the elevator up. When we got to Denali's apartment, Doorman used a security key to let us in. Then he and Muscle boy took a post outside the door. Despite the bright morning sun, the room was shaded because there was no way to open the vertical blinds. I couldn't hold back a faint smile.

"Sit," Keeper said.

I eased into a leather chair while Keeper stood with his back to the door. We waited.

It wasn't long before Anton Denali appeared from the bedroom. He was smaller than I expected. His tar-black hair was pulled back against his scalp into a short ponytail and his dark skin fit well with his mouse-like features: thin lips, high cheekbones and the penciled thin mustache he kept under his beak-like nose. He wore a red satin bathrobe over white satin pajamas and brown suede slippers. I felt uncomfortable just looking at this guy. I could sense the inherent evil in him. He looked me over through dark beady eyes as he walked to the leather sofa and sat. When he crossed his legs, I couldn't help noticing there were no hairs near his ankles.

"That was a foolish escapade you pulled yesterday," he said. "Did you think I would be amused?"

"I was," I said.

I could tell he didn't like being talked to that way by the way he tightened his eyes and the muscles in his lower jaw. When he recomposed himself, he said, "I'm a vengeful man, detective, and don't frighten easily."

"You went over the line by going after my girl."

"It was a warning for you to stay out of my business."

"I'm not interested in your business. I'm looking for my friend, Ray Deverol. Do you know where he is?"

He removed a silver cigarette case from his bathrobe pocket. As he lifted a cigarette from it, Keeper rushed to him with a lighted match. Denali leaned into it and drew on the cigarette delicately. He took his time blowing the smoke through his pursed lips.

"Deverol was a fool," he said. "He panicked and ran when he discovered the police were asking questions. He was an amateur trying to get rich quick."

"Then you know Ray is still alive."

"How would I know that?"

"You said, he panicked and ran."

"A logical assumption."

"How do I know you didn't kill Ray?"

"What motive would I have?"

"Maybe you figured he might drop your name."

"I'm smarter than that, detective. I'm well protected from that liability I don't venture into things without thinking ahead."

I didn't believe him. He just said he'd gotten mixed up with an amateur.

"Then, you have no idea where Ray is?"

He took another draw on his cigarette and let the smoke out easily, allowing it to encircle his head. "Frankly," he said, "I don't care if he ever shows up." He fanned away the remaining smoke from his face and then pointed a threatening finger at me. "Ray's not a threat," he said, "but you've uncovered enough information to tie it all together."

He took his time smothering out his cigarette in a small silver ashtray on the table beside him, then stood and walked back toward the bedroom as abruptly as he had entered. I got the feeling his business with me was over. On his way, he threw Keeper a portentous look. I knew what it meant.

"You're out of your mind if you think you can kill a New York City cop," I said.

He turned and looked back at me, undisturbed. "You'll simply disappear like your friend," he said. Then he stepped into the bedroom and closed the door.

Conversation over.

What was Denali saying? Did he mean he'd made Ray disappear, or was he simply using an analogy to describe the particulars of my elimination?

Keeper had his hand in his jacket pocket around his gun. He motioned for me to get up. As I did, he wrapped on the door, and it was unlocked from the outside. Muscle boy locked Denali in and remained at his post while Keeper and Doorman escorted me out of the building. It had been a long while since I felt helpless and short on ideas. I remember thinking: *If Drew were here, I'd ask him how Poe would write his way out of this one.*

***

I was in the back seat of the Crown Vic with Keeper. Doorman was behind the wheel again. We were traveling south on the Garden State Parkway. I had no idea where we were headed. It was beginning to look like I wouldn't get to enjoy the biscotti I'd left on the front seat of my Chevy. I wasn't satisfied that Denali knew nothing of Ray's disappearance. He claimed to have no motive, but I could think of one valid one, like keeping Ray from implicating his name to the police. Ray might have conveniently disappeared due to other circumstances, but if he hadn't, I'm sure Denali would have made it happen sooner than later.

We drove for more than an hour until Doorman took an exit off the parkway. I saw a sign which read: WHARTON STATE PARK and knew we were somewhere in the New Jersey Pine Barrens, a million acres of trees, foliage, rivers, and lakes. A person could get lost out there and never be found. We continued on a paved road for another twenty minutes until we turned onto a dirt road. We bounced around for a few more miles until Doorman pulled under a canopy of tall trees and cut the engine. He waited behind the wheel while Keeper got out. Keeper motioned for me to get out too. I did. The mid-morning sun was bright but did little to penetrate the abundance of trees and closely tangled limbs, leaving the area where we stood in heavy shadows. Keeper took a .45 from his pocket and pointed it at me. "Move, wise guy," he said. "That way." I walked over a bed of fallen pine needles toward a thicket of undergrowth with Keeper close behind me. The air was cool but heavy with moisture, and I could feel dampness forming on my face and neck. When we were out of sight of the Crown Vic, Keeper said, "Far enough. Turn around."

I knew I had to make a move now, or I was finished.

Keeper kept the .45 pressed hard against my back, which was a mistake for him and an opportunity for me. I spun around and knocked it from his hand. In the time it took him to realize what had happened, I reached down, scooped up his gun and turned it on him. He put his hands in the air quickly. "Don't kill me, Graham," he pleaded.

Keeper fit the bill perfectly. I'd seen plenty like him, heartless tough guys when they had a weapon in their hands but sniveling cowards when the possibility of their own death was imminent.

"Turn around," I said.

He did. I reached into his jacket, found my .38 and dropped it into my front pocket.

"Now it's my turn," I said. "That way."

I led him behind a tree and told him to keep his mouth shut. We stood there for a while, listening to a symphony of birds and insects. When enough time had passed, I fired a shot into the air that reverberated through the treetops. A crescendo of screeching birds and flapping wings filled the air and ended in dead silence. It wasn't long before I heard Doorman's voice. "Let's go, Jake."

I put the .45 to Keeper's head. He stood quietly.

Doorman's voice rang out again. "Come on, Jake. Let's get outta here."

I heard the car door slam and footfalls crunching dried leaves and pine needles. When I peered around the tree, Doorman was pushing his way through the undergrowth. I saw him remove a snub nose revolver from behind his jacket as he moved cautiously toward us, waving the gun nervously in front of him. "Where are ya, Jake!" he shouted. Half hidden by a large shrub, he stopped, crouched low and craned his neck to look around. I pulled my head in behind the tree, but not before he spotted me and fired a shot in my direction, splintering the bark on the tree inches from my head. I ducked. So did Keeper. "Don't shoot!" Keeper shouted. "He's got my gun!"

Doorman didn't hear or didn't care and let off a second shot. This time Keeper took the round to his temple, spraying blood onto my sweatshirt. He slid down the tree trunk like the slime he was and laid motionless at my feet.

I kept low and moved around the tree, keeping an eye on Doorman. I watched him move through the foliage, darting a look in every direction, trying to spot me before I spotted him. When something rustled the brush ahead of him, he aimlessly fired off two more rounds and threw himself to the ground. I came up behind him and put the .45 against the back of his head. He dropped his gun and extended his arms in front of him.

"On your feet," I said.

He stood up with his hands in the air. He was breathing heavily. Perspiration glistened on his face and ran down his temples and dried leaves and twigs clung to the front of his black suit and the red patch of hair on his chin.

"Where's Jake?" he said.

"He's dead."

"You kill him?"

"No, you did," I said.

I prodded him back to the car.

"How'd I kill him?"

"You fired at me and missed and hit him. Denali's not going to like that."

"Take off your belt and give it to me…slowly."

"What?" he said.

"Give me your belt," I repeated.

He unbuckled his belt and slid it from around his waist. It never occurred to me that Doorman might be smart enough to use his belt as a weapon and swing it, buckle first, at my head, but that's exactly what he did. When I ducked, he kicked at my gun hand, knocking my gun to the ground. He dove for the gun to get to it before I could. When I dove after him, I found myself on his huge back. As he tried to reach the gun, he wiggled and squirmed beneath me. I felt like I was riding a bull. His sausage fingers were only inches from the weapon when I grabbed his forearm and pulled his arm away but he lifted his arm quickly and my fingers slipped from his flabby skin allowing him to slide his forefinger into the trigger guard. I was able to get my arm under his three chins and pull his head up and back in a chokehold. He offered little resistance, but I applied steady pressure until he relented, and I felt his body slacken. I reached out and picked up my gun and got to my feet. "Get up!" I said. He moved into a sitting position and sat there for a while to get his breath back. which gave me time to steady my own breathing?

"It was a stupid move," he said, "but one I had to take."

"I know," I said. "Give me your tie."

"My tie?"

I pointed to the knot in his tie with the barrel of my gun. He got the message, undid the tie and handed it to me.

I told him to turn around and put his hands behind his back. I wrapped the tie around his wrists and secured it tightly with a double knot. "I've learned a lot about knots lately," I said.

"What are you gonna do, Graham?" he said.

I ignored his question and said, "Did your boss have Ray Deverol killed?"

"Never heard the name," he said.

"Don't lie to me," I said. "I don't like being lied to and I don't have time to stay here and beat the truth out of you."

"I swear. I never heard of the guy," he said.

He was probably telling the truth. Under the circumstance, he would be a fool to lie, and I don't think Doorman had the degree of loyalty that Denali would like to think he had.

I walked Doorman back to where Keeper was lying with a hole in his head. I ordered him to sit beneath a group of nearby saplings. I chose one with a small diameter truck that looked sturdy enough for my purpose. Doorman looked down at his ex-partner and grimaced. "Nice shot," I said. He looked away, then slid down to the base of the tree and sat with his legs extended. I put the belt around his chest and the tree and pulled the end through the buckle. I cinched it tight, using the last hole in the belt. Then I walked to where he had dropped his gun and picked it out of the pine needles, using my handkerchief to avoid getting my prints on it. I walked back to him and carefully slid it back into his shoulder holster.

"What are you gonna do to me?"

"What you and your partner were going to do to me," I said.

I walked a short distance away from the area and threw Keepers's .45 into a cluster of heavy brush. Then I walked to the Crown Vic, got in and started the engine.

"You can't leave me here," Doorman shouted.

"You were going to leave me," I said, "with a bullet in me."

"For God's sake, Graham, there are animals out here."

"You're getting a better chance than you were giving me."

As I drove out of the thicket toward the dirt road, Doorman shouted my name a few more times, but it was difficult for me to hear over the rumblings in my stomach. My breakfast had been interrupted, and I hoped my biscotti hadn't gotten stale.

On my way back up the parkway, I stopped at the Cheesquake Service area and phoned the New Jersey State Police. Without identifying myself, I told them where to find Keeper and Doorman. I was sure Doorman wasn't dumb enough to mention my name when he tried to explain to the police what he and Keeper were doing there and how a bullet from his gun wound up in Keeper's skull.

***

It was a two-and-a-half hour ride back to Tortolla's Bakery where I'd left my car. I ditched the Crown Vic in an empty lot across the street, wiped my fingerprints from the steering wheel and door handle and anyplace else I could think of that I might have touched. Then I walked across the street to where I had parked the Chevy. There was a parking ticket on the windshield, and someone had stolen my biscotti from the front seat.

It was after two when I got back to my apartment. I checked the voice mail on my kitchen wall phone and found a message from Drew. He said he would call back. I threw my bloody sweatshirt in the garbage, peeled off my clothes and scrubbed myself clean in the shower. Then I put on a tee-shirt, a pair of sweatpants and my fuzzy slippers. Even though it was late afternoon, I was determined to have my breakfast. I started some coffee and went to work on a cheese omelet.

Drew called back.

"Thought I'd touch base," he said.

I held the phone to my ear with my shoulder while I broke some eggs into a bowl.

"Ray's officially a missing person," I said. "I had to give it to NYPD."

There was a short silence.

"Is that the right thing to do at this point?" Drew said.

"It's the only thing to do at this point," I said.

There was another short silence.

"What can I do?"

"There's not much either of us can do for now. There's just not much info on Ray to follow. That's why I gave it to the department."

There was a long silence.

"What about his connections on the West Coast?"

"I haven't dug that deeply," I said. "I want to see if things play out here first."

"But we know he took a flight."

"There's no record of it," I said.

"We saw it on his notepad."

"There's no record of it," I said again.

Another short silence, then, "There must be some way I can help?"

"Keep reading those Poe mysteries," I said. "Maybe you'll come up with a solution to finding Ray."

I hung up the phone and began to slice some cheese. I cut up a green pepper and dropped the pieces into the bowl. Drew was showing his usual concern for Ray, although I wasn't entirely convinced it was authentic.

Things were getting more complicated every day: I had gotten involved with Denali and his henchmen, risked Sandy's life and my own, got myself suspended, and so far, there had been one accidental death and two murders. Denali was right. I was the only one that had enough on him to put him away for a long time. He wanted me out of the picture and that meant, dead. Trying to find Ray had introduced me to a ruthless adversary, and I still didn't know where Ray was. Denali just couldn't understand that finding Ray was all that mattered to me. From now on, I'd have to have two pairs of eyes.

Chapter 20

"Here matters again took a most unfavorable turn."
Edgar Allan Poe—Thou Art the Man

I brought my breakfast to the coffee table and sat on the sofa to watch the four o'clock news. The violence and adversity they were reporting seemed pale by comparison to what I had been through these past weeks.

When I finished eating, I kicked off my slippers, stuffed a pillow under my head and stretched out comfortably. I closed my eyes and let myself sink into the thick cushions. Three hours later, I was jolted from a deep sleep by the ringing of my cell phone. I jumped up, hit my shin on the coffee table and hopped across the living room floor to my bedroom where I had left the phone. "Hello," I said.

"Help me," a woman's voice said. "I'm afraid."

"Who is this?"

"It's Carla." Her voice was almost a whisper.

"What's wrong?"

"They're after me."

"Who?"

"A couple of Denali's goons."

"Where are you?"

"An alley near my apartment. They're trying to kill me."

My instinct of self-preservation told me to be careful. Why would Carla call *me* for help? I reached down and rubbed my shin.

"Call the police," I said.

"No time," she said. "You got to come."

The quiver in her voice told me she was genuinely terrified. But if this were a set-up, I'd kick myself for walking into it; if it weren't, this girl's life could be on my head.

"Calm down," I said. "Is there someplace you'll be safe until I get there?"

"The parking lot across from my apartment," she said. "I'll hide in my car. The red Taurus two-door."

"What's the plate number?"

"I don't remember," she said.

"Okay. I'll be there as soon as I can, but if you call the police, they'll get there sooner."

"Just hurry," she said.

***

It was almost eight o'clock when I turned onto Carlyle Place. I drove to the end of the block and parked on the opposite side of the street, facing Carla's apartment. The parking lot Carla mentioned was directly across from her building. If it had lights, they weren't working and the few street lamps at the curb didn't do much to illuminate the area. I got out and stood beside the Chevy. The street was dark and still. A silver Cadillac was parked in front of Carla's place with the lights off and the motor idling. A guy in the driver's seat lit a cigar. I could see he was the only one in the car.

I walked along a tall hedgerow toward the parking lot, my eyes darting in every direction, trying to spot something that might tell me I was walking into a trap. At the end of the hedgerow, I turned into the gravel parking lot and stopped inside a dark shadow to look around. There was no movement. A dozen cars were parked randomly, and it was difficult for me to discern color. I continued along the perimeter until I saw the red Ford Taurus parked alone in a corner. Its rear window was fogged, which was a dead give away. I pictured Carla crouched on the floor behind the front seat.

I moved behind some shrubbery along a wooden fence until I came up behind the Taurus. I looked into the back seat through a small area on the side window that wasn't fogged. Carla wasn't there. I edged closer to the windshield and looked again. The car was empty. Carla said she would hide until I got there. Maybe I was too late. I glanced at the Cadillac across the street. It hadn't moved, and the guy behind the wheel was enjoying his smoke. I decided to check him out. I took my gun out and moved along the back wall of an adjourning garage. As I got closer to the sidewalk, I heard movement behind a metal garbage can. I stepped back into a shadow and watched Carla crawl out from behind the can on all fours. I put my gun away.

"If I can see you, so can he," I said.

I helped her to her feet and pulled her back into the shadows next to me. She threw her arms around my neck and buried her face in my chest. She was trembling.

"You're supposed to be in the car," I said.

"I got scared," she said.

Across the street, the sound of footsteps echoed in our direction. I pulled Carla back against the garage wall where the shadows were darker. When the footsteps became louder and increased to a running cadence, I knew we'd been spotted. I took Carla's hand and dashed the hedgerow. When I looked, I saw two figures in the street running toward us, having a hard time of it in their suits and dress shoes. They looked pretty worn from having chased Carla all over the neighborhood, but I wasn't taking chances. We'd have to get to the Chevy before they got to us. I ran along the hedgerow with Carla beside me. For a heavy smoker, she had no trouble keeping up and reminded me of the running competitors I'd had at college.

Before we got to the end of the hedge, Carla rushed ahead of me. "This way," she said. I followed her through the hedge and across the street into an unlit alley. The opposite end of the alley opened to the next block, which was dimly lit by several street lamps beyond the opening. I could tell we hadn't lost our pursuers by the sound of their leather heels echoing on the blacktop not far behind us. I hoped they wouldn't get tired of running and start firing shots at us.

I followed Carla through the alley, losing her in the total darkness more than once. Instinctively, I was able to follow her toward the lighted opening at the far end where I could see the silhouette of a staircase with several trash cans and boxes beneath it. When we reached the staircase, Carla grabbed my jacket and pulled me down beneath the stairs beside her. We crunched down behind the cans in the deep shadows and waited. "This is where I was when I called you," she whispered.

Our pursuers ran passed the stairs just a few feet from us and stopped at the end of the alley. Frustrated and out of breath, they looked around in every direction, until one of them said, "We lost 'em."

His partner turned and looked back into the alley, scouring the shadows through squinting eyes. "No way," he said. "They're still in there, somewhere."

Carla was trembling again and breathing heavily. I put a comforting arm around her shoulder. At the same time, I rested my right hand over my holstered gun. We sat quietly and watched the dark figures stealth their way back into the alley toward us.

"Spread out," one of them said.

They moved away from each other, groping their way through the semidarkness. The one closest to us reached inside his jacket, pulled a gun from his shoulder holster and held it at the ready. As he approached the stairs, he stopped and squinted into the blackness where we were hunkered down. Carla put her hand over her mouth to muffle her breathing. I wrapped my hand around my gun grip, slid my finger closer to the trigger and held my breath. The chaser craned his neck in every direction and looked hard into the darkness. I could feel his eyes burn into mine as he looked directly at me; unaware I was but a few feet in front of him. He stood deathly still, moving only his eyes to scan the area beneath the stairs, listening, sensing, and searching. I released the safety on my gun and sat motionless. Like a coiled spring, I was ready to react if he discovered our presence. *Someone could die here in the next thirty seconds,* I thought.

Christie and Justine came to my mind.

After seconds that seemed like a lifetime, our pursuer lowered his gun and started away from us down the alley. I let myself relax a bit. Carla had been sitting with her head buried between her knees. She looked up cautiously, her frightened eyes scanning the darkness.

"Wait till he gets further away, then we'll make a break for the opening," I said.

I waited until they were both deeper into the alley and lost in the darkness before I maneuvered around the trashcans. Carla kept close by, holding on to the back of my jacket. We moved quietly along a brick wall, trying not to silhouette ourselves against the streetlights beyond the alley. If we could turn the corner and make it up the block, we could get to the Chevy safely.

We weren't that lucky.

A gunshot reverberated through the darkness at the same moment a muzzle flash brightened the alley like daylight. The wall exploded close to Carla's head, spraying red brick dust into the air. She let out a short scream, dropped to her knees and covered her head. I crouched low and got her to her feet. She was shaking and almost hysterical. I helped her along the brick wall toward the light at the end of the ally. Once outside, we started up the block at a rapid pace. I looked behind but didn't see our pursuers emerge from the ally. I hoped they hadn't doubled back and was waiting for us up in the street. If we could get to the Chevy unnoticed, we'd have a chance.

We ran along a chain-link fence until we reached the sidewalk on Carlyle Place. The street was quiet except for the low rumble of the Cadillac's idle. I looked down the block. The Caddy was still in front of Carla's apartment with the driver behind the wheel. The Chevy was parked not far from us, across the street. If we could get to it without being seen, we might get away. I took my keyring from my pocket and found the ignition key. Carl took the key from me and started to bolt across the street, but I grabbed her shoulder.

"Not yet," I said.

I looked down the street and saw our chasers emerge from the shadows. They stood beside the Caddy and appeared to engage in an argument. When the big guy waved his arms in protest, I gave Carla a nod. She ran for the Chevy. I was right behind her. With one quick motion, she opened the driver door and slid across the seat. I jumped in behind the wheel. When I turned the ignition key, the Chevy sputtered and choked before it started, which didn't help our cause. As I put the car into gear, shouting voices broke the silence up ahead. I looked down the block and saw our chasers climb quickly into the Caddy. They had spotted us and were "pissed". The Caddy's headlights snapped on, cutting through the darkness and sending a blinding light in our direction. It was too late to escape *quietly* but *quickly* was still on the program. I stomped on the accelerator and spun the Chevy into a one-eighty. I hoped her tires would hold as she squealed and fishtailed, leaving a billow of rear-end smoke. Through the rearview mirror, I saw the Caddy pull away from the curb and roar down the street toward us. I gripped the steering wheel and punched the accelerator again. The front end shimmied, and the windows rattled, but the Chevy got up with what spirit she had left.

It wasn't important where we were going. The idea was to get away. I took a sharp right as the Caddy came up close to our rear, its high beams lighting the interior of the Chevy with a blinding intensity. Carla leaned forward and gripped the dashboard.

"The seatbelt on that side doesn't work," I said, apologetically.

A gunshot rang out and whizzed passed the window on Carla's side. She slid down in the seat. "Thanks for your concern," she said.

The Caddy stayed close. I knew the Chevy couldn't outrun the Cadillac, but I was sure it could outmaneuver it because of its smaller size.

A second shot rang out.

These guys weren't playing.

I made a left, then a sharp right. Traffic was light on these side streets and I was able to zigzag through the dimly lit secondary roads, making us less of a target. I didn't have time to check the speedometer, but I guessed we were doing eighty. *Where are the cops when you need them?* I hoped the Chevy would hold out. I knew if I could get to a highway and get lost in traffic, we'd have a chance.

"We need to get to the highway," I said to Carla.

She sat up in her seat just enough to look out the side window. "Make a left," she said. "I think."

"*You think?*" I said.

I took the left but couldn't see a highway.

"Go right here," Carla shouted. "The on-ramp is on the other side of the underpass."

The Caddy bumped our rear again, harder than before. Carla slid down again. I took a quick right and saw the lights of the highway entrance on the other side of the underpass. I kept the pedal to the metal, but the Caddy stayed right on us as we came out of the underpass. I could see the on-ramp to the highway, and made a hard right, but the Chevy couldn't make the turn at the speed I was pushing her without flipping over. Her front end swayed, and her tires screeched. I turned the steering wheel back to the left and missed the ramp. In the rearview mirror, I watched the lights of the highway becoming more distant and the Cadillac gaining on us. I made a quick left into the same block we'd just exited. I made another left and then one more, working my way back to the on-ramp. The Caddy made each turn with me, fishtailing and smoking its tires and keeping closer than I hoped it would. Carla was crouched down now with her head between her knees. I could see her body shaking with fear. I slumped forward as much as I could without losing control of the vehicle, hoping I wouldn't take a bullet to the back of my neck. I peeked over the steering wheel and saw the on-ramp coming into view again. I slowed the Chevy down and made the hard right. As I did, another shot exploded and took out the side-view mirror on my side, spraying glass and plastic onto the windshield. The Chevy struggled up the ramp with its engine roaring until we finally merged into flowing traffic. When I looked in the rearview mirror, I didn't see the Caddy. I eased off the pedal to give the Chevy and myself a breather. I checked the rearview mirror several times to see if the Caddy would show. It didn't.

"We're okay now," I said.

Carla sat up and looked around. "Are you sure?"

"No," I said, "but I think we lost them."

"*You think?*" she said.

"Are you all right?"

She took a deep breath and said, "I guess."

I stayed in the right lane, keeping tight with the traffic and frequently looking into the rearview mirror to be sure we weren't being followed. I figured the Caddy wouldn't be back, but that didn't mean they weren't still looking. I gave Carla time to settle down.

"Whenever you're ready, tell me what this is all about," I said.

She took another deep breath and brushed her long hair away from her eyes.

"Denali thinks I ratted him out to you."

"And he wants you dead."

"Those guys weren't bringing me flowers," she said.

"How'd he find out you talked to me?"

"My guess is Bernie put the idea in his head."

I had been wrong about Carla; she hadn't ratted me out. She was too afraid. Denali felt the noose tightening around his neck and decided to do the simplest thing—get rid of Carla and me. So far, he'd failed both times. I learned one thing for sure about this guy. He might be a small-time operator, but he was ruthless and would stop at nothing to get what he wanted.

"What do I do now?" Carla said.

"Is there someplace you can stay?"

"I don't know anyone who'll put me up."

"You could stay with me," I said, "but my girlfriend wouldn't appreciate it."

"I won't tell," she said.

"I'm in enough trouble," I said.

She looked out the side window at the lights of the traffic. "I'm afraid," she said. "You don't know what it's like knowing somebody wants to kill you."

She brought her hands up to her face and began to sob. When she removed them, her cheeks were glistening with tears. "I don't know what to do," she said. "I don't even have a tissue. I left everything at my apartment."

"Some in the glove box," I said, "but open the door carefully or the whole thing will fall to the floor."

She found the tissues, blew her nose and wiped her face.

"Can you give me the details?"

She blew her nose again, took a deep breath and stuffed the used tissue in the waistband of her pants. "I was making myself something to eat when there was a knock on my door. I opened it and—"

"Do you always open your door before finding out who it is?"

"I wasn't thinking."

"Living alone, you should know better."

"I—wasn't—thinking," she repeated, articulating each word slowly with a flawless exhibition of feminine indignation.

"You should be more careful," I said.

She waited to be sure I didn't have more to say about it, but I knew better. She continued:

"Two guys pushed their way in. The big guy—"

"Lot of muscles?"

"He was wearing a suit—just big."

"Balding with a red goatee?"

For a moment, I wondered if Doorman could have survived the Pine Barrens.

"Dark hair, straight to his shoulders."

"Go on."

"The big guy grabs my arm and twists it behind my back. I let out a scream and the other guy slaps a piece of duct tape over my mouth."

"What'd the other one look like?"

"Skinny," she said.

"Silver earring in his left ear?"

"I was too busy to notice."

"Everything happens fast. They never say a word, just take me down to the street to a waiting car. Another guy is behind the wheel with the motor running. When they try to shove me into the back seat, I kick skinny in his balls. He melts to the sidewalk like ice cream on a hot skillet. I break away, pull the tape from my mouth and run down the block. When I look back, the two of them are chasing me, although the skinny guy is holding his balls and hopping along behind his partner trying to keep up. I gain a pretty good distance and duck into an alley. Lucky for me, my cell phone was still in my pocket. That's when I called you." She looked at me apologetically. "I'm sorry. I was afraid to call the cops, and you were the first one I thought of."

"It's okay," I said.

I turned into a Rite Aid parking lot and parked by the front entrance. I took a twenty-dollar bill from my wallet and gave it to her. "Get whatever personal items you'll need for the night. I know someone who'll put you up till tomorrow."

She took the bill, leaned over and kissed my cheek. "Thank you," she said. "You saved my life." She got out of the car and went into the Rite Aid. I wiped the kiss from my cheek, out of a sense of guilt, and punched up Sandy's number on my cell. I explained the situation and asked her if she would put Carla up at her place for the night. She said she would, but it would cost me a night of carnal pleasure. I had no choice but to accept her terms.

As I ended the call, I looked up and spotted the Cadillac pulling into the Rite Aid parking lot. I guess we weren't as lucky as I thought. They had somehow followed us to this location. The caddy pulled into a space about five down from where I was parked. Two guys got out and headed my way, the driver and a big guy, guns drawn. The lead guy was as big as a gorilla. His arms hung down past his knees. His legs were short and bowed, and he had no neck. I put the Chevy in reverse and mashed down on the gas. Her tires raised a cloud of dust and debris as I fishtailed onto the street. My pursuers ran after me, but stopped at the sidewalk and ate my dust as they watched me disappear down the street.

I worked my way into traffic and drove around the block. I hoped Carla had seen them and had enough sense to stay as inconspicuous as she could inside the Rite Aid. When I came around the block, I pulled into a service station that was closed. I parked alongside an unlit building, which offered the vantage point of seeing the front of the Rite Aid and the Cadillac. I watched as one guy got back behind the wheel and Gorilla guy entered the Rite Aid. I wondered what happen to skinny. Maybe Carla put him out of commission when she "drop-kicked" his balls.

I waited.

It didn't take long before I saw Carla and gorilla guy walk out of the Rite Aid and head for the caddy. I could tell he had a gun pressed into her back. He escorted her to the rear side door of the car, opened it and pushed her in, then got in beside her. The Caddy's engine roared, then backed out of the parking space and headed out into traffic.

I followed.

We drove on the secondary roads until the Caddy took the on-ramp for the highway. I stayed as close to them as I could without giving myself away. The Chevy was having a hard time keeping up with the power of the Caddy, but she was doing a good enough job for me. I patted her dashboard as a gesture of appreciation.

We rode for several miles on the highway until they took the first off-ramp exit. I found myself driving through poorly lighted Suburban Street. We drove for another ten minutes until the Caddy pulled to the curb in front of a large colonial house. I parked at the curb a good distance away and watched. The driver stayed behind the wheel while gorilla guy got out and pulled Carla out with him. He led Carla up the porch steps to the front door. He unlocked the door with a key and they disappeared inside.

I got out of the Chevy and walked in the shadows in the direction to where the Caddy was parked. I could see the silhouette of the driver. He was puffing on a cigar, smoke billowing out the driver's window and partially filling the front seat area. I knew his peripheral vision would be obliterated by the smoke as I crept up to the rear of the Caddy. I held my gun at my side. I crouched low and moved along the driver's side of the car until I was at the driver's side window. Before he was aware of my presence, I put my gun to his temple. "If you move, you're dead," I said. He stiffened and exhaled a long stream of cigar smoke. I reached in, snatched the cigar from his lips, and tossed it into the street.

"Get out easy," I said. "Bring the keys."

He pulled the keys from the ignition switch as I opened the door for him. I took the keys and patted him down. He was carrying cannon. I put his gun in my pocket and directed him to the rear of the Caddy.

"What's going on?" he said.

"Shut up," I said, as I unlocked and opened the trunk. "Get in."

He hesitated, looked down into the wide expanse of the Cadillac's trunk.

"Plenty of room in there for you and the spare," I said, as I prodded him with my gun. "You can thank GM."

He climbed in and rolled onto his back. I slammed the trunk lid in his face.

I turned my attention to the house. There was no movement or sound inside and only a yellow light coming from the front windows. The house had a wrap-around front porch, which made it easy for me to get close to the windows and look inside. As I peered through a front window, my vision was obscured by the sheer curtain hanging on the inside, but I could see well enough to identify Carla sitting in a chair at the corner of a large living room. Her wrists were secured to the arms of the chair with rope. There was a handkerchief tied around her head, covering her mouth. On the other side of the room, gorilla guy was leaning against a doorframe talking on his cell phone.

I crouched low and made my way around the porch to look through a side window. There were no curtains on this window and I could see the living room clearly from this perspective. I could also see a short hallway and a large kitchen. There appeared to be no one else in the house.

As I turned away from the window, a shot rang out shattering the window glass nearby head. Gorilla guy had spotted me. I hit the deck and crawled along to the front of the porch, keeping below the window ledge. I peered through the corner of a window and saw gorilla guy standing behind Carla's chair. I couldn't take a shot without risking hitting Carla.

Gorilla guy was smarter than he looked.

I crawled back to the side window where I had been. I peered cautiously over the sill. From this angle, I was looking at a rear view of Carla and Gorilla guy. He was watching the front windows intently, moving his gun nervously from side to side, hoping to get the shot he'd need to take me out. I could take him out him easily from this angle, but shooting a guy in the back wasn't in my game book. Besides, I didn't want to hit Carla.

I had to think fast before gorilla guy thought to bring Carla out to the front porch at gunpoint and take the high ground. I'd have to give up my gun under the threat that he would kill Carla if I didn't.

I had to get into the house unnoticed and overtake gorilla guy. Although I didn't look forward to a physical confrontation with a guy this big.

Where are you, Chestnut, when I need you?

There was no access to the back door of the house from the porch, without having to climb over the porch rail and run the risk of being seen. Going around to the left side of the house was too risky. I'd have to expose myself as I passed the wide windows and front entrance door.

Beside me was a rhododendron flower in a ceramic planter sitting inside a wrought iron stand. The planter was big and weighted heavily with soil. I lifted the planter out of its stand and edged closer to the window. I thought I'd use the old "distract and attack" tactic. I looked through the window again. Nothing had changed. My chance was as good now as any.

I tossed the planter through the broken window and followed it in. Gorilla guy reacted quickly and fired a shot in my direction. I fired a shot well to the right of him, which I thought would divert him to the right and away from Carla. Instead, he dropped into a crouch position and ducked behind Carla's chair. He wrapped his long arm around her throat and pushed his gun barrel hard against her temple.

"Give it up," he said, "or she's dead."

I had no choice. I left my gun on the floor and got up slowly. He got to his feet and kept his gun pointed at my chest.

"Get your hands up," he said.

I raised my arms and laced my fingers behind my head. He indicated for me to move to the sofa and sit. I did. When he was satisfied I was not an immediate threat, he moved to the front window and looked out through the curtain. He craned his fat neck in every direction and looked intently into the Cadillac out front, searching for his partner. He couldn't see him, anywhere.

Guess he disappeared with a puff of smoke.

I was sitting there, enjoying the fragrance of Rhododendron when I notice unusual movement in Carla's eyes. She was trying to message me. Her eyes were darting obliquely in the direction of the floor where a large piece of broken ceramic from the planter had landed by her chair close to her leg. I wasn't sure what she was up to, but had no choice but to follow her lead.

Gorilla guy was still at the window, waiting as if expecting someone to arrive soon. He looked over at me every few seconds. I could see he was edgy, not sure of himself. He was breathing heavily and sweating profusely. I could tell he was not comfortable in his current position, but trying not to show it.

"You won't kill the girl," I said. "Your boss wouldn't like it."

Resignedly, he gave up looking for his partner and took a few steps to the center of the room. "Maybe, but I can kill you," he said.

He removed a handkerchief from his trouser pocket and began to wipe the sweat from his face and forehead.

When he wiped his eyes, Carla saw her chance. She kicked the ceramic piece hard with her foot. It slid across the wood floor in the direction of gorilla guy's feet with a loud scraping noise. Startled, gorilla guy instinctively looked down at the floor. When he did, I dove for my gun, but he was quick and fired a shot at me. I snatched up my gun, spun around and fired one round into his massive chest. He dropped his gun, grabbed his chest and went down hard.

I moved quickly to Carla, untied her wrists and removed the gag from her mouth. She threw her arms around my neck and pressed her face against my chest. "I thought I was dead," she said.

"It's okay now," I said. "Let's go."

As we walked toward the front door, I stepped over gorilla guy. He wasn't going anywhere.

***

It was almost midnight when we got to Sandy's place. I called Briggs from my cell phone and explained what went down earlier. I gave him the address and told him to find *one* inside the house, dead, and *one* in the Caddy trunk, maybe, dead.

After introductions, Sandy offered Carla the use of her shower and a place to freshen up. When she disappeared into the bathroom, Sandy and I sat at the kitchen table and I told her about Carla's former relationship with Ray and her involvement with Denali.

"Is she sorry or stupid?" Sandy said.

"She's lucky she's not floating down the East River," I said.

"What are you going to do with her?"

"Try to convince her to come with me to see Briggs tomorrow. A charge of 'accessory' is a lot better than dead."

"What if she doesn't want to go?"

"Then I'm counting on you to convince her with some legal talk, counselor."

"And if that doesn't work?"

"I've done my good deed. I'll dump her in Briggs's lap."

"Has she offered any information about Ray?"

"She says she hasn't seen him since they broke up. I believe her."

Carla came out of the bathroom looking fresh but tired. She was wearing one of Sandy's bathrobes and a pair of flip-flops. Her hair was wrapped in a towel around her head like a turban. She sat down at the table between us. "Thanks a lot," she said to Sandy.

"It's nothing," Sandy said.

I asked her if she was feeling better.

"I'd feel a lot better if I knew what to do next."

I looked at Sandy, who looked at Carla.

"As an attorney, my advice to you is to turn yourself into the police," she said.

"Turn myself in? I haven't done anything. I'm the victim here."

"Not completely true," I said. "You're also complicit in a crime."

"What crime?"

"You knew about the criminal activities of Anton Denali," Sandy said.

"And?"

"It's the law. If you fail to tell the police what you know, that's a crime in itself."

"I don't understand. I'm in trouble because I kept my mouth shut?"

"More or less," I said.

"If I open my mouth, they want me dead. If I keep it shut, they want to put me in jail. There's no way out."

"There is one," I said. "Come with me to see Chief Briggs tomorrow, I'll explain everything, tell him you passed the information along to me. There may not be charges."

"You'll be safer in the custody of the police," Sandy said.

Carla stood and walked into the living room and began pacing. She stopped in front of a window and looked out into the night.

"What if I don't go?" she said, without turning.

"Then you'll be looking over your shoulders," I said, "until Denali's men find you."

***

I watched Briggs studying Carla from behind his desk. He was leaning back in his chair reading her face, trying to ascertain how much of her story he believed, and how much, if any, she had embellished. He was good at that. She was sitting in a chair opposite him. I was leaning against a filing cabinet with my hands in the front pockets of my jeans, listening intently. I'd instructed Carla earlier to tell the truth; no more, no less. She had done a good job, but I wasn't sure Briggs was satisfied. He sat up in his chair, rested his elbows on his desk and laced his fingers in front of his chin. He looked at me with an expression that said: *Do you believe this woman?* I hoped my return look said: *Yes, I do.* He looked back at Carla. "How long have you worked for Denali?" he said.

"Couple of years," she said.

"As a hairdresser?"

"Yes."

"Besides keeping his secrets, have you ever done anything else for him?"

"You mean like sexual favors?"

Briggs looked at me, then back at Carla.

"I mean has he asked you to do any other work for him?"

"Break the law?"

"Anything," Briggs repeated.

"No. I just cut hair."

"You say this thing's been going on for almost a year now?"

"That's when Ray came to me with it."

"And you're willing to testify in court with this information?"

Carla looked at me. I didn't say anything. Then she looked back at Briggs and said, "Sure."

"You did the right thing by bringing this to the attention of Detective Graham," Briggs said. "The department appreciates it."

He looked at me again. I got the feeling he wanted to say, "Nice job," but he didn't.

In my efforts to find Ray Deverol, I had given Briggs his entire case on a silver platter. But the question remained, where was Ray and was he dead or alive? From the point of view of solving this case, it mattered little to Briggs whether Ray was still drawing breath. He had Hamlin's testimony, and I'd given him Carla. With my report and subsequent arrests, this case was sewn up. Nonetheless, I was determined to find out what happened to Ray.

"What happens to me now?" Carla said. "I have no job and no place to live."

"As of now," Briggs said, "you're in protective custody as a material witness. The city will put you up until the trial. Afterward, we'll work out a more permanent arrangement to suit you."

"It's like a witness protection program," I said. "The city will see to your every need. They even have people who'll help find you a job."

"As long as I'm safe," Carla said.

"You will be," Briggs said. "A couple of my men will escort you to your apartment so you can collect your personal belongings. When you get back, we'll take your official statement and iron out the particulars."

Briggs excused himself and walked out into the main squad room.

I pushed away from the filing cabinet and walked closer to Carla. I could see she felt uneasy and unsure, which was only natural. I took her hand in mine and squeezed it gently.

In less than a minute, Briggs was back. Through the glass partition, I could see Danny Nolan and McClusky waiting outside the office door. Briggs indicated them with a hand gesture. "These men will take you to your apartment now," he said.

Carla looked at me with an uncertain smile.

"You'll be okay," I said. "You're doing the right thing."

"Will you be here when I get back?" she said.

"I'll keep in touch," I said.

She nodded and walked out of the office with McClusky and Nolan.

Briggs closed the door and sat behind his desk again. He leaned his chair back and laced his fingers behind his head.

"I'm sure you have more pieces to this puzzle," he said.

"I'm on leave, remember?"

He gave me a "Don't be a wise guy" look and said, "The only reason I'm not chopping your head off is because you've gone this far. I'd be stupid to tie your hands now."

"Does that mean I'm back to work?"

He looked at me for a long moment, then brought his chair down and unlocked his desk drawer. He removed my gun and shield from the drawer and put it on the desk without ceremony. I clipped my gun to my belt and put my shield and ID in my pocket. It made me feel whole again.

"I'll need a comprehensive report from you," he said.

"Give me forty-eight-hour, Chief," I said. "I'll hand you this case wrapped in red ribbon."

I watched him wrinkle his brow with reservation, but *I* knew *he* knew—I would.

I left Briggs and drove to the New York Public Library on Fifth Avenue. I was playing a hunch. If I could obtain the information I needed from the library, I was pretty sure I'd know where to find Ray, although a large part of me wanted my hunch to be wrong.

As I walked through the library's main entrance, I'd forgotten just how big the place was. I felt lost before I began. With all the people in this enormous space, you could hear a pin drop. I was grateful when I saw the information desk in the center of the room and headed straight for it. There were more than enough employees behind the desk, some tapping keyboards, some carrying books and others shuffling papers. I walked up to a young lady who was sipping a latte as she read from a computer screen. She looked like a college kid. Her brown hair was pulled tight into a ponytail which hung almost to her waist. I stood and waited. She knew I was standing there but took the time to finish what she was reading before she looked up at me. I got the feeling she thought I had interrupted her and was being a pain in the ass. "How can I help you?" she finally said.

"Do you supply road maps for this place?" I joked, smiling.

She didn't think that was funny, and said, "What are you looking for?" Her face was completely without expression.

"If you point me to the fiction section, I think I can navigate the rest myself."

She stood, pulled a pencil from her hair and used it to point to the far corner of the room.

I thanked her and headed in that direction. I don't think she liked her job.

When I entered the maze of shelves, I found myself in the alphabetical section labeled: "K". I continued to the end of the row until I came to the letter "P". As I expected, there were numerous books available for what I needed. I scanned a few volumes and chose one entitled: *Selected Works*. I was sure this was where I would find what I was looking for. I carried the book to a nearby table and sat in front of a reading lamp. I opened the cover and read the table of contents. It listed twenty or so stories, and although I wasn't certain which one I wanted, I was pretty sure I could narrow it down to a few. On the table in front of me was a small wooden box filled with short yellow pencils and a stack of notepaper. The pencils had no erasers. What good was a pencil without an eraser? I jotted down three-story titles, one of which I believed would corroborate my hunch. I turned to the first one and began to read.

I left the library two hours later and headed for Greasy John's. He'd had enough time to dig up anything on Drew or Ray if there was anything. I parked across the street and dodged my way through Eighth Avenue traffic toward the newsstand. Greasy was sitting on a stool, sipping a cup of coffee and flipping through the Daily News. When he saw me, he closed the paper and looked up quickly.

"I thought you were a customer," he said.

"I am," I said. "I want to return this pack of stale gum." I retrieved the opened pack I had in my pocket and dropped it on the counter.

"No refunds on personal items," he said.

He slid off his stool and leaned over-the-counter closer to me, then took his time looking up and down at the sidewalk traffic. When he was satisfied the time was right, he said,

"*Nada* on Deverol, but your doctor friend carries a heavy gambling debt."

My first thought was: *that doesn't make sense. Drew was a millionaire several times over and certainly didn't need to gamble for the money.*

"How heavy?" I said.

"Six digits."

"A.C. or Vegas?"

"Strictly underground," Greasy said. "Your boy likes it under the covers."

"Who takes his action?"

"Too high up for me to find out."

He saw the quizzical look on my face and said, "What's up?"

"This guy's got mountains of money," I said. "Why would he put himself into a hole like that?"

"The monkey," Greasy said.

I showed him another quizzical look.

"Gamblers get hooked for lots of reasons," he said. "Each one carries a different monkey on his back. But they all have one thing in common. They don't gamble for profit. It's an addiction. It's not the win. It's the uncertainty of whether they're gonna win that gives them the kick."

"But he's got the bucks to pay the debt, anytime," I said.

"Man, these guys don't pay off with their own money. They just keep playin', hopin' to win enough to pay what they owe, but they only get in deeper. It never works. I know."

"Is that all?"

"His closet's clean except for that skeleton."

"Thanks," I said. "Keep your head down."

"Yeah. Watch your back," he said.

As I walked back to my car, I wondered what kind of monkey Drew carried on his back.

Chapter 21

"I saw clearly the doom which had been prepared for me..."
Edgar Allan Poe—The Pit and The Pendulum

It was past noon when I left Greasy John. My stomach was rumbling. I stopped at a Burger King and ordered a Whopper with cheese, fries and a large lemonade. I sat in the Chevy in the parking lot and went to work on the Whopper. Just as I reached into the bag for a handful of fries, my phone began to ring. I couldn't find a napkin, so I wiped my hands on the paper bag before I answered it. It was Allan Deverol.

"I received a call from Ray," he said.

I almost swallowed my pickle.

"Are you sure?" I said, trying to gulp down the remainder of what I'd been chewing.

"Of course."

"How can you be sure it was Ray?"

"I know my brother's voice."

I hoped he was right and had to contain my anticipation.

"What did he say? Is he all right?"

"He sounded okay. He said he wants to turn himself in."

"At least he's thinking straight," I said.

"But he'll only turn himself into you."

It made me feel good that Ray still had confidence in me.

"Where is he?"

"Maybe, outdoors. I could hear what sounded like traffic behind him."

"What does he want me to do?"

"He gave me an address. If you meet him, he'll go with you to the police."

I wasn't comfortable with that.

"I don't like it," I said.

"I don't understand," Allan Deverol said.

"Could be a set-up."

"What do you mean?"

"Are you sure it was Ray?"

"I'm sure. Why do you doubt it?"

"We have to be careful."

"Of what?"

"Of everything."

There was a short silence from the other end until Allan Deverol said, "I'm sorry. I don't think like a policeman."

"When does Ray want to do this?"

"Tonight, he said to meet him at seven."

"Give me the address," I said.

"I'd like to be part of this," Allan Deverol said.

"I don't advise it."

"I might be helpful."

"You could get hurt if things don't turn out the way they're supposed to."

"I can take care of myself,"

"Think of Melissa," I said.

After another short silence, he recited the address to me without further protest. I found a pen in my glove box and wrote the address on the Burger King bag.

"What do you want me to do?" Allan Deverol said.

"Stay by the phone. If Ray calls again, call me immediately, otherwise, I'll be at the designated time and place."

As soon as I got back to my apartment, I phoned Sandy. I needed to be sure she was okay. I knew Denali wasn't through with me, but if Ray's call was the real thing, I wanted to be there for him.

Sandy said she had made lasagna and was planning on having me over for a dish. For an Irish girl, she could cook great Italian food. She'd been a waitress in an Italian restaurant while she helped work her way through college and had picked up a few cooking tips from the resident chef. I'd told her once that she cooked better Italian than my mother. At the risk of having a wooden spoon broken over my head, I told her I would deny that I'd said that if my mother ever found out.

It had always been important to me to be truthful with Sandy, but now, I thought it best to tell her I had an appointment with Briggs to discuss my report and would have to make it another time. To tell her what I was getting into would only cause her undue stress and worry, and she didn't need any more of that. When she promised to freeze a square of lasagna and keep it for me and assured me she would be home all night, I told her I'd call her in the morning.

I hung up and called Chestnut. I wanted him with me. I could be walking into a trap, but if that phone call was the real thing, it could mean getting Ray back. I explained to Chestnut what was happening and asked him to meet me by six. He said he would.

Chestnut arrived at my apartment before six. It was already dark, and there was the usual chill in the October night. He was wearing sneakers, jeans, a navy blue sweatshirt, and a black leather waist-length jacket. A black knitted cap was stretched tightly around his shaved head. He waited by the front window while I finished dressing. I slipped into a pair of jeans, laced up my Rockport boots and put on my brown leather jacket. At the kitchen table, I loaded my gun with hollow points and loaded a second clip that I put into my front pocket.

"Lot of firepower," Chestnut said as he watched me load the weapon.

"Enough for both of us," I said.

I was confident Chestnut could go up against almost any adversary, but he didn't carry a gun and if bullets started to fly, I felt an inherent obligation to protect him. I holstered my gun and zipped my jacket around it. We left the apartment, not sure of what we were getting into.

***

Chestnut drove a late model Ford Mustang, black with chrome wheels. He'd insisted we take it, and I didn't disagree. I had no idea what Chestnut did for a living, and didn't care to know, but I was glad he could immerse himself in a bit of luxury. As we drove east on Route 78 toward Jersey City, I couldn't help thinking about my Chevy parked in front of my apartment whenever Chestnut pushed on the gas pedal and the power of the Mustang surged beneath us. In her day, the Chevy seemed to get up like the Mustang, but the years have taken that from her. Now, she was an old friend resisting retirement. She had taken care of my family and me over the years, and now I was taking care of her. Besides, I couldn't afford a new car.

"Which way now?"

Chestnut's baritone voice broke my reverie. I took the sheet of paper from my pocket, clicked on the overhead light and followed the lines of the map I had printed off the Internet.

"Grant Street," I said. "It should be right off this main road. Look for a bar called The Blue Crab."

"Never saw a blue crab," Chestnut said.

I gave him a look and clicked off the light.

Although the main road was well lit, the side streets were in shadow. I could smell the river even though we were several blocks away. I counted the streets until we came to Grant. "Make a right," I said.

As soon as we made the turn onto a cobblestone street, I could see the cracked and partially lit sign for "The Blue Crab" at the end of the block.

"Drive past and park on the other side."

Chestnut drove the Mustang to the end of the block, made a U-turn and parked two doors away. He cut the engine and lights. We had a clear view of the bar from where we were without being conspicuous. I was feeling uncomfortable about this whole thing now that we were here. I knew Ray liked to drink, but I kept asking myself, why would he frequent this place? There were plenty of watering holes between here and his apartment.

"What now?" Chestnut said.

"I go in."

He reached for the door handle but I stopped him with: "I said, 'I go in'."

He looked confused.

"I'll need you to stay here and watch."

"Watch for what?"

"Watch for me. If Ray's in there, I'll bring him right out."

"And if he's not?"

He waited for my answer, but I had none.

"Just wait here and keep your eyes on the front door."

I pulled the Colt from my holster and checked the magazine. I was sure it was fully loaded but checked it out of habit, something I'd always done whenever I felt uneasy about a situation. I returned it to its holster and pulled my jacket down to conceal it. I crossed the street diagonally and headed for the bar. The area was quiet except for the muted music coming from inside the bar and the voices of a few men lingering by the front door, smoking cigarettes. I passed them without incident, opened the barred door and walked through the entrance into the brightly lit bar. I scanned the tables to my

The Stillness Broken

left and the bar on my right but didn't see Ray. Multi-colored lights flashed from a jukebox in a corner where a female patron gyrated to the music blaring from its speakers. A group of men sitting at nearby tables threw dollar bills on the floor at her feet. She swooped down and picked them up without missing a beat. I wondered how well she could dance if she weren't half crocked. I squeezed my way up to the crowded bar and ordered a beer. I looked at my watch. Ray was to meet me at seven. The fact that it was nearly seven-thirty made me more cautious. Had Ray changed his mind when I didn't show on time? Was he late? Had I walked into a trap? I had no choice now but to wait.

The floor dancer began to sing along with the music, and it wasn't long before the men at the table joined her. Several patrons at the bar turned to watch the show and began to sing along too. The volume of noise became almost deafening. I finished my beer and turned to look out at the crowd. Among all the bloated faces, there wasn't one I recognized. I checked my watch again...seven forty-five. I ordered another beer and decided I'd wait until eight. If Ray were going to show, there would be no reason why he shouldn't be here by then.

The bartender brought my beer. As I raised it to my lips, I felt something hard press against my side. It was that familiar feel of a gun barrel being pushed into my ribs. I hoped I was wrong. I put the glass to my lips and took a swallow. There it was again, harder this time.

"Don't turn around," a voice said, close to my ear. "Out the back door."

"I'm not finished with my beer," I said.

The gun barrel pushed deeper into my ribs. This time it hurt. I set my glass on the bar and headed for the unmarked door between the restrooms, my unidentified escort discretely kept his gun at my back as we made our way through the crowd. I opened the door. We passed through an unlit hallway that led to the rear entrance and a parking lot. As soon as we stepped out into the lot, I spotted the Crown Vic that had been my ride once before. Bernie was behind the wheel, slouched low like the weasel he was. We stopped by the rear side door of the car. The guy behind me spun me around, pulled my gun from its holster and dropped it into his jacket pocket. No one said a word. A big guy got out of the front seat, walked around and gave me a quick frisk. When he found the extra magazine in my front pocket, he tossed it into the bushes and secured my hands behind my back with a plastic zip-tie. He took a roll of duct tape from his pocket, tore off a length and placed it over my mouth. My escort opened the rear door of the car and shoved me inside. All three men were well-dressed, business suits but no ties. The only one I recognized was Bernie, who was trying hard to avoid eye contact with me. I guess he wasn't as scared as he pretended to be that day at the park. I owed him for that, and one for Carla. My two escorts sat in the back seat on either side of me. Bernie started the engine and pulled out of the parking lot, spinning the rear wheels and spraying gravel up into the darkness. As we drove down a side street, I wondered if Chestnut was still watching the front door like I'd asked him to.

We made a right, then a left onto Grant and headed out to the main street. As we took the turn, I could see the Mustang parked across the street. Chestnut's head was back against the headrest and I hoped he hadn't fallen asleep. We drove the main street for about twenty minutes in silence. By now, I was pretty sure Ray wasn't going to show—if there was a Ray? It was obvious this was Denali's *coup de grâce* to me. When Keeper and Doorman went missing, it would have been a cinch for Denali to figure out I was still breathing and his men had botched their mission. I had humiliated him twice. I was sure he wouldn't let it happen a third time. I wanted to believe Ray made that call to his brother, but I'd underestimated Denali's creativity and walked into his trap. Even though I knew I might become a victim, I had to follow through with the phone call lead. I owed it to Allan Deverol and his daughter...and to Ray.

I was unfamiliar with the area, but it was easy to see we were driving closer to the waterfront. I looked back through the rear window, hoping I'd see the Mustang following, but all I got was a blinding glare from an onslaught of headlights.

When I looked forward again, Bernie was turning into the parking area of a marina. The shimmering lights on the water revealed the silhouettes of a numerous of boats berthed along the perimeter. Bernie pulled into a parking spot and killed the engine. I was yanked from the backseat and led down a narrow wooden dock toward several sailboats and large yachts. We stopped by a cruiser whose cabin was well lit. The name in gold letters on the stern read: *Mia Amore*. I made a note of the license number on the bow, although it wouldn't do me any good if I wound up at the bottom of the Atlantic, which was a distinct possibility.

Bernie climbed on board first, removed a key from his pocket and unlocked the cabin door. We followed him down a short stairway into the living quarters. The big guy pushed me onto a cushioned chair in a corner. It was obvious they were under strict orders from Denali and were afraid to make any slip-ups. Bernie locked the cabin door, put the key in his pocket, then sat at a small table with the others and opened a bottle of Dewar's. He pulled on his nostrils a few times, then filled his glass. No one spoke. The only sounds were the water slapping the sides of the vessel and the clinking of glass as each goon poured himself a drink, then passed the bottle. Between twitches, Bernie kept looking at his watch. The bottle was passed one more time, then set in the center of the table. I looked at a clock on the wall. Somehow, behind a picture of a flock of seagulls encircling a lone lighthouse painted on its face, I was able to decipher that it was 8:30. It had been an hour since I'd left Chestnut in front of The Blue Crab, and I hoped he wasn't still waiting there.

A few more minutes passed before Bernie got up, unlocked the door and climbed the stairs to the upper deck. I could hear him lock the cabin door from the outside. His cohorts settled in with a deck of cards and started a game of Gin, just as the cabin floor began to rumble with the sound of the engine starting. Bernie was on the bridge. I was sure now; the plan was to take me out and dump me in the ocean. The sound of the engine continued for almost a full minute, but the yacht remained anchored. Then, as abruptly as it had started, the engine stopped. In the returning silence, I could see the concern on the faces of the goons at the table as they stopped their game and listened. Something wasn't going as planned. The big guy pushed his chair away from the table and went to the door. He rapped on it a few times and shouted up to Bernie. If Bernie responded, the big guy missed it when the cabin door exploded inward with shards of mahogany wood and Chestnut's huge body. The guy went down against the bulkhead. Chestnut made sure he stayed there with a sidekick to his abdomen, followed by a quick chop to his Adam's apple. The guy grabbed his throat in a desperate search for air. His face turned purple-blue as he slid down to the cabin floor. His buddy at the table jumped up and went for his gun. I managed to kick his chair back against his legs with my foot. He lost his balance and fell backward, but not before he cleared his gun from his holster and fired at Chestnut. The bullet missed and shattered the clock on the wall, sending seagulls flying everywhere. Chestnut retaliated with a roundhouse kick to the shooter's chest. The shooter hit the floor, and Chestnut finished him off with a merciless chop to his windpipe.

In the ensuing calmness, Chestnut took time to examine the resulting carnage. There was no doubt in my mind that both these guys were dead. Chestnut was that thorough. Satisfied, he turned to me with a broad smile. Then, without warning, he reached out and yanked the duct tape from my mouth. It hurt like hell and I let out a howl.

"Real funny," I said.

"It's the best way to take it off, my mon," he said, smiling.

"What took you so long?"

"Black cars are hard to follow at night," he said. He was still smiling as he cut the zip-tie from my wrists with his knife.

"A few more minutes and I'd have been in Davy Jones's locker."

Chestnut gave me a puzzled look.

"Never mind," I said.

I got to my feet and walked over to the shooter on the floor and took my gun from his pocket. I felt for a pulse but found none. His partner's face was as purple as an eggplant. I knew there'd be no pulse there.

"Where's my friend, Bernie?"

"The one upstairs?"

"Yeah."

"He had a gun, but I fixed him."

I wasn't sure what Chestnut meant by "fixed him" as images of what he'd done to Keeper, Muscle boy and Doorman came back to me. I holstered my weapon and climbed the stairs to the main deck with Chestnut behind me. Bernie was slumped over the wheel on the bridge.

"Is he dead?"

"No, mon, I only fixed him." Chestnut took Bernie by his shoulders and shook him a few times until his eyes fluttered open. When Bernie saw Chestnut, his eyes widened. He must have thought he'd gone to Hell and was looking at the Devil.

"Don't kill me," he said.

Now that was the Bernie I knew.

"I should've killed you in the park," I said.

"I—I was only doin' what I was told."

He tried to stand, but Chestnut pushed him back into the seat.

"You set me up, Bernie, and tried to get Carla and me killed."

"No! I swear. Denali knows everything. He's got people."

"Does he know where Ray Deverol is?"

"Who?"

It was worth a second try, but I was sure Bernie knew nothing about Ray.

"What do we do with him?" Chestnut said.

"Throw him in the ocean."

Bernie's eyes almost popped out of their sockets when he heard that. I took a pair of handcuffs from my belt and secured his hands in front of him. We walked up the dock toward the parking area where Chestnut had left the Mustang. The night was quiet and calm, with plenty of stars and a full moon. It was almost pleasurable standing by the Mustang while Chestnut searched in his pockets for his car keys...until Bernie got stupid, shoved me against the car and bolted down the dock toward the birthed boats. I wondered where he thought he was going. The dock had to end somewhere and unless Bernie could fly, or run on water, he had no place to escape. I started after him, with Chestnut behind me. When I got close enough, I reached out and grabbed Bernie's shoulder and spun him around, then hit him with a right to his jaw. He staggered backward but came back at me with a butt head to my solar plexus. I lost my breath for a few seconds as I buckled over at the waist. When I looked up, I could see Bernie clearly in the moonlight. He ran past the line of boats and climb onto the *Mia Amore*. He picked up his revolver from the deck where it had fallen and crouched low in the shadows. Chestnut and I ran down the dock and took cover behind a small tackle shed at the end of the dock. When I peered around the corner, Bernie fired a shot in our direction. He was playing tough. When he let off another shot, I shoved Chestnut into a shadow and pressed myself against the side of the shed. "Stay here," I said, "and keep low."

"I'll go around the other way and fix him," Chestnut said.

"Stay here and keep low," I repeated.

Sometimes Chestnut thinks he's superman.

I took out my gun, crouched low and began crawling along the wet dock boards closer to the *Mia Amore*. Although Bernie was down in the shadows, the yellow light spilling out from the cabin illuminated him enough to give me a clear shot. I fired one a few feet from his head, hoping I could convince him to give up. I didn't want to kill Bernie unless it meant saving my own life or Chestnut's. Bernie panicked and began throwing shots wildly in my direction. I ducked behind a metal trash bin. A couple of bullets whizzed by my head, close enough that I could feel their velocity. I crouched in the shadows, and waited while Bernie continued to fire sporadically. One-shot...two shots...three shots. I knew it was over when I heard the hammer on his revolver dropping on empty chambers. Bernie was out of bullets—and luck.

I stood up and moved closer to him. "It's over, Bernie," I said. "Give it up."

"Fuck you, Graham," he shouted.

He threw the empty gun at me and started running down the dock.

Chestnut came up behind me. "Where's he going?" he said.

My answer was cut short by Bernie's scream and the sound of churning water.

It's not impossible to fire a gun with your hands cuffed together in front of you, but nearly impossible to run on a slippery dock at night and not lose your balance. It sounded to me like Bernie was in the drink.

Chestnut and I hurried to the end of the dock. We stopped where the dock met the water and stood staring down into the swirling foam. We couldn't see Bernie, anywhere. After a while, Chestnut said, "Mon can't swim without arms."

***

It was nearly eleven when Chestnut dropped me off at my apartment. I was dirty and sweaty and too exhausted for a shower. The morning would have to do. I poured some milk into a pot and left it under a low flame on the stove, then went into my bedroom and stripped down to my shorts. My bed looked inviting, but I was too wound up to sleep. If I tried now, I'd toss and turn all night and feel lousy in the morning. Now that I was off administrative leave, I was back on a regular schedule and due to work the dayshift tomorrow. I didn't want to do anything to get Briggs upset again. The warm milk would help me sleep. It always did. Back at the stove, I poured the milk into a mug and carried it to the sofa in the living room. I eased into the deep cushion and put my feet on the coffee table, stretching my legs out and nearly knocking over the flowered vase Sandy had given me to add ambiance. The warm milk relaxed me. Before I knew it, my mug was empty. I placed it on the table, dropped my head back on the sofa and closed my eyes. I'd give myself a few minutes, then head for my bed. My mind immediately went to Sandy. I was still concerned about her safety. Danger was a part of my business, but when my danger became Sandy's danger, it was time for me to tie loose ends and finish this thing. I'd been pushing it for Ray's sake, and there had been too many close calls.

It was time for me to confront Drew.

Chapter 22

But two, they fell: for Heaven no grace imparts
To those who hear not for their beating hearts.
Edgar Allan Poe—Al Aaraaf

The following day went pretty well for my first regular day back on the job. Briggs hadn't given me any new assignments, so I was able to catch up on the few cases I had pending. Danny Nolan had taken over a couple of my cases while I was on leave, which made it a lot easier for me. He was always there in a pinch. I wouldn't tell him to his face, but the guy had become invaluable to me.

When I got home, I found Sandy at my apartment whipping up something over my stove. I was always glad to see her, but seeing her now was unexpected, and I hoped she hadn't planned a long night with me. My mind was on what I had planned to do, and I didn't want any diversions, although Sandy certainly was a *pleasurable* diversion.

I had phoned Drew from work that afternoon and told him I wanted to discuss some new ideas I had about Ray's disappearance. He sounded eager to meet with me and suggested I come by the mansion about eight. That gave me just three hours to accommodate Sandy, without making her suspicious, and make it to Drew's on time. I hoped she wasn't feeling frisky. That wouldn't make things easier for me.

From the aroma of basil and parsley that permeated the apartment and the steam I saw rising from the pot of water on the stove, I concluded she'd been putting together a pasta dinner.

"Something smells Italian," I said as I closed the door behind me.

"I felt like spaghetti," she said, "but didn't want to eat alone. You up for it?"

"Always," I said.

"I figured we'd celebrate your first day back with a good meal," she said.

I came up behind her and kissed her neck.

She slid some spaghetti from the box, snapped it in half and dropped it into the pot of boiling water. I went into the bathroom to wash.

"How's it feel to be back?" she said.

"Like I never left," I said.

I went into my bedroom and slid into a pair of sweats and a tee-shirt. I put on my fuzzy slippers and shuffled back into the kitchen. I looked like I was in for the night. Sandy had set the table and was opening a bottle of wine as I took my usual seat. I poured the wine while she dished out the spaghetti onto our plates and then sat down opposite me.

The spaghetti was good, as I knew it would be. After my first mouthful, I said, "Any Italian bread?"

"I forgot," Sandy said.

"It's okay," I said, "The spaghetti is delicious."

We ate in silence for a full minute until she said, "I guess your mission with Chestnut was a success."

I nodded with a mouthful.

"I supposed as much," she said.

"How would you know?" I said.

"Because I don't see any cuts or bruises on your face."

"You're an alarmist," I said.

We continued to eat in silence for another full minute until she said, "Any progress on your friend, Ray?"

I wasn't sure how much information I wanted to give her and tried to be honest yet selective with my wording. I knew she'd worry no matter what I said, and I didn't want to take her down that road. I'd been trying to distance her from any further involvement. The less she knew, the better off she'd be. I'd placed her in harm's way once and wasn't about to let it happen again. I wasn't going to tell her I was on my way to see Drew and force his hand. Besides, the hunch I had was based on my theory and might have proven meaningless. I hoped my visit with Drew would finish this thing.

"I'm closer than I have been," I said.

"Do you know where Ray is?"

"If my hunch turns out to be right, the conclusion of this case won't leave me with any sense of satisfaction."

"Do you think Ray is dead?"

"Yes."

"Based on the facts you've uncovered thus far."

"Yes."

"But you could be wrong?"

"Yes."

I stopped eating and looked up at her. "Hold on, counselor," I said. "Is this an official interrogation?"

"I'm just asking questions," she said.

I put my fork down and looked hard at her across the table. I was trying to make her understand without hurting her feelings.

"I've been through hell this last month," I said.

"Nobody knows that better than me," she said.

"If things work out, this will be over in a few days. We'll know all the answers and we can put this thing behind us. Can we just enjoy our spaghetti for now?"

"Okay. I'm sorry for asking," she said.

I felt like a jerk and reached over and took her hand. "No, *I'm* sorry," I said. "I don't mean to shut you out. It's just that I'm trying to keep things straight in my head and don't want to confuse myself with unnecessary questions and answers."

"I'm trying to be a part of this," she said. "Offer what help I can."

"You've already been too much a part of it," I said, "and all because of me. I don't want you in harm's way again,"

"I'm not out chasing criminals, Max. I'm just offering you advice."

"I appreciate it," I said. "But I don't want you involved, not after what you've been through. I won't run the risk of getting you hurt because of me."

"Look who's being an alarmist now," she said.

I took a sip of wine and tried to change the subject. "This sauce is almost as good as my mother's," I said.

She ignored that and looked at me seriously.

"You're keeping something from me, Max," she said.

"I'm not," I said. "I told you, with any luck, this thing will be over tomorrow."

"Then that means something's going down tonight. Something you don't want me to know about."

"I'm asking you to trust me."

"I do."

"Then let's enjoy our dinner and the rest of the evening."

There was a half-minute of silence between us, until she said, "You're meeting Chestnut tonight, aren't you?"

"Sandy, please."

"Okay," she said. "I'm sorry."

"Stop saying you're sorry," I said. "There's nothing to be sorry about, although you did forget the Italian bread."

She stopped talking and went back to eating her spaghetti.

I remember thinking how many times I had played this same scene out with Marlene. I was doing to Sandy exactly what I had done to my ex-wife. The suspicion and worry she'd endured eventually cost me my marriage. I knew how important it was not to let that happen again, and I was trying with every ounce of fiber in my body to prevent it. But tonight, for the first time, it manifested itself over a dish of spaghetti. At the risk of losing Sandy, I had to continue on my current course and hope things worked out. Sandy was savvy about the law and police procedures, and I hoped she would understand more than Marlene had. I'd have to trust her as I'd asked her to trust me.

We continued our dinner without anything more on the subject. It was 6:30 by the time we cleaned the table and washed the dishes. Sandy made herself comfortable on my sofa, and it looked like she wasn't going anywhere soon. She picked up the remote and clicked on the TV. I thought I was done for. If she planned on staying a few more hours, my only option would be to tell her the truth.

I sat down beside her and watched her channel surfing. She flipped through the usual news and movie channels but didn't seem very interested. I put my feet up on the coffee table and laid my head back on the sofa pillows. I closed my eyes when I was sure she noticed. After a few seconds, I heard her click off the TV. I felt her cuddle next to me and put her arms around my waist. She leaned in and kissed my cheek, and then ran her lips down the side of my neck.

Oh, God, she's feeling frisky, I thought. *I'm doomed.*

It wasn't easy, but I kept motionless. When she released her hold on me, I opened one eye and watched her walk away from me and toward the kitchen. She removed her jacket from the back of the chair and slipped into it, then grabbed her purse from the counter. I sat up quickly as she walked back toward me.

"Are you leaving?" I said.

"I think you've had enough of me for tonight," she said.

I stood up and took her by her waist. "I can never get enough of you," I said, and kissed her forehead. She gave me a smile which didn't seem genuine.

"I've got a full docket tomorrow," she said. "I'll turn in early."

"I'll walk you out," I said.

I kept my arm around her waist as we walked down the stairs and out to the street where her car was parked. She took her keys from her purse, pressed the remote, and unlocked the door. Before she got in, she looked up at me. "Be careful," she said.

I didn't know what to say without feeling like a liar. She knew something was going down, despite what I'd told her, and she was afraid for me. I felt as guilty as hell for not coming clean with her, but I had no choice.

I watched Sandy drive away and then went back upstairs It was a quarter to seven. I still had time to make it to Drew's by eight. I left my fuzzy slippers on the floor next to my bed and put on a pair of jeans and my sneakers. I slipped into my leather jacket and clipped my Colt to my belt. I hoped I wouldn't have to use it.

Chapter 23

"But evil things in robes of sorrow,
Assailed the Monarch's high estate."
Edgar Allan Poe—The Haunted Palace

The grounds were dark as I pulled off the road and parked by the front entrance to Drew's mansion. I got out and looked around. The place was even more foreboding at night. I couldn't see a light anywhere inside and wondered if Drew had forgotten our meeting. A full moon peeked out from behind a procession of clouds after each passed in front of it, throwing metallic light patterns onto the shadowed landscape as I walked to the front door and pushed the chime button. The familiar chimes resounded throughout the house, but no one came to the door. I tried again and waited. No response. I expected the door to be locked, but when I turned the knob, the door opened easily. I walked through the darkened vestibule, opened the inner door and found myself within the shadows of the main corridor. I stood quietly and listened. The silence was eerie, and I was already beginning to feel uncomfortable. *Where was Drew? Why hadn't he come to the door?* At the far end of the corridor, I could see the flickering flames from the library fireplace spilling out through the double doors, illuminating the framed portrait of Monica Flannery, her luminous eyes watched with dispassionate interest as I walked through the semidarkness toward the library. The library was dark, other than the generous fire crackling in the hearth and the silver-blue moonlight coming through the wall of windows. As I stepped through the double doors, I saw Drew in an armchair absorbed in a book, bathed in the orange glow of the fire. He was wearing his black clothes again. I sensed he knew I was there but continued to read. "I've been waiting," he said, without looking up. As I walked further into the room, he closed his book and placed it on the arm of his chair. I could tell it was his Poe volume by the leather cover and the gold ribbon bookmark separating its pages. He got up and walked to the bar, poured himself a drink and made a gesture of offering, which I ignored. The November night had turned raw, and I moved closer to the fireplace to warm my hands.

"I'm glad you came," he said. "I've been completely baffled by all this and hope you've made some degree of progress."

"I've followed enough leads to come up with a picture," I said.

He sat down in his armchair again, crossed his legs casually and began sipping his drink.

"Where do you go from here, then?" he said.

"I'm not sure," I said, trying to sound convincing. "Maybe you can tell me."

"What could I tell you that you don't already know?"

"You can tell me something current about Ray, something you might've forgotten to mention. The two of you had been re-acquainted for a while before I came back into the picture."

"I already told you," he said. "Ray came to the hospital looking for a new account and was fortunate enough to run into me. I put him in touch with the right people—you know, help out an old friend."

"But the relationship wasn't strictly business?"

"Of course not, he's been here for dinner."

He held his glass up and swirled it around to melt some ice, studying its contents longer than he had to. I could see he wasn't comfortable with my line of questioning by the way his eyes kept avoiding mine.

"Did your wife join you for dinner?"

He looked suddenly annoyed. "What does my wife have to do with this?"

I was hoping I wouldn't get that reaction. I let it go and walked to the armchair, picked up his leather-bound Poe volume and opened its cover. I walked back to the fireplace, turning pages. It was time to push a bit harder.

"I think you know," I said.

"I'm sure I don't," he said. He set his drink down and walked to the fireplace and began to warm his hands over the hearth. While he did, he watched me skim through the pages of the book and said, "Hoping to learn from the master?"

"Mr. Poe has been as much a part of this case as I have," I said. "He's been more than helpful."

I could see he was beginning to feel uneasy, not sure of himself. I let a few moments of silence pass between us before I said, "Your wife came to see me. She told me about her involvement with Ray."

His demeanor quickly changed, his face hardened, his eyes showing both betrayal and surprise. He stopped warming his hands and turned to face me.

"And so now you know," he said. "I've been trying to save my marriage for months but ran out of options."

"Except one," I said.

He glared at me for an explanation.

"The option of getting rid of Ray," I said.

He gave me a surprised look that I didn't buy.

"Are you suggesting I had something to do with Ray's disappearance?"

"Do you know where he is?"

"Certainly not," he said.

"I think you do."

"You can't be serious? Why would you think that of me?"

I let the hammer drop. "Because I think you killed him," I said.

I wasn't ready for his reaction. He snatched the shovel from the hearth and swung it like a major leaguer at my head. I raised the Poe book to my face, and the blow knocked it from my hands and into the fire, causing me to lose balance and fall against the mantle. The pages and binding caught quickly, sending black smoke up and over the hearth. Drew watched the burning with frantic eyes, helpless to stop the destruction. In the same instant, my eye caught movement above me. I looked up in time to see the Poe bust teetering forward off the mantel. I jumped back quickly enough to watch it crash to pieces at my feet. Drew looked down at his shattered idol in disbelief. Panic-stricken, he looked up at me, his face convulsing in spasms of horror as I readied myself for a second assault. Instead, he turned and ran from the library, taking the shovel with him. I followed him into the dark corridor. There, I could hear his running footsteps echoing on the terrazzo floor until they faded to silence. I was unable to tell their direction. I made my way to the front vestibule and checked the inner door. My guess was Drew hadn't had time to unlock the front door and leave the house, but made his way down the main corridor and into the darkness of the myriad rooms. Was Drew trying to make his escape? Or was he waiting for me, somewhere in the darkness? I slid my hand along the wall next to the doorframe until I found a light switch. When I flipped it up, the corridor remained dark. I walked across the hall and groped the wall where I thought there should be another switch. I found and tried a second switch, but to no avail. For whatever reason, Drew had disconnected the main power breaker, keeping the house in total darkness. Maybe he had a premonition of what might be ahead and planned his escape accordingly. The prisms hanging from the crystal chandeliers in the high ceiling reflected moonlight like a thousand stars but offered no light below.

I walked past the front vestibule, keeping close to the wall and squinting through the darkness at every recess and corner. I kept my gun holstered, hoping Drew wouldn't give me cause to use it. I was being careful. The way Drew swung that shovel, told me he had no compunction about smashing in my skull, and in a house this size, he could easily hide or make his escape, especially since we were playing on his turf. I felt like a mouse in a maze.

I made my way cautiously through the corridor, half hoping Drew would choose to confront me rather than try to escape. After a few futile minutes of trying to find my way and not being able to see much of anything, I stopped and listened. Within, the house held the same quiet stillness I had experienced on the grounds outside, a stillness broken only by the occasional whistling of the wind over the rooftops.

I was fooling myself. There was no way I could search for Drew without becoming entangled in a web of uncertainty. The advantage was his. I decided to make my way back to the more familiar surroundings of the library where there was light from the fireplace, hoping Drew would confront me there.

I walked back passed the vestibule at the main entrance. Only the faint moonlight penetrating the stained glass windows above me, casting colored rectangles on the terrazzo floor, afforded me enough light to continue. As I felt my way along the paneled walls, I was suddenly struck by Drew's full weight as he hit me from behind, knocking me to the floor. His hands came up around my throat quickly. I grappled with his fingers, but he was stronger than I'd expected and I couldn't stop the pressure of his thumbs against my windpipe. I couldn't breathe and felt my face go from crimson to purple before his sweaty fingers slipped away. I managed to roll myself free and got to my feet. He jumped up quickly and threw a punch wide in my direction. I feinted and blindly shot a right cross to his face, hoping it would hit its target. It did! He staggered back against the wall, but reached down and picked up the shovel lying by his feet and swung it at my head. As I ducked, I could hear the sound of the blade cutting through the air. It missed my head by inches. He followed through with a second swing, this time bringing the shovel down like an ax. When I sidestepped the swing, he turned and ran down the corridor and into the library, swinging the shovel in the air like a mad man. I ran down the corridor after him and turned into the library in time to see him hurry through the French doors and out to the rear grounds. I jogged through the doors not far behind him. He scrambled over a low stone wall surrounding the patio and ran across the open lawn. I vaulted the wall without losing my stride and although he had the advantage of knowing the grounds; I knew he couldn't match my speed.

I could see his dark figure in the moonlight about twenty-feet ahead of me. He was running hard, but the weight of the shovel wasn't helping his balance or speed. I knew he couldn't keep his pace up for long. My breath came short, and I cursed the flabbiness around my waist as I ran, but I sucked in a lungful of night air and pushed harder; pacing myself and using the same running technique I'd learned at college. I followed him down one side of a grassy slope and up the other, across an expanse of open lawn and along a length of hedgerow. He stumbled a few times but regained his momentum and was able to continue. I could see he was breathing hard and having a tough time of it.

When we reached the rear grounds, he changed direction quickly and cut diagonally in the direction of the tennis court.

He ran along the high fence and then bolted across an acre of freshly cut lawn toward the perimeter fence. If he reached the array of shrubbery there, I might lose him in the cover. I had no choice but to increase my stride and give it all I could or risk losing him. When I started to gain on him, he sensed I was close and began swinging the shovel wildly behind his back. I saw my chance and dove for his legs. I went down on top of him. As we rolled in the damp grass, he grabbed my throat again and began to squeeze. I pried his clammy fingers away easily this time, and cracked him hard in the jaw with a right, then cracked him again with a left. Each time my knuckles met his face, long suppressed images of Sherilyn flashed across my mind. *Payback! Payback! Payback!* Despite the barrage I had given him, he got to his feet, snatched up the shovel and came at me swinging. I ducked and went for his legs, bringing him down a second time. One more rap to his jaw and he fell limp. I picked him up by his shirtfront and brought him to his feet. My heart was pounding, and I was short of breath, but I felt good. While he shook himself from his stupor, I removed my handcuffs from my belt and secured his hands behind him. I picked up the shovel and prodded him back to the library.

***

I shoved him down into the armchair. He was breathing heavily and staring at me with a look of defiance and disbelief. On the floor of the hearth lay the broken pieces of his treasured Poe bust. He looked down at the shattered remnants, then back at me. I got the feeling he blamed me for its destruction. Untouched on the mantle, the perched Raven sat watching and listening in indifferent silence.

"You think you know the answers?" he said.

"I do now," I said.

"You know nothing," he said. "It's difficult to prove a murder without a body." A trickle of blood oozed from one corner of his mouth and he swiped it with his tongue periodically as he spoke. "Ray could be on the other side of the country visiting a sick aunt for all we know, or he may have *dropped out* like he did once before to get away from it all. Maybe he doesn't want to be found. A district attorney would have a hard time believing otherwise."

"Maybe," I said. "I'll admit I was dead-ended for a while until your wife came to me. It was clever of you to invite Ray and I here for a good time, fill him with booze knowing his weakness for alcohol; then suggest I drive him home, making me the last person to see him alive. And your phone call to me—duly concerned about our mutual friend but designed solely to remove suspicion from yourself."

He glared at me with an arrogant smile. "You never could match my cleverness," he said.

"When Ray told you the police were asking questions, you knew it would only be a matter of time before the investigation led to him, and then to you. He was the only one that could link the two of you together. Your wife couldn't say a word or she'd go down with you."

"Monica's a whore," he said, "an ungrateful whore. I gave her all this, and she betrayed me for a salesman."

"In your sick mind, you blamed her for ruining the perfect life you had planned. But in reality, it was her life you ruined. She became your Golem; trying to be the perfect person you wanted her to be, constantly in fear of saying or doing something that might not meet with your endorsement."

"You'll need a motive," he said.

"When Ray showed an interest in her, that put you over the edge and you devised his murder. With him out of the way, you'd be safe from the prying eyes of the police and have your revenge against your wife, as well. There's your motive," I said.

He looked at me, cocky and self-assured. "You can't prove any of this?" he said. His sense of invincibility was based on the fact that he believed he had planned the perfect crime.

"And then there's your gambling debt," I said. "You became possessed with making money quickly to pay that down. Ray's proposition could easily make that happen."

"My finances are none of your business," he snapped.

"They become my business when they include murder."

He laughed aloud. "You're prefabricating something in your mind that even *you* don't really believe," he said.

"You had means, motive, and opportunity," I said.

"But no corpus delecti," he said.

"We'll see after tonight," I said.

He'd remained confident throughout all this, but now regarded my last statement with an expression of concern.

"That evening you went to Ray's apartment and forcibly brought him back here before he could sober up. But not before you snatched his car keys so you could plant that phony note in his glove box to make it look like Ray had split. I checked the handwriting against Ray's invoice signature—not even close. Not much cleverness there."

I saw a flash of contempt in his eyes, but he said nothing.

"After you killed Ray, you took your time with the necessary sordid details. What simpler solution was there than for you to get rid of him before the questioning started? You included me in your twisted plan to avert suspicion from yourself by pretending to be an integral part of the search for our mutual buddy. That was your first mistake."

"You're nearly as smart as that inept detective that followed me for a week," he said. "He thought he had the answers, too."

"He had more answers than you wanted him to have."

"I tried to buy his silence, but he was naively honorable."

"So you killed him."

"You'll have to prove that, too," he said.

"Maybe I can," I said. "And that you also killed Evangelista."

"Blackmail is an ugly business," he said. "Ray had loose lips when he drank too much—which was all the time. When Evangelista learned about our thing, he wanted a part of it. When Ray refused him, he came to me. When I turned him down, he threatened to go to the police. I couldn't let that happen."

Evangelista had lied to me. He'd given me a false date and claimed he hadn't seen Ray since his arrival here. But he had been with Ray long enough to learn what Ray was into and tried to get a piece of the pie. He got more than he could swallow.

"For a man who is dedicated to saving lives, you have no problem taking them," I said.

He smiled and quoted Poe. "'The *boundaries which divide life and death are at best shadowy and vague. Who shall say where one ends, and the other begins?*'" And then, adding his own philosophy, he said, "I deal with life and death every day, just like you do."

"But the difference between us is, I respect it," I said.

"How do you know what I feel," he said. "You don't know me."

"I use to," I said.

"You make judgments on me just like the others," he continued, "on this house, my wealth, my reputation. The everyday demands are brutal, trying to stay at the top, trying to be what everyone expects you to be, trying to please everyone and trying to keep the life you've built from falling apart. There's never enough time."

"One needs to be pragmatic to survive," he said. "When things don't work out one way, one must try something else."

"Like lies and murder," I said.

I lifted him out of the chair by his shirtfront, grabbed the shovel, and walked him out of the library. Holding him by the cuffs, I led him down the corridor to the archway that led to the wine cellar. We descended the stairs, and I turned the key in the lock and pushed the door back. Inside, I pulled the light string.

"Do you expect to find Ray down here?" he said.

I pushed him into a corner and stepped back to the center of the room. He stood in the shadows, his face glistening with perspiration. I could see the madness in his eyes. The good doctor had reduced himself—through his own deeds—to a pathetic being, frightened and confused, alone in desperation. The standards and ideals he had chosen for his perfect life became too much of a burden, pushing him beyond reason. Despite my loathing of him, I couldn't help feeling sympathy for the scholarly young man I once knew.

"You won't find anything here," he said. "Ray is gone."

I hesitated and took a couple of deep breaths to engender the courage I knew I would need to continue. I walked to the center of the room and put the point of the shovel between the floorboards. I pushed down on it with my heel. A board came up easily, telling me I'd found the right spot. I reached down and pulled up a two-foot length of board, exposing a dark hole in the floor.

Drew began to recite Poe again as I got on my knees and pulled the second board up with my hands. *"'I was never kinder to the old man than during the whole week before I killed him,'"* he said, and then he laughed, a shrill, manic laugh that sent a shiver up my spine.

I yanked out the third and then the fourth board. Before I pulled up the next board, I could see what I'd expected, and inwardly feared—partially concealed beneath the opened floorboards, wrapped in a clear plastic trash bag and bound with duct tape, lay the dismembered remains of my once best friend, Ray Deverol, just where Drew Flannery had concealed them. I looked away in a rush of disgust and sadness.

Chapter 24

Let my radiant future shine
With sweet hopes of thee and thine.
Edgar Allan Poe—Hymn

Sandy and I were having lunch at Branigan's. It was a Saturday afternoon, and the place was packed. We were sitting in a booth by the front window. I was enjoying a Cheeseburger Deluxe with bacon, lettuce, tomato and a thick slice of raw onion. Sandy was nibbling a chicken salad on toast with a side of coleslaw. We both drank Cokes. Sandy's was diet.

I was feeling pretty good. The trial against Anton Denali and Drew Flannery was underway. I had given my testimony and felt certain Denali was finished. Drew's defense team had entered a plea of not guilty by reason of insanity, which seemed viable to me. As far as I was concerned, he was definitely off his rocker. The judge had ordered a psychiatric evaluation of Drew and his fate was still in the air. He could be charged criminally for the murder of Ray, or his involvement with Denali, or both, or ordered to mental rehab. Either way, he'd be away for a long time, if not forever. Anyway, I was glad it was almost over. It all seemed like a bad dream, finding Ray again after all those years, regaining his friendship, and then losing it again so quickly.

"Influenced by Poe's fiction, Drew believed he could get away with murder," I said to Sandy. "He hid Ray's body where he was sure it would never be found. Without a corpse, it would be difficult to get a murder conviction."

"Difficult but not impossible," Sandy said.

"The blueprint for the crime is detailed in one of Poe's most famous stories, and Drew followed it precisely, but there was one factor he overlooked.

"Which is?" Sandy said.

"In college, I'd read Poe too."

"Then your hunch was right on?"

"Unfortunately."

"A clever piece of detecting."

"Not clever enough. I wasn't able to save Ray's life."

"How could you know the big picture?" she said. "Drew's sick plan was in motion before you were involved. You were drawn in as an integral part of it."

She was right, but it didn't make me feel any better. I was satisfied that I had paid a small debt to Ray but felt a deep sadness at losing him, which I supposed I'd never get over.

"There'll be no problem getting convictions," Sandy said. "I've been involved in cases more complicated than this, that the DA has won. With Carla Darling's testimony, yours, and the testimony of Monica Flannery and the Hamlin kid— Denali's toast."

She took a bite of her sandwich and followed it with a sip of Coke, then said,

"Monica Flannery would be smart to make a deal with the D.A. to save herself and spill everything she knows."

"Maybe," I said, "but she's not being charged with conspiracy to commit murder. She had no knowledge that her husband killed Ray, even though she suspected it."

"True, but she has first-hand knowledge of what Ray was into and his connection with Denali. Her testimony could send Denali and his bunch away for a long time."

"Monica Flannery will spill her guts one way or another," I said.

"What happens to Carla Darling now?" Sandy said.

"Carla will be okay," I said. "She's a talented hairdresser and won't have a problem finding work. She'll start a new life, and if she's lucky, find some semblance of happiness."

Sandy's mood suddenly changed. She looked at me solemnly, then reached across the table and took my hand. She rubbed her thumb across my knuckles tenderly and said, "Max, I'm sorry for the way things turned out with Ray."

"And I'm sorry for what I put you through," I said. I placed my other hand over hers as an offering of strength and unity. "Ray was a good guy but made a bad decision trying to do the right thing."

The afternoon sun angling through the front window bathed Sandy's face in a warm yellow, turning her eyes a sensuous hazel-green and sparkling her auburn hair. She looked almost angelic. I felt tender looking at her and thankful that I could turn to her for comfort.

"I keep thinking about Ray's niece," she said. "What will happen to her now?"

"All's well that ends well," I said. "Ray named his brother beneficiary in his will. Ray wasn't rich, but his brother will inherit a good chunk of money. He'll see that his daughter gets that operation."

"I guess Ray accomplished what he wanted to after all," Sandy said,

"At the expense of his own life," I added.

Sandy wiped her mouth with her napkin and pushed her dish away. She put on a big smile as she reached out and took my hands in hers and squeezed affectionately. "Let's go back to your place," she said. "I intend to spend this entire weekend with you."

"Sounds promising," I said.

I slid a twenty-dollar bill under the saltshaker and helped Sandy on with her coat. As we turned to leave, we spotted

Pete Branigan at the end of the bar at the same moment he spotted us. I expected him to come over, but he didn't. Instead, he began waving his arm in front of his face to catch our attention. He looked like he was swatting flies. When Sandy and I waved back, he gave a thumbs up and mouthed something we couldn't understand. We kept smiling and nodding as we walked out the front door.

On the sidewalk, Sandy hooked her arm through mine as we walked around the corner to where I had parked the Chevy. The afternoon was cold and breezy, and we could see our breath in front of us whenever we spoke. When we reached the Chevy, we slid into the front seat quickly to escape the chill.

"My kingdom for some heat," Sandy joked.

"By the time this car heats up, we'll be at my place," I said.

I removed the car key from my pocket and slid it into the ignition switch.

"I need to stop by the food mart and pick up a few things for tonight," she said. She was rummaging through her purse and pulled out what looked like a short grocery list.

"Sounds like someone's planning a candlelight dinner and a night of romance," I said.

"Not quite," she said.

"No romance?"

"I'm making another batch of chocolate chip cookies," she said, and then added with a suggestive smile, "You can help me mix the dough."

I smiled back at her and turned the key.

It was going to be a great weekend.

The end

Made in the USA
Monee, IL
11 January 2021